Pr[illegible]
the Diva's Dead

5 Stars: "The fun in this entertaining amateur sleuth is observing the humorous goings-on behind the scenes of a local opera company. The cut-throat competition is not just about roles on stage. Whereas Debbie is the star holding the tale together, the support cast is solid with a range of egomaniacal personalities at the opera house and zany (insane may be more descriptive) friends and family of the heroine. Fans will appreciate A Night At The Opera."

—Harriet Klausner, The Mystery Gazette

"Debbie is smart, quick-witted and self-deprecating. Her interactions with her parents, mostly her mother and her agent, are wickedly funny .... The setting of this story is fun and interesting, as the reader gets to see what life is like backstage behind a stage production .... *Ding Dong the Diva's Dead* is a fast-paced mystery full of passionate characters who will stop at nothing to advance their careers and love lives .... Even if you're not an opera fan, you will be entertained by this dramatic book."

—Clea R. Gellar, BookWenches.com

4.5 out of 5—Top Pick: "This is a quirky and perky mystery with an operatic background. Things move along quickly throughout the story and each character is unique and different .... Overall, I liked this book and didn't want to put it down. Deborah's adventures interested me. I also had to wonder how many times poor Deborah would be found naked and in public. As for who was causing all the problems, it sure wasn't anyone I was thinking it might be ...."

—Terri, Night Owl Reviews

"I loved this novel! It introduced me to a world I knew nothing of, and gave me a new perspective on murder mysteries. I really enjoyed the humor and the rollicking parody of the very genre she is working in."

—Peter G. Beidler, Author of *A Reader's Companion to Salinger's The Catcher in the Rye*

"A good ol' bodice ripping sexual fever dream and an easy-reading page burner. Self-deprecatingly funny, sophisticated, and observant."

—Tim Askew, CEO/Founder, Corporate Rain, International, and former operatic tenor

"An entertaining romp through some of the unglamorous parts of being a professional musician, with intrigue to boot."

—Sara Jobin, Opera Conductor

"Cat Melodia knows the score ... the opera score, that is. Her witty debut as a mystery writer sparkles, with backstabbing divas, clever repartee, backstage antics, budding romances, and enough background color to leave her readers—as well as dyed-in-the-wool opera fans—shouting 'Encore!' "

—Nanette McGuinness, Lyric Soprano

"I read it straight through—very entertaining (and I hardly ever read fiction anymore)! It really kept me turning the pages, and I could 'see' the action—it would make a fun movie. Singers will find it amusing from an inside-baseball viewpoint, and non-singers get a glimpse of the (albeit elegant) sausage factory of regional opera along with the mystery story—and maybe develop a bit of sympathy for us struggling artistes!"

—Andrea Matthews, Lyric Soprano

"Who the hell are all these people? If you don't care if you can keep track of characters in a classical opera, and you'd like some inside dirt on mezzo-soprano vocal stylings, this is the book for you. It's Bloody Backstage At The Opera. Wonderful fun, and just as snotty as any theatrical company can be."

—Donna Barr, "The Desert Peach"

"Thoroughly entertaining—particularly because I recognize that the author is herself an expert on the topic of opera, opera production, operatic personalities and all the gruesome, behind the scenes antics so wonderfully captured by her pen."

—Lisa Bergman, Pianist and Executive Director, Northwest Opera in Schools Etcetera

"*In Ding, Dong, the Diva's Dead* Cat Melodia has given us a delightful romp—full of juicy gossip and innuendo and propelled by lust, envy, pettiness and murder. Her characters stride, stumble or waddle into our lives, by turns seducing, entertaining or repelling us. The relationships rock on this taut little ship of fools. It's a great ride."

—John Lowrie, Actor, Singer, Musician and Author of *Dancing with Eternity*

"The operatic elements ... are presented in an entertaining manner, and some readers will no doubt delight in the madcap adventure Debbie seems to be on."

—Mysterious Reviews

Ding Dong
the Diva's Dead

Ding Dong the Diva's Dead

CAT MELODIA

CAMEL PRESS
SEATTLE, WA

CAMEL PRESS

Camel Press
PO Box 70515
Seattle, WA 98127

For more information go to: www.Camelpress.com

This is a work of fiction. Names, characters, places, brands, media, and incidents are either the product of the author's imagination or are used fictitiously.

Cover design by Sabrina Sun
Cover illustration by Stasia Burrington

Ding Dong the Diva's Dead

ISBN: 978-1-60381-807-0 (Trade Paper)

Printed in the United States of America

To my wonderful mother, who laughed at all my jokes and supported all my follies.

Acknowledgments

Special thanks to all the early readers of this book, especially my sister, Laura Puckett, and friends Karin McCullough, Tina Dietz, Bob Tangney, and Colleen James.

Thanks, also, to the Pacific Northwest Writers Association, which selected *Ding Dong the Diva's Dead* as a finalist in the Mystery/Thriller Category of the 2007 Literary Contest. I may not have won, but I was greatly encouraged.

The earliest reader of this book was my mother, who has now been gone for over two years. She dreamed of being a published novelist herself, and her belief in my ability as a writer prompted her to read and critique every draft of every manuscript that I ever gave her. My dear father, a distinguished professor who died in 1994, read cozy mysteries for relaxation and often passed them on to me. He is responsible for my love of classical music; almost every evening he turned on the classical radio station or played his favorite symphonies or operas on the phonograph. I like to think that some of his wry sense of humor rubbed off on me as well. This book is also for him. Surely there is reading in the afterlife.

TALES OF HOFFMANN

Opera in Three Acts
Prologue and Epiloque

Music by Jacques Offenbach
Libretto by Jules Barbier and Michel Carré
(Based on stories by E.T.A. Hoffmann)
English Version by Cat Melodia

Stage Director
Corabelle Swift
Chorus Master
Ignatius Poubelle
Costumes
Mary Jo Perlmutter

Conductor
Juergen Kopfschlager
Artistic Director
Hubert Silvertone
Set Design
Jason Bell

Councillor Lindorf	Bass-Baritone	Angelo Capellinerino
Andres, *a servant*	Tenor	Hugh Rainier
Luther, *an innkeeper*	Baritone	Chorus
Nathanael, *a student*	Tenor	Chorus
Hermann, *a student*	Baritone	Chorus
Nicklausse, *Hoffmann's Companion*	Mezzo	Deborah de Lille
Hoffmann, *a poet*	Tenor	Sven Gorsson
Spalanzani, *an inventor*	Tenor	Bob Alter
Cochenille, *a servant*	Tenor	Lawrence Hottenbolt
Coppelius, *friend of Spalanzani*	Bass-Baritone	Angelo Capellinerino
Olympia, *a doll*	Soprano	Lisette Samson-Ellis
Giulietta, *a courtesan*	Mezzo	Camille Parquet
Schlemil, *her protector*	Tenor	Hugh Rainier
Dappertutto, *a magician*	Bass-Baritone	Angelo Capellinerino
Pittichinaccio	Tenor	Lawrence Hottenbolt
Antonia	Soprano	Ulrika Mannschliesser
Crespel, her father	Bass	Jim Sod
Frantz, a servant	Tenor	Lawrence Hottenbolt
Dr. Miracle	Bass-Baritone	Angelo Capellinerino
Voice of Antonia's mother	Mezzo	Deborah de Lille
Stella/Female Understudy	Soprano	Teresa Belladonna

1.

As Alexander Pope once wrote, though not with aspiring opera singers in mind, *hope springs eternal.* Beneath March skies the color and texture of laundry lint, the Seattle landscape was coloring up nicely. Pink cherry and white apple blossoms, yellow daffodils, blue-bells, and purple and yellow crocuses. The universe offered kaleidoscopic possibilities, if only I could keep my eyes on the road ahead instead of reaching for the sky with my head in the clouds. Not easy, when your chosen path is more convoluted than the Los Angeles freeway.

At least I was alive, which was more than I could say for the late Juanita Macaree-Smith, whose busy career had been the envy of every struggling lyric mezzo on the West Coast. That very morning OperaChatter.Com had posted the following item:

> **Life Is More Tragic than Opera:** As you may recall, we were the first to report the tragic death of mezzo soprano Juanita Macaree-Smith after her car "failed to negotiate a turn." The raven-haired firebrand, who scorched opera stages west of the Mississippi with her irresistible portrayal of Carmen, was killed en route from her latest engagement as the teenage lothario Octavian in *Der Rosenkavalier* (ironically, an opera where her character is alive and kicking at the end). A little songbird told us Juanita Makes-Me-Stiff was upset over reviews that fell short of her usual raves. Unbelievably, the consensus was that she failed to titillate as a man. We say, Juanita, in trousers or bustier, you were a hottie. We don't believe a tough chick like you would let a few lukewarm reviews drive you over the edge. (Yep, that was the coroner's finding!) No, we think the gods were too impatient for your company. Nuestro Juanita, we will miss your lush voice and full-steam-ahead, passionate commitment to your art!

Juanita channeled the iconic temptresses of old to heat up the stages of West Coast "B" opera houses. I, on the other hand, regressed daily to a non-existent boyhood to play Hansel for high school assemblies in a G-rated, Cliff's Notes version of Humperdinck's *Hansel and Gretel.*

That very morning, my tenth-grade French teacher had caught me in the act. "Is this what you're doing now?" he said, eyeballing my jaunty knee breeches and vest as if he had discovered me panhandling on Skid Row. Fifteen years had passed, and he was still teaching high school French. How was that so superior? And yet I said nothing. Don't get me wrong. I was equal to the task of defending my brilliant career. Those galley years in New York paying to perform in opera workshops had made me a pro at polishing up fools' gold.

Only, why bother? I could see his point. In his eyes, I was a thirty-two-year-old woman dressed as the Lonely Goatherd prancing across cafetorium stages for a skeptical audience of middle-school students. He couldn't appreciate that this was my first paid opera gig since moving back to my home town, fresh from earning a Master of Music from the University of Southern California.

Getting an MM had meant chucking a fledgling career in public relations—my coward's choice, fresh out of college with a Bachelor's in Music from Barnard. Cutthroat fellow students and a jaundiced voice teacher had convinced me my career prospects as an opera singer were slim to none.

I had dreamed of being a diva since the age of ten. My first opera was an uninspired staging of Delibes' Lakmé, featuring a linebacker of a soprano and a tiny, spherical tenor. If she had sat on his lap, he would have imploded. That experience had been enough to make a convert out of me. My mother bought me the recording, and from then on all my Barbie dolls were opera singers.

Corporate life had driven me to anti-depressants, a new voice teacher had cheered me on, and USC had given me a scholarship, so here I was, thanking my lucky stars to be mock-salivating over plastic gingerbread cookies.

Besides cookies that could have doubled as fake dog poop, the Hansel and Gretel set was basic enough to dismantle and reassemble up to four times a day. Mainly it consisted of three interlocking wooden panels—on one side a wooden cottage, on the other a gingerbread house Velcro'd with cookies and lollipops. Three chairs, two baskets. The Metropolitan Opera it wasn't.

It was 7:30 p.m. at the close of a three-show day on the fourth of March. I had just returned from yoga, which I practiced three times a week at various community centers. I had been sampling different yoga paths for two years now, and the enlightenment part still eluded me. On the other hand, I was getting lots of compliments on my arm development.

I lay draped across the sunken couch in the living room of my one-bedroom apartment, located on the frowsy boundaries of the seedy University District. I was the very picture of dejection, and no wonder! What in blazes was I going to do once the final curtain fell on this gig? Then the phone rang and snap! Everything changed. It was as if God really was the Johnny-on-the-spot, on a par with the Tooth Fairy and Santa Claus, I had pictured in Sunday school.

2.

"Debbieeeee!" a voice trilled into the phone, getting stuck on the final "e" vowel like a defective compact disc.

"Frankieeeee!" I sang back. It was my buddy Frankie Donato in Los Angeles, now a musicians' agent, also my agent, according to an informal arrangement. No contract. Frankie didn't have the heart to take ten percent of the paltry fifty bucks a show I made with AHOO, An Hour of Opera. His one agent-esque service to date had been questionable advice regarding the cover art of my one and only compact disc. In a misguided effort to sex it up, we had called the CD *Love for Sale*. This isn't quite as tasteless as it sounds, being the title of a Cole Porter tune. The cover makes it look as if I have just enjoyed a roll in the hay. I'm lounging seductively, straight blond hair arranged in a golden aura, jeans tighter than support hose and blouse unbuttoned to reveal the modest swell above my Wonder Bra. All that was needed to push the image beyond the pale was straw in my hair and a post-coital cigarette. Someone had been messing with the farmer's daughter, either the equine Mr. Ed or an incubus, a nasty spirit that ravished Victorian women while they slept. Considering the months that had elapsed since my last romantic encounter, this was the most likely explanation. As I aged, the dating pool had gotten too hot for me. I was in danger of being poached.

"You there, Babe?" The serrated vocal cords of Frankie Donato twanged. If Pixar ever needs a voice for a mosquito, Frankie is a shoo-in. Looks-wise, think animal, not insect. The only reason Frankie doesn't have a partner is that, unlike me, he won't take any crap. We met in the same Master's program at USC, but he stashed his cello in a storage closet about the same time he came out of the proverbial closet. His extended Italian family in the Bronx hasn't disowned him, though they pray daily for his redemption. "What's up, girl?"

"Not much. Still trying to pass myself off as a fourteen-year-old boy to the real thing."

"Cruising schoolboys, eh?"

"No, I am one. I told you ... I'm doing Hansel for school kids."

"Question is, who's doing you?"

"Let's say I'm in no danger of getting knocked up and losing my boyish figure."

"Well ..." He stretched the word out to its snapping point. "You're not what I call the motherly type."

"Who says? I can't play boys forever."

"If you wanna be a mom, babe, get crackin'. Your eggs ain't no spring chickens, if you get my drift. What about Winston?"

My heart sunk at the mention of my ex-boyfriend. My brain knew he was a creep, but the rest of me hadn't gotten the message. "What about him?" I said, blithe enough to convince myself. "I only hear from him between girlfriends."

"Ouch!" Frankie said. "Funny, I keep having these Winston sightings. Every time a black Mercedes convertible goes by, I'm sure it's him. Probably some other slick, self-important guy in a suit."

"He cultivates a generic look of well-groomed prosperity. A Hollywood divorce attorney has to look the part."

"Well, the next time he calls, tell him Frankie Donato says he's pond scum, and that your still waters run too deep for the likes of him."

Hmm ... For once Frankie had actually mixed a metaphor in a way that sounded intentional. I kept my voice steady, although—damn it—a tear prickled in my eye. "Sure thing. Maybe he'll marry again. That would occupy him for a year or so."

"Girl, you need to get a life, and I'm just the guy to help! Won any major competitions or been wait-listed for Chicago Lyric's Apprentice Program?"

"Very funny! As you have so kindly reminded me, I'm a little stale for that gambit. Thirty-two, honey, going on thirty-three in June. *When I was a child, I spake as a child, but when I became a man, I put away childish things.*"

"Ooh, the Bible. Always gets me hot. You've been doing too many church gigs. But back to Hansel ... I bet you look cute in Lederhosen."

"You know, Frankie, you're awfully sweet to keep believing in me against all odds, but let's face facts. At my age, without having won the Merola Competition or the Met Regionals, and with only one apprentice program under my belt, I'm hardly your dream client. So you can't work miracles—"

"Aha! That's where you're wrong. Screw San Francisco Opera and the Met! Move over Annie Sullivan, I am THE MIRACLE WORKER."

"Huh?"

"Look ... lyric mezzos never win competitions. Those rackets are all about high notes and volume. Discovering Pavarotti II or the next Brünnhilde. So it's not expected. Besides, I have connections. I also have a new client. Guess."

"Um, Placido Domingo?"

"The Three Tenors are so last century! Brace yourself … Sven Gorsson! Whadaya think of that?"

"Terrific, Frankie. What does it have to do with me?"

"Gimme a chance! How do you feel about Nicholas?"

"Jolly old Saint Nicholas? Don't believe in him."

"Nah, you know the one, from *Tales of Hoffmann*."

"The one that's pronounced Nick-louse, like the bug that nests in hair?"

"That's the guy."

My heart started doing jumping jacks. "Are you kidding, Frankie? I'd love to play Nicklausse!"

"And so you shall!"

3.

"It's with a new-ish company," Frankie continued. "I told 'em, if you still want Sven, you gotta hire Debbie, too."

"Oh, Frankie, I wish you hadn't strong-armed them! Whenever Mom forced my brother to let me tag along with his friends, I always wished I had stayed home."

"Come on. You will be fabulous, and they will adore you. They were crazy about your CD!"

Well, color my world! Things were looking up, after all. Nicklausse, though not a major character, was pivotal and appeared in every act. Like Hansel, it was a trouser role, a young man's part intended to be played by a woman, in this case the tenor's sidekick and conscience. "What's the company?"

"Vile d'Horror Opera."

"Huh?" He spelled it. "Oh, *Ville d'Aurore*," I said with the proper French accent.

"That's what I said. Only it's pronounced Vile d'Horror, cross my heart. This is America, toots."

"Where is it?"

"Idaho. Land o' lakes, like the buttuh. You can hike, you can bike, you can swim. Of course, if you wanna do any of those things, you'll do them alone or with a local. The only way to get a singer off his or her fat butt is to pay 'em."

"When does it start?"

"May 12th. Perfect timing, right? You told me the babysittin' gig is over at the end of April. Two weeks of rehearsal, three weeks of performances. Wednesday, Friday, Saturday evenings. The understudies do the Sunday matinee."

"Don't they book these things years in advance?"

"Usually. They hired Sven three years ago, before he won the Franco Corelli Competition. He's got gigs up the yin-yang. With New York City Opera, Seattle Metro Opera, Santa Fe, you name it. This is his last small-potatoes thing. A week ago I get the word that their Nicklausse died."

"Died?"

"Tragic accident. She drove off a cliff on the way home from a gig."

"Wait a minute … you can't be talking about Juanita Macaree-Smith?"

"Why not? I mean, I definitely am."

"Oh, no! It's like hiring Jennifer Aniston to replace Angelina Jolie. And, for your information, the coroner declared Juanita's death a suicide."

"Suicide, Shmuicide! That kid was harder than a bed of nails. She was hell on wheels, and not just in a car. What a pain in the rear! Besides, this role doesn't need a busty babe with sex vibes in overdrive. You'll be a helluva lot more believable."

"Frankieeeee," I groaned.

"Shuddup and listen. So … the company put out an all-points bulletin for replacements. I say, have I got the girl/boy for you. I send 'em a CD. They say, nice voice, no credits. I say, take her or lose Sven."

"Can you do that?"

"Sven wanted out. Fortunately for you, they caved."

"Thank you for that."

"You're welcome. You're in-like-Flynn. Sven's not so thrilled. He sang Don José not so long ago in the company's first production. It left a bad taste in his mouth. He didn't say what went down, but he wanted out of his contract real bad."

"So, why did he sign with you again?"

"If you mean, am I bangin' him, the answer is, I wish! They don't call him Gorgeous Gorsson for nothing. Six foot five. Flaming red hair. That's one burnin' hunk of Swedish meatball."

"Hmm."

"Don't get any ideas. He doesn't swing in your neck of the jungle."

"Please! I wasn't barking up that tree. Anyway, how would you know? He's been linked with women."

"The linkage was purely virtual, take my word. He had a thing going with one of my baritones for a week or two. But don't let that stop you. Go for it, Babe! You got five weeks with nothing else to do. Nicklausse ain't exactly the Mount Everest of opera roles. You could probably sing it in your sleep."

"Tell you what. After I seduce Gorgeous Gorsson, you can spread the word that he and I are a team. Dallas Opera will hire him to do another Don José, but this time I'll be Carmen. My Mom will die of a heart attack, happy at last, and my father and I will finally be at peace."

When he stopped laughing, Frankie said, "Dream on, Debbie. Debbie does Dallas, huh? Get real. That's kinda rich for your blood type. Take my advice. Get someone to christen those eggs of yours before they go to egg heaven."

4.

A year earlier my New Yorker and Angeleno buddies had groaned over my unbridled enthusiasm for Seattle and its stunning natural beauty, perky sales people, and laid-back motorists.

That was then. Now I was itching to wipe the Seattle mud off my character shoes. At least once a day my bicycle drew a barrage of verbal abuse from demonically possessed drivers. My career prospects had bleakened and my love life had stalled. Eligible single men my age were elusive, at least in my microcosm. They did not attend church, classical song recitals, children's operas, or church oratorios. And making a living as a singer in this town was proving to be one hell of a rocky row to hoe, as foolhardy as trying to cultivate wine grapes in the soggy rainforest town of Forks, Washington.

I could already picture idyllic Ville d'Aurore, a friendly Our Town peopled with rugged, liberal-minded Sportsmen.

My landline phone was ringing. I sprinted the staircase leading up to my third-floor walk-up apartment just in time to answer. "Hello!" I gasped.

"Debbie?" It was my mother, her voice pitched low and theatrical. Without the visual of generous caftan-draped curves, she sounded like a drag queen. "You're out of breath," she said. "Are you getting enough exercise?"

"I just ran up the stairs," I said. "Are bike riding and yoga enough, or do I need to start training for triathlons?"

She clicked her tongue disapprovingly. "Must you always be sarcastic?" Recognizing this as a rhetorical question, I let it lie. We were off to our usual contentious start.

My parents live in Port Smelton, located northwest of Seattle on the Olympic Peninsula—home to new age artists and unemployed loggers. Lillian and Harold are in their sixties and newly retired, thanks to a goldmine in the form of a house in Windermere that sold for about a hundred times its original value before the economy tanked. (I exaggerate, though not by much.) My mother, a former legal secretary, has fully embraced the Venusian culture that surrounds her, a strange brew of Zen Buddhism, Goddess Worship, and Enlightened Episcopalianism, the one with a lot of female and gay priests and congregations peopled mostly with same-sex couples.

By marrying my father, my mother became Lillian de Lille. Her name is an endless source of amusement at cocktail parties, at least for her. Mom drapes her no-longer-dangerous curves in voluminous tents of hemp and other earth- and animal-friendly materials and is teaching herself to read palms and Tarot cards. Otherwise her taste runs to crime fiction, the more blood-thirsty the better. She's read every John D. MacDonald paperback featuring the indestructible Travis McGee. Now I'm hooked, too. Three-quarters of the way through, you can depend on Travis to be beaten to a bloody pulp. Twenty pages later, he magically reconstitutes, as if made of foam rubber, to his devilishly handsome self, the accumulating scars more fetching badges of masculinity on his furry Neanderthal pelt.

With a few glasses of wine in her, Mom is fond of proclaiming her lust for Sean Connery's James Bond, whom she often remarks looks exactly like my father. In dim light and from certain angles, Dad might well be mistaken for the likewise aging Sean, only with more hair. The illusion is spoiled when he opens his mouth—kind of like that scene in *Diamonds are Forever* when James Bond uses the voice-altering machine. Until recently Dad worked at the post office. His line of postal customers was always the longest and most unruly, and who knows whether he ever succumbed to what must have been formidable temptation? Now that his glory days as a postal pinup have ended, he sighs and adapts. He never did speak much, and that's a boon for the marriage, because Mom has a lot to say.

Mom and I have our squabbles, but when she isn't trying to

improve me, she is my biggest fan. It would be nice to tell my news to someone who would receive it with genuine pleasure. I would have phoned Sheri, my college roommate, but she has four sons under the age of eight and lives in Minnesota. Relaying good news to her feels unfair, like telling someone who is serving an indefinite sentence of penal servitude in Siberia about your upcoming vacation in Bermuda. Sheri is my first choice when I need to commiserate. There's also my good buddy Beth, whom I used to hang out with in New York. She now works on Wall Street, and I definitely look forward to catching up with her when she retires—a bitter, exhausted, but wealthy woman—at the age of fifty. (Come to think of it, was she even still employed? Well, either way, we weren't close enough anymore for spontaneous phone calls.)

Then there is my big brother Roland, an MBA from Harvard and Chief Financial Officer of a well-established company in Silicon Valley that sells computer-related parts beyond my powers of comprehension. Roland receives news of my career successes with pursed lips of displeasure, as though I were a gambler who cannot shake the habit because of an occasional win at slots. He's not married, either, much to my parents' chagrin. Although roughly my height, paunchy, and balding, Roland goes through attractive, well-educated women in their twenties as if the supply were limitless. His own promiscuity leads him to write off every man I date as being after only one thing.

"Mom, I have terrific news," I said, eager to get us back on a more positive footing. "I've been hired by a professional opera company!"

"That's grrrreat!" my mother burbled, Tony-The-Tiger style. "Did you hear that, Harold? Debbie is a real opera singer now! Our daughter, a DIVA!"

"Mom, mezzo sopranos aren't divas," I said. "That's reserved for prima donnas."

"Who says? Carmen's a diva."

"I'm not playing Carmen."

"But you could!"

"Technically."

"Isn't that fabulous, Harold? Harold?!" A pause, faint mumbling in the background. "Your father says it's fabulous."

"His exact words, I'm guessing."

5.

"Have you told Winston the good news?" My mother asked.

"Mom, Winston and I haven't spoken in months. For all I know, he's on Wife Number Three. The man may be rich, but he's a creep. Stop hoping he'll see the light and realize I'm the one woman on earth who could fill that tiny, empty place where they forgot to put a heart." I said this more for my own benefit than Mom's. She stubbornly refused to stop believing in the original myth of Winston—the one rich and successful man I had ever dated.

"Well, you are," she insisted. "And someday he'll figure it out."

"Mom, please, you're negating months of therapy."

"What's that, honey? Why yes, eventually he'll tire of dating, and there you'll be!"

"Excuse me?" *Ther-a-py* equaled *there you'll be*? This was farfetched, even for her. Mom is only hard of hearing when the subject is hard for her to hear.

"Hello, hello?" Mom sang out, as if testing a microphone. "Do we have a bad connection?"

Yes, most definitely, but I love you anyway. Aloud, I said, "Enough about me! Mom, how are things?"

"Peachy. Shall I read the cards for you?"

"No, thank you."

A loud exhalation of air into the phone. "Piffle."

"I can't stop you. However, if it's bad, I'm not changing my plans."

"It won't be bad. How could it be bad? Here's your father."

"Hello, dear."

"Hi Dad. What's up?"

"You always say that," he groaned. "I never know what to say." Even more than making idle chitchat, Dad hates talking on the phone. He attributes his avoidance of the danged contraption to post-traumatic stress left over from a college job that required him to make cold calls to strangers, pitching accidental death insurance.

"Are you ... reading anything interesting?"

"War and Peace."

This gave me pause. "Uh, cool. Anything else?"

"Harry Potter."

"Dad, a better question might be, what are you drinking?"

"Hi, Honey, it's Mom again. Don't give your father a hard time. He really is reading *War and Peace*, the graphic novel version. And that *Harry Potter* series is delicious, at any age. You should read it. You're too cynical."

"He wasn't kidding?"

"Honey, your father is not a kidder. So what part are you playing?"

"Nicklausse."

"Mickey Mouse? This isn't another children's opera, is it?"

6.

"Not Mickey Mouse, *Nicklausse*," I told her. Next time I was in Fort Smelton, I had to show Mom how to turn up the volume on the phone. "Nicklausse is a boy's name. Another trouser role. He's like, the tenor's best friend."

"His lover?"

"Mom, this opera was composed in the late nineteenth century. No one wrote about gay relationships then."

"A secret attraction might have been in the subtext. You don't know. When do you get to be the love interest? It's a shame. You're so pretty. Some rich patron would see you in your attractive costume and—"

"Mom, the rich patrons are all dragged to the opera by their wives or attending with male partners."

"There are heterosexual men who like opera."

"Not under sixty."

Another audible huff of air. "Sixty isn't old!"

"No, you're right. It isn't. Unless you're thirty-two."

"Dear, you are so negative. You must work on that. No one likes negativity."

"No, I mean, YES!"

"What was that?"

"That was me being positive."

"No one likes a smart-aleck, either."

After this, I promised myself, I would treat myself to a dry martini and crack a new mystery, preferably one that depicted a universe even kookier than mine. Roland was the only normal one in our family. No wonder he never brought any women home to mother.

"How's Roland?" I asked. One of these days I hoped to ask this question and hear something surprising, such as that he was engaged to a woman his own age or had quit his job to join an ashram. Not this time.

"I think he's on a business trip," Mom said.

"Roland is always on a business trip. That's what he does."

"He's took a woman along."

"He always takes a woman."

Mom sounded shocked. "Really?"

"Yes really. Beautiful, unmarried women in San Francisco are as plentiful as blackberry brambles in Seattle. He likes the berries but only puts up with the prickles until they snag his thousand-dollar suits."

"Dear, be nice. Roland has a few things to say about your choices as well."

"Yes, I know." I covered the mouthpiece of the phone and heaved a monstrous sigh. Having got that out of my system, I said, "Mom, It's been great talking to you. Hugs and kisses to you both."

"Hugs and kisses. Do take care. I'll let you know what the cards say."

Forty-five minutes later, the phone rang again. I was stretched out on the couch, listening to Renaissance lute music, sipping a dry martini, and reading *A Deadly Shade of Gold*, filched from Mom's bookcase.

"Don't go."

"I'm not going anywhere, except to bed."

"I said, don't go! These cards are terrible. The hanged man! Death!"

"I thought that meant change."

"And the tower!" she sobbed. "The nine and ten of Swords!

"Mom, calm down. I told you, I'm not going to turn down this opportunity because of inauspicious tarot cards."

She calmed down enough to add, "At least you're going to meet a handsome stranger." (Sob) "IF YOU LIVE LONG ENOUGH!"

7.

I harnessed my bike onto the rack and departed for Idaho a day early, just in case my aged Civic broke down halfway across Washington State in some tiny, isolated hamlet like George, Washington, where not even the buses stop anymore. Was I worried about Mom's warning? Nope. She had predicted disaster for me before. And, although my love life might be considered disastrous, I was alive and kicking.

So far my luck was holding. I had found another singer to stay in my apartment and cover a month's rent and utilities. To ensure that this stranger didn't run off with my only valuable possessions—my collection of opera scores—I boxed them up and left them with one of my colleagues from AHOO.

It was a perfect Seattle May morning. A wispy film of cirrus clouds drifted artistically through mostly clear skies. The drive was a straight shot over I-90, unimpeded by road work or traffic snarls.

Until the pass, the road was forested with a variety of evergreens. Snow crowned the peaks, and countless lakes punctuated both sides of the highway. After Snoqualmie Pass, dryness prevailed. Long stretches of farmland were interspersed with isolated farmhouses and barns, clumps of shade trees, and Ponderosa Pine forests.

Five hours from my departure time, it started to rain, the sort of downpour that requires windshield wipers to run at warp speed, or at least faster than my Honda's. Even that was lucky. If I hadn't been driving slowly in the right lane, I'd have missed the Ville d'Aurore exit.

I soon had cause to wonder if my luck had run out.

I telephoned the stage manager, Peter Haas, and arranged to meet him at an address along Main Street. The rain had stopped by then, but clouds still loomed, low and ominous. I emerged warily from my car, expecting to be blasted again at any moment like a cartoon cockroach in a Raid commercial. Then, from the gloom, a ghost-boy emerged, deathly pale as though recently released from a sanitarium. His chin sported a few days of blond stubble, and his hair was concealed beneath a baseball cap. He wore a gray hoodie with *Ville d'Aurore Opera* emblazoned across the chest and black cargo shorts, beneath which boney white knees glowed like dimly lit bulbs. "Peter?" I said doubtfully.

"Deborah, hi! I'm glad you arrived in one piece." This was said a little too fervently to pass as the usual pleasantries. After all, the remains of the last Nicklausse had probably required some reassembling for the sake of her Catholic relatives. I tried to dismiss the grisly image as Peter silently led the way to my future habitation.

The building looked like a motel, and what was worse—judging from the greasy-haired, strung-out, scrawny denizens smoking in the doorways of their rooms—a *welfare* motel. Either I wore an expression of naked alarm or Peter was also surprised by the scene before us. At least he had the grace to be embarrassed. "There's been a snafu," he stuttered, "I mean, this ... I'm sorry. *We're* sorry. Don't unpack anymore than you have to." He unlocked the door to my room, which reeked of stale cigarette smoke. I checked the motel sign again. "0% non-smoking rooms," it advertised.

Hardly a reason to brag! "Is this a smoking establishment?" I asked Peter.

"They assured us not!" Peter blurted out, after confirming the sign's message. "Wait a minute!" He ran, in a weird, loopy gait, to view the other side of the sign. "It was a typo," he reassured me. "The other side says '100% non-smoking rooms.'"

I tried to keep my cool. "That's nice. It doesn't change the fact that my room smells like the Blue Moon Tavern at six a.m. Sunday morning. Clearly all these nice people smoke." I nodded in their direction, not wanting to piss anyone off by pointing. "Whether or not they smoke in their rooms, they carry that smell around with them."

"Point taken," Peter said, avoiding my eyes. "I'm going to get right on this. Why don't you ..." He checked his watch. It was only 3:30. "Uh, go for a walk, maybe? I'll call around."

8.

The clouds had retreated, so I decided to take my bike out for a spin. The row of Hitchcockian motels gave way to a neighborhood straight out of a 50s sitcom. Quaint, modest homes, their front porches shaded by ornamental plum trees, oaks, and maples. At the stretch of Main Street favored by tourists, I walked my bike. I passed a Starbucks, an overpriced boutique, and two stores selling equestrian and hunting gear. The boxy commercial buildings and curlicued wrought-iron lampposts fit the kind of frontier town where Clint Eastwood might burst through swinging saloon doors and paint the town red. Although in this case, the city elders would have insisted on burnt sienna. Flower baskets hung at every corner, and whimsical fountains portrayed smiling moons and stars, card-playing deer and beavers, and fish dancing on their fins.

On the other side of Main Street, Lake Ville d'Aurore

beckoned, vast and gray, reflecting the dense cloud cover. On the banks of the lake stood the majestic Ville d'Aurore Lodge, a longhouse massive enough to accommodate Tecumseh's tribal confederacy. The lodge had been constructed of logs peeled and polished to perfection, then pimped by an admirer of European castles. At each end there stood tall turrets with crenellated, circular tops. Rapunzel would have felt right at home.

After the marina, I passed a curiously stylized park, an approximation of Paris's Jardin du Luxembourg. No potted palms but lots of fruit trees. Also gravel paths, towering hedges, circular ponds, and scantily clad statues of gods and goddesses. Beyond the park, the evergreens were overwhelmingly Ponderosa Pines, although here and there stood a random Douglas Fir, improbably symmetrical, like a sheared Christmas tree replanted after the holidays. As I was about to reenter the forest, I heard my cell phone resound with the rising scales that signaled an unidentified caller.

Peter had found me another motel room—at the Pine Tree Inn, where the chorus was quartered. With the smell of Pine trees filling my nostrils and visions of rustic knotty Pine and cheerful window boxes dancing in my head, I rode back to my car, packed up my things, loaded my bike back on the rack, and drove to my new and improved digs.

The motel's name had cruelly raised my expectations. It couldn't have been grimmer if you had barred the windows—a yellow stucco exterior with no contrasting trim, balconies, or decorative eaves. It was a square lemon pound cake of a building, in the same state of decay as Miss Havisham's, left to rot after she was abandoned at the altar. The interior was no improvement. Dingy white walls and curtains, bedspread, and carpet in shades of gray—no doubt to camouflage the filth. The dappled gray fibers of the rug crackled disagreeably beneath my feet. Who knew what living and nonliving organisms lurked and roiled about in this petrified, primordial soup of a carpet?

"Bummer," Peter said, shaking his head dolefully.

"At least it doesn't reek of cigarettes," I said, sniffing

experimentally. No, not of tobacco smoke. More like mold.

Peter helped me unload the car. Since there were no open parking places in the immediate vicinity, Peter described a spot on the street several blocks away where I could leave my car for days on end with no risk of being ticketed or towed. He insisted I wouldn't need a car to travel to and from the Bragelonne Opera House, located on the other side of Bragelonne Park.

"Bragelonne," I repeated. "Any connection to the novel by Alexandre Dumas?"

"Huh?" Peter said. Foolish of me. Hardly anyone read *The Three Musketeers* anymore, much less the multi-volume sequels, *Twenty Years After* and *Le Vicomte de Bragelonne*.

"Ever heard of *The Man in the Iron Mask*?" I said. "There was a movie version several years back starring Leonardo DiCaprio."

"Yeah? Never saw it. There was a Count de Bragelonne," he explained. "Not a real count. That's what he called himself. Struck it rich as a prospector in silver and gold in the 1880s. He built the lodge and the opera house. Also designed the park. Reade owns most of it now."

"Reade?"

"Reade Phillips, the general director of Ville d'Aurore Opera."

Okay, so I had heard these names, but pleading ignorance would allow me to hear Peter's version. "Who's Aurora? Was there an Aurora de Bragelonne?"

"There's no Aurora," Peter laughed.

"Oh," I said, reluctantly abandoning the fantasy I had concocted featuring Aurore the Whore, who had serviced the entire town and later become mayor.

"Aurore, as in the French word for daybreak," Peter explained. "City of the Dawn. It was named by French-Canadian fur trappers. They harvested nocturnal critters from the traps at dawn. That's when the town was at its best, with the skies all pink and the birds twittering away."

"Vile d'Horror," I said, exaggerating the American pronunciation. "*Ville d'Aurore* is a distinct improvement, don't you think? But then, everything sounds better in French. Vile d'Horror would be a good setting for *Psycho, the Opera.*"

Peter didn't laugh. I must have struck a nerve, considering the untimely death of the woman whose role I had inherited. He turned tail and dashed away, helter-skelter.

9.

After parking my car in the recommended location, I returned briefly to my squalid quarters to open all the windows. Then I set out in the Pine-scented evening air in search of dinner. Too hungry for caution, I ended up in one of those homey restaurants with huge portions of heavy, gravy-laden vittles. This kind of fare would have hit the spot after a two-day, thirty-mile hike. Not five hours in a car. I opted not to order salad after observing the iceberg-lettuce-based one my neighbor was eating. No matter. The food was edible, and the waitress was a congenial, folksy bottle-blonde.

While I ate I amused myself with the place mat, a map of Ville d'Aurore. The miners, loggers, and trappers who had founded the town had invented a passel of colorful names. Jack Ass Junction, Loco Luke's Last Stand, Gold Fever Gulch, Nugget Valley, Hard Rock Ridge …

Sedated by mega-carbs and a generous pour of cheap cabernet, I slept tolerably well that night, despite my lumpy mattress. I now had a fair idea of what it might be like to sleep on top of a kitchen range. Let's just say I was intimate with the bedsprings. As a result my neck went on strike, refusing to pivot to the left.

I was on my own until the get-acquainted gathering the following afternoon, so I headed over to the Ville d'Aurore Lodge to ask the desk clerk about leisure activities. Entering the luxurious lobby, I felt familiar pangs of regret regarding my jettisoned business career. I might eventually have afforded to treat myself to this sort of luxurious rusticity. Or, if I hadn't been so stubbornly independent, I might have married a wealthy entrepreneur who stayed in luxury hotels like this one when he wanted to rough it.

The hotel owed its hunting lodge ambiance to peeled log railings, stone floors, an oversized hearth, and the trophy heads of two stags and a moose. My attention was drawn away from these eternally livid beasts by a living, breathing display of ire in the form of a pissed-off hotel guest. The droopy-eyed clerk regarded the man with the placidity of a cow contemplating a small, yapping dog—which, incidentally, the man did not in the least resemble. Other than his flushed face, he was a well-groomed, nicely muscled male representative of the human species. He spoke in a low, threatening voice, so I caught only a few words: *confirmed reservation, lake view, incompetent.* I got the gist.

The man, who must have sensed my curious regard, turned to face me. Yes, he was a jerk, but since when had that stopped me from admiring a man's physical gifts? Embarrassed, I fixed my attention on the angry moose. *High-tail it out of here, you idiot girl,* the animal seemed to say. This is the type of man who killed me! Reluctantly I obeyed. I had observed enough to note a strong resemblance to Stewart Granger's Allan Quatermain in *King Solomon's Mines.* He had a Hollywood tan and healthy thatch of salt-and-pepper hair, a scalp that would have made a dandy trophy in frontier times. I also admired his thin, aristocratic lips and boyish brown eyes.

Rattled, I decided not to hang around. The desk clerk didn't look like an authority on outdoor activities in any case. I picked up a map of bicycle trails from a rack of brochures and chose the most convenient path. By now the sun had burned away the clouds, and the lake sparkled in the sun as it lapped against the shore. While I pedaled, I sang softly through my scenes in the *Tales of Hoffmann* score.

10.

A half hour into my trip, the trail headed inland and ended abruptly at the highway. I consulted my map. True to my lousy sense of direction, I had taken the wrong fork in the road. Chilled and hypnotized by the monotony of the scenery, I retraced my route.

In the *Tales of Hoffmann*, the character of Nicklausse, while constantly on stage, is mostly a hanger-on. The singing part is scanty, consisting of one forgettable aria, a famous duet (the Barcarolle, one of the most recognizable tunes in opera) and a lot of recitative, or sung dialogue. I knew the original French but had needed to learn the English translation commissioned for this production. The young company obviously had more money to throw around than your typical B-house.

The opera combines three supernatural novellas by the nineteenth-century German author ETA Hoffmann, mostly known as the author of the story, "The Hard Nut," dramatized by Tchaikovsky in his *Nutcracker* ballet. The opera revolves around the poet Hoffmann (a tenor), who is drawn to femmes fatales. The prologue finds him waiting in a bar for his girlfriend Stella, a prima donna, to complete the evening's performance of Mozart's *Don Giovanni*. Meanwhile the barfly students ply him for details of his romantic exploits. He obliges with three tales, each unfolding in a separate act. Eventually he drinks himself comatose. When Stella arrives to keep their rendezvous, she ends up going home with the villain. The villain's main advantage? He is still standing.

Nicklausse is Hoffmann's best friend, conscience, and artistic muse. It is his thankless job to convince his buddy to stop drinking and womanizing and fulfill his artistic potential. The kid is basically a killjoy. Whatever the character's drawbacks, I was planning to enjoy myself. It was always a challenge to find that ideal balance of androgyny, neither too butch nor too girly, that might appeal to audience members of both sexes. Not easy, in Nicklausse's case. Nobody likes a nag, as Mom would say. Nicklausse's unhummable bauble of an aria lacks sustained high or low notes and meaty emotional hooks. Also, how can a tiny role like that hope to make an impression in an opera dominated by three leading ladies and their inflated egos?

My bicycle started to buck like a rodeo bull, jolting me out of my reverie. Had I wandered off the pavement? No, the path remained smooth. Someone had turned the level on my stationary bicycle up to 20! Oh, right. I wasn't on a stationary bicycle! Suddenly airborne, I flailed for a nonexistent handhold.

11.

I hit the pavement chin first, the impact of my fall partially broken by both outstretched palms and one knee. I communed with the pavement for several minutes, feeling like the victim of a rock 'em sock 'em robot.

Finally I lifted my head experimentally. At least my *block* was still in place. My palms, skinned and gritty, stung, but my wrists rotated easily. When I stood, my gashed knee sustained me. I was basically in one piece. Gingerly I manipulated my jaw, which was sore but mobile.

Thank God I was nearly in shouting distance of the Lodge. The object that had caused the puncture still protruded from my front tire. It looked like jewelry—gold with an embossed head. The now-mangled antique might have been worth something prior to its unfortunate run-in with my bike. I slipped it in the pocket of my polar fleece. Like this once-precious piece, my bike had fared worse than me. It lurched to the left as I guided it along the path. Just what I needed—an expensive repair bill.

I left the abused bike leaning against a young birch tree. This time, upon entering the majestic lobby of the Ville d'Aurore Lodge, I attracted curious glances from an elderly couple, who averted their eyes with alarming speed. Apparently I looked worse than I felt.

The bovine desk clerk recoiled slightly. "What happened to you?" he enquired with undisguised horror.

"I fell off my bike," I said.

"Are you okay?" he said, his eyes fixing on my chin. Following his gaze, my hand flew to the rising lump. Hell, it was more like a tumor.

"Nothing serious," I said, voice quavering. It had suddenly dawned on me that I would be attending tomorrow afternoon's get-acquainted shindig sporting half of Dudley Do-Right's protruding cleft chin.

"Do you need a doctor?" the clerk said with genuine concern.

"No," I insisted, "but I could use a bicycle repair shop."

After consulting the wall clock, he said, "It should still be open. Head north on Main Street. There's also a clinic—"

"It's okay," I interrupted. "I'm fine, really." He opened his mouth, as if to protest, then thought better of it. His eyes said, *It's your funeral.*

While dabbing at my wounds in the Lodge's feng shui-ed public restroom, I confirmed that my injuries weren't pretty, particularly the swollen and lopsided chin. The chunk missing from my knee might cause alarm in someone susceptible to infection, but I was generally hale and hearty. Thanks to a daredevil childhood, my knees were already chewed up. My palms were merely crusty.

The buff young man who presided at Bison Bicycle Repair avoided my eyes, preferring to focus on my bike. "It's not too bad," he assured me. "Should I patch the tire while I'm at it?"

"That would be great," I said. Normally I patched my own tires, but I was too defeated to care about the cost.

He seemed to be reading my mind. Or perhaps it was my welling eyes. "Don't worry," he said, "It won't set you back much. I can tell you've had a rough day. Do you know what you rolled over?"

I fished the offending antique out of my pocket and laid it on the counter.

"What is that?" he said, taking a closer look.

"Jewelry, I think," I said. "A broach or a hat pin."

"Looks old," he said, nodding. "Might be worth something."

"Maybe before my bike had its way with it," I said. "It's not much to look at now."

"You never know," he said. "It could have belonged to someone famous. Although this is Ville d'Aurore. How famous could they be?" I slipped the piece back in my pocket. "The bike will be ready tomorrow," he said. Now that the ice was broken, he stared at me more openly. "You must have been going pretty fast."

I shook my head wearily. "My mistake was that I kept trying to pedal. I rarely have flats. Knock on wood." I knocked on the counter, and we both laughed.

"That's locking the barn door after the horse is gone," he said.

"It's preventative," I explained. "I'm warding off future bad luck."

"Good luck with that!" he said.

12.

The next morning I tanked up at Starbucks (still ascendant in chichi places like Ville d'Aurore that ban McDonalds and its McCafés) then prowled like a caged rock wren (the only flightless songbird left on earth) around my grim chamber. My quarters reminded me more and more of an airport lounge located in some impoverished township in New Jersey before smoking bans.

While I paced, I crooned softly to myself, reviewing my part with the help of a recording made with my coach. Coaches don't teach vocal technique; they help you learn your role, correct faulty rhythms and entrances, and polish diction. Since I'm a decent pianist with a good ear for languages, I rarely spring for coaches—only when I need to test my memory. They charge $50-60 per hour (compared to top teachers, who charge anywhere from $90 to $150 and up), so it pays to prepare as much as possible on your own. Factoring in the cost of coaches and teachers—usually well-established musicians whom singers choose with an eye toward cadging an introduction to a conductor or agent—financing a career often feels like tossing gold ducats down a wishing well.

The Pine Tree Inn sounded like a music conservatory, or rather, the holding tank for the preliminary rounds of *American Idol*. The entire chorus was warming up, and the individual voices, as far as I could make out, were not going to make it to the next round. What if the chorus stank? Not my problem. This turkey was going to sound better than anything else on my résumé, no matter how raucously it gobbled.

My chin tumor had continued to blossom, despite hours of icing. I tried to disguise it with a special green foundation especially formulated to counteract redness. It could be that I lacked the skill of a makeup artist like Kevyn Aucoin, but the end result resembled half of the Wicked Witch of the West's plastic prosthetic chin. Finally I gave up and decided to let its freak flag fly.

My heart sank. I wasn't a party girl under the best of circumstances.

13.

At around 4:00 p.m. I plodded reluctantly over to the house of the chairman of the board of directors, Hubert Silvertone, for our casual Cocktail Party and Buffet. This event was a chance for the muck-a-mucks—the major contributors—to take stock of the stock. A petting zoo for opera patrons.

Not all these events are a downer, especially in cases where the host genuinely likes opera, has no singing aspirations himself, and has many like-minded friends—although, on the whole, opera does tend to draw its share of snobs. On a scale of 1 to 5, 1 being Santa Claus and 5 being the Grinch, Silvertone & Co. rated a 4.75. The looks I received as I crossed the threshold into the fussy, overstuffed parlor could have frozen liquid Nitrogen.

Perhaps I was the problem. I did have this giant chip on my shoulder—I mean, my chin—and I was justifiably apprehensive about stepping in for the legendary Juanita Macaree-Smith.

I wore black dress pants, boots, and a plain, cream-colored silk blouse—an ensemble that, under normal circumstances, would have allowed me to blend into the woodwork. With a few adjustments I might have passed as a waiter. In any other crowd I'd have been practically invisible. Here I would have stuck out even without the extra chin. Among the women, I was THE tall, slim one. Call me a swan among ducks—Muscovy Ducks with lacquered tips on the end of their webbed toes and jewels in their crests and tail feathers.

Why oh why hadn't I worn a little black dress? At the very least I could have sprung for a manicure and chosen a darker shade of lipstick and higher heels.

I spotted a likely candidate for small talk—a small, fish-faced woman, standing alone, her ropy neck glinting with diamonds. "Hello," I said, jovially, "I'm Debbie de Lille."

She leaned in and said with some irritation, "Excuse me? Who did you say you were?"

Hmm, deaf, I thought. "DEBBIE DE LILLE," I said in my stage voice.

"I HEARD YOU," she replied, offended. "I just didn't recognize the name."

"I'm sorry," I said, feeling my cheeks heat up, "It's just that it's loud in here—"

"Why are you here?" she said, looking me up and down and no doubt calculating the cost of my ensemble.

"I'm in the cast," I said. "I'm playing Nicklausse—you know, Hoffmann's muse."

"I do know," she said. "I saw Flicka play that part at the Met. A hard act to follow, I can tell you. As is Juanita." Her eyes kept returning to my chin, although not even she was rude enough to mention it.

"Yes," I said, desperate to please, "I love Frederika von Stade, and I hear that Juanita was just terrific."

"Where would I have seen you perform?"

"Um, probably nowhere. I was in school in California, and now I'm living in Seattle." This was ridiculous. Why hadn't I devised a canned answer to this question, which came up at every party?

"I do get out, occasionally," was her arch reply.

"Um, Sea View Opera?" I said. No sign of recognition. "Seattle Metro Opera?"

She brightened at the mention of Seattle's one International opera company. "In which role?"

"Just previews, I'm afraid," I said, too disheartened to lie.

"Hmm," she said. "Did you know Juanita?"

"No, I never met her," I said. "Her death was a real loss for the opera world."

She patted my arm, as one might comfort a child whose game piece had just landed on Boardwalk, already owned by another player and occupied by one hotel. "I'm sure you'll do fine," she said. With that small concession to manners, she headed purposefully into the other room. Not an auspicious beginning. I looked at my watch. Would anyone notice if I left?

On my way toward the exit, I practically plowed down a tiny gentleman wearing an ascot. "Hi, I'm Debbie De Lille," I said. The way he was staring up at my chin prompted me to add in the same breath, while gesturing to my new appendage, "I had a bicycle accident." He clicked his tongue sympathetically and introduced himself in an unintelligible voice. "You need a drink," he said, giving me a little push in the direction of the bar. "You'll excuse me?"

This time I didn't dare raise my voice, ask him to repeat his name, or make further attempts to revive the conversation. The rows of white wine glasses at the bar beckoned.

I had planned to abstain entirely. Alcohol isn't easy on the vocal cords and can leave them dry and swollen the next day. However, I was suddenly in dire need of liquid courage.

14.

Although I am shy by nature, I can fake outgoingness convincingly for brief periods. One of my friends calls this trait *loud shy*, not uncommon in performers who are more comfortable onstage than off. We tend to overcompensate. Among these party guests—predisposed toward my predecessor—I wasn't at my best. A mouse might as well attempt to befriend barn cats.

One glass of wine blunted my mortification. The second almost made me forget my disfigurement. The woman next to me had a harmless, pleasingly plump Aunt Bee façade. *Once more unto the breach!* I thought, bravely extending my hand.

It turned out to be none other than our host's tarnished-trophy wife, Madeleine Silvertone. Madeleine wasted no time in coming to the point. "My dear, what did you do to yourself?" she said, as if I had somehow committed a breach of contract by damaging the goods.

"I fell off my bicycle," I said, making no attempt to turn the incident into an amusing anecdote. Would you joke around with a disapproving headmistress?

"You fell off your bicycle," she repeated.

"Yes, I'm afraid so," I said. "I was lucky," I quickly added, gesturing to my chin. "It's nothing."

Her skeptical squint said that, if this was luck, she'd prefer to be cursed. She changed the subject. "Are you related to the de Lille's of DeLille Wine Cellars in Woodinville?" she asked.

"Their family name is actually Lill," I said, "No 'De' and no 'e' at the end. L-I-L-L."

"Oh," she said, moving right along. "What role are you playing?"

"Nicklausse."

"Oh?" she said again, patently bored.

"You have a great stage name," I said, clinging in vain to the ice floe as it broke free and started to drift off to join with some other frozen landmass. Slippery and biting as this handhold was, at least I wasn't actively drowning.

"Yes," she gushed, coloring with satisfaction. "Isn't it wonderful? Our ancestors were singing hymns at Plymouth Rock! Well, I won't monopolize you further. Have fun!" She waved to one of her friends and was off. I shivered. From here on out I would think of Madeleine Silvertone as Aunt Vee, for viper.

I moved on to a succession of ultra-brief encounters, some of them almost pleasant. A gangly Jimmy-Stewart type with an English accent said, "Capital!" when I told him I would be playing Nicklausse. "You have the figure for it. Juanita was a fine Carmen, but a little broad in the beam to play a man, if you ask me." He winked. He was on the sleazy side, but I was grateful to encounter friendliness in any form.

Then his wife intervened. With her ample girth, she would have made Juanita look like a beanpole. Not bothering with introductions, she stepped in and claimed his arm. "Darling," she said, lips curling upward in a slight smile. The rest of her face did not join them. "You didn't object to her curves at the time, did you?" The husband smiled sheepishly. She turned to confront me. "Juanita had a stellar reputation. You have big shoes to fill." Staring at my size nine boots, she concluded, "Your feet look to be about the right size. Is your voice?"

Another woman, a close cousin to a manatee, had apparently been eavesdropping. She remarked, "It must be nice to have the sort of schedule where you can be available at a moment's notice."

15.

How many glasses of wine had I drunk? At least three. I needed to eat something before the alcohol made me do something foolish, like tell someone off. I had run the gauntlet for nearly an hour. Surely I had done my duty?

The room with the buffet, separated from the main parlor by a hallway, appeared to be occupied entirely by singers. How could I tell? They were younger than the guests, more flamboyantly dressed, and their firm cheeks had muscles peculiar to singers, muscles that help place the voice in the sinuses. Forward or nasal resonance is one of the main reasons opera singers don't need amplification.

The only cast member I recognized at first glance was Sven Gorsson. He was impossible to miss, with his flaming red hair parted in the middle and swept dramatically back in thick, feathered wings like the god Mercury. His impeccable posture made him seem taller than his purported 6'5", and his large white teeth gleamed savagely. As I watched he threw back his gigantic head and guffawed. A harsh laugh can shred your vocal cords, so singers learn to produce a resonant, "Ha! Ha! Ha!" that would fit right in the middle of an aria.

I scurried over to the buffet and helped myself to crackers and cheese. The fat and carbs would help metabolize the alcohol. I overheard an enlightening exchange before anyone registered my presence. Not only do singers laugh too loudly, they also project their speaking voices with maximum efficiency, usually without realizing it.

"Poor Juanita! What gruesome news," said the first soprano.

"I never heard the whole story," said the other. "All I know is that she drove off a cliff while returning home from Denver."

"They think she swerved to avoid an animal."

"That doesn't sound like the Juanita I knew. Driving too quickly, yes! I mean the part about avoiding the animal. She mowed down anything that got in her way. They say it was suicide, but I don't believe it. She was too tough for that."

"I don't know. Her reviews really stunk. Do you remember? Octavian is hardly the dream role for a true mezzo. Wicked tessitura. It wasn't her finest hour."

"So I heard. Do you remember what the reviewer said?"

"Hmm ... Who could forget? The Octavian of Macaree-Smith could have used a shot of Viagra. Her acting was limp-wristed, and her high notes did not rise to the occasion."

Silvery operatic laughter, soon stifled. "I'm sorry. That was heartless of me. Only ... I had forgotten just how bad the review was! I think that was a little harsh, don't you? She does—uh, did—have a pretty universal appeal, at least sexually. But that's a tricky role. I mean, a woman as the main male love interest! Thanks a lot, Richard Strauss. If you can't carry off the opening bedroom scene, the entire premise falls flat."

"Who's replacing her? Didn't that happen, like, a month ago?"

"Some nonentity from Seattle. Her agent bundled her with Sven in a package deal. Sven says it was supposed to get him out of his contract. No such luck."

Judging from their rich, musical voices and overweening egos, these women were two of the soprano leads. Before I fled, I caught a glimpse of the one who was well-informed as to the fate of Juanita. A few inches taller than me and a good deal chunkier, she was a drag queen's take on an opera singer. Fluffy clouds of white-blond hair fell to her broad shoulders, and her makeup was exaggerated enough for the stage. A vintage wrap-dress showed her hourglass shape to best advantage. As for her companion, all I could see was her broad backside and jet-black hair. Like me, she was wearing black dress pants—only with stiletto heels and a sparkling cashmere sweater.

In the classic short story "The Lady and the Tiger," the protagonist must choose between two doors. Behind one is a beautiful lady, behind the other a deadly tiger. At least that guy had a chance. My choices were two lethal ladies vs. a scary tiger in the form of Sven Gorsson. As in the wild, before I could act, he had already pounced.

16.

"Good eats?" Sven boomed.

"Uh, I don't know," I said, silver-tongued as ever. I indicated what was left of the spread. "Don't let me stop you. You look hungry." I stood aside.

The onceover he gave me was hunger-free. "How do you fit into all of this?" he asked, thumping me playfully on the shoulder.

I held my ground against the unexpected force of his gigantic paw and said, voice unsteady, "I'm Debbie de Lille. I'm Nick—"

"—lausse," he interrupted. "Ha! Ha! HA! You're the one who wasn't terrible enough to get me out of my contract."

"Gee, Gorgeo–, I mean, Sven, you have a way with words." I decided not to be offended. It was the truth, after all.

"So you know who I am." Was he looking down his nose at me, or was that just what you had to do when you were six feet five inches tall with superb posture?

"Who else could you be?" I said. I was trying to place his accent. It reminded me of Cary Grant's, in the sense that it sounded like his own invention. But then, opera singers usually sound affected. Their speaking voices are too well placed, as if they're always on the verge of breaking into song.

"You're a feisty one. Come with me to the Casbah. When I get through with this buffet, there might be nothing left. Ha! Ha! HA!" He practically shoved me into his path, as if expecting me to run interference. How I longed for body armor, or, at the very least, a cloak of invisibility. If ETA Hoffmann had written this, he might have given me one. Unfortunately, association with Gorgeous Gorsson had suddenly thrust me front-and-center stage. Now everyone turned to face us, including the dark-haired soprano. Next to her, the wasp-waisted drag queen looked like the town hooker. Imagine Snow White, twenty pounds heavier, after ten years of arguing with the prince: lips red as blood, hair black as ebony, and skin white as snow that, between her brows, had two cross-country ski tracks.

Have you figured out yet that I spent too much of my childhood reading fairytales and too much of my adolescence watching old movies?

17.

"Deb-or-ah de Lille," Sven intoned. "That has got to be a stage name!" He leaned close to my ear and crooned softly, in a tone too acerbic for flirtation:

De-bo-rah de Lille
Her name has star appeal,
And when she dresses as a man,
The gay boys cop a feel!

"Say!" he added, stooping to take a better look at my chin. "Are you injured?"

"I fell off my bike," I said, wearily.

"A wounded warrior," he proclaimed. "Chins up!" He chuckled at his little pun. "It's a doozy, but it will soon heal, and you'll be back to your dapper self." As if reading my thoughts, he continued, "Yes, I know, tough crowd. You'll find no compassion here. These people are looking for ways to put us in our places.

"Lisette, Camille!" he called out. The women exchanged wary glances, as if to say, *How much did she hear? Why, nothing at all*, my bright smile assured them. "Meet Lisette Samson-Ellis and Camille Parquet," Sven said. His gestures identified Lisette as the Drag Queen and Camille as Snow White.

"What a pleasure," I said, with all the sincerity I could muster.

"Yes, it is," Camille remarked. *For you*, she might have added.

"Hello, there!" Lisette said, more convincingly genuine.

"Now be nice," Sven warned. "She's been injured by a rogue bike."

"At least she knows how to take it on the chin!" Lisette joked, not unkindly. "That's important in this business."

"You must be the one who's going to play Nicklausse," Camille said, looking pointedly at my chest.

"How can you tell?" I said, wickedly. I was curious as to how she'd wriggle out of this one.

"Your voice, of course," Camille chirped. "That plummy mezzo resonance is a dead giveaway."

"And she looks the part," Sven added. After a prolonged pause, he added, "I mean, of course, those endless legs." He gave the ladies a courtly bow. "You'll excuse us now, I hope? Debbie and I are both in dire need of sustenance. If you ladies have eaten your fill, that is." He surveyed the buffet with comic dismay. Though not exactly stripped by locusts, it might have been nibbled to shreds by aphids. "Not a moment too soon, I see," he commented. Wow. I really liked this guy.

The ladies' smiles no longer reached their eyes. "Be our guests," Camille said, with the sort of broad, sweeping gesture that accompanied a high C.

"Which one is Olympia?" I asked him when we were out of earshot. "No, let me guess. Lisette."

"Very good," he said, helping himself to a generous slab of smoked salmon and a hunk of bread. "She has the right look for it, don't you think? Mattel could use her as the model for Opera Singer Barbie." To appreciate Sven's insult, it helps to know that Olympia is a doll. Hoffmann falls in love with her, believing her to be the daughter of Spalanzani, a character tenor. In truth she's Spalanzani's creation, a clever automaton. Her eyes, however, are the work of the villainous inventor, Coppelius, who destroys her when Spalanzani tries to stiff him. "The perfect voice, as well," Sven added, as if to gloss over the previous dig. "Stratospheric high notes and amazing vocal agility. Care to guess Camille's role?" He shoved a large forkful of salmon into his mouth.

"Giulietta," I said without hesitation. Giulietta was the expensive courtesan, in league with the devil to steal Hoffmann's soul.

"Good for you." He helped himself to a baby carrot. "So, are you a dyke?"

"Do I look like a dyke?" I dipped a shrimp in cocktail sauce and bit it in half.

"You might be a lipstick lesbian." He popped the last shrimp in his mouth and chewed it slowly.

I stalled by eating one of the fancy, unidentifiable hors d'oeuvres. Ugh. Anchovy paste. "You don't pull any punches, do you?"

"Well, are you?" he said, inserting an entire slice of cheese-slathered bread between his pantherine jaws. "Lesbians are drawn to these roles."

I popped an olive in my mouth. You may be wondering if this duel of tongues and teeth had sexual undertones. *Tom Jones* it wasn't, and if you don't know what I'm talking about, see the movie, the original with Albert Finney. It contains one of the sexiest eating scenes in film, next to the consumption of figs in *Women in Love*. In other words, it was hot. This was not. The sheer ludicrousness of the situation—or was it the wine?—inspired me to take three olives and juggle them. I figured this was one talent I had over the rest of them. "My sexual preferences," I said blithely, "are none of your concern."

"So you *are*."

"I'm *not*."

"Gotcha." He grabbed one of my olives and popped it into his mouth. The other two slipped through my fingers and rolled under the buffet. Sven worked the olive deliberately, spit out the pit, then swallowed. "Go ahead," he said, "don't let me stop you. You'll find two easier to manage."

"They've chosen their own path," I said, referring to the olives, I think.

18.

The cryptic exchange with Sven ended abruptly when a man roughly my height and just as lanky approached the buffet. He claimed the one remaining olive and said, "I'm determined to get my share." With a curt bow, he said, "Lawrence Hottenbolt, at your service."

"Debbie de Lille." Lawrence stood next to Sven, making comparisons inevitable. The word elfin comes to mind.

"Debbie," Sven repeated, in a falsetto that mimicked my voice with disturbing accuracy. "It's simply not you. I prefer, De-bo-rah."

"De-bo-rah de Lille," the other man repeated, drawing the syllables out English-Butler-fashion, as though announcing the next dish in a multi-course feast. "Are you related to the wine-making family?"

"No," I said, too tired of the question to elaborate.

"May I call you Dee-Dee?" He tilted his head, cockatoo-style.

"Only if you want people to think you stutter."

"No, that would be D-Dee."

"Well, then, only if you'd rather be singing soprano."

"Deborah."

"Debbie, please."

"Debbie it is!" Lawrence said, slapping his thigh decisively. "I like it. It's so un-diva-like. Speaking of un-diva-like, what did you do to your …" He reached out to touch my chin extension.

Sven slapped his hand. "Lawrence, don't be rude."

"Abusive boyfriend?" Lawrence inquired.

"Rogue bicycle," Sven said.

"Ooh, nasty," Lawrence said. "I hope your jaw isn't fractured. Are you clumsy?"

"Lawrence!" Sven remonstrated.

"I ran over something sharp," I said, a tad defensively. "It's a piece of jewelry, maybe a hat pin." I reached into my purse, where I had stashed the object. "What do you think?" I held it out for them to view.

"Hmm," Lawrence said. "Definitely jewelry. And old." He looked to Sven for confirmation. "Stray costume piece?"

Sven shrugged. "Could be."

Slipping the object back in my purse, I asked Lawrence, "Is your name really Hottenbolt?"

"Yes, it's awful. I keep meaning to change it. It underwent some terrible sea change at Ellis Island, I think."

"You don't know?"

"I'm illegitimate." He shrugged. "It's my mother's name, and she wasn't one for keeping track of family history."

"He's lying," Sven said. "He chose that name. He's a comprimario tenor. If he was competing with me, he'd have chosen a name like …" He pursed his lips and fluttered his fingers, "de Somptuaire."

"No, if I were competing with you, I'd call myself Lawrence Hottotrot. Get it? Hot-to-trot."

"Ha, ha," Sven responded dryly. "That would suit you to a T." They glared at each other.

"So," I said nervously. "What about the third soprano?"

"Sounds like a Hitchcock film," Lawrence said. "*The Third Soprano: A Tale of Violence and Intrigue.*"

"What transpires in this murder mystery?" Sven asked.

"It revolves around a performance of *Tales of Hoffmann*," Lawrence said, flexing his hands and wrists as if limbering up for a traditional East-Indian dance. He was more at ease by the minute, leaving no doubt as to his sexual proclivities. Thanks to Frankie, I didn't need to guess Sven's. "The original Nicklausse dies. Each one of the three leading sopranos is known for her colossal ego. There is, ironically, only one understudy for all the women, including the replacement Nicklausse. The plot is afoot. One down, five to go: you, Camille, Lisette, Teresa, and ..." He floated his index finger around the room like a divining rod. "Eureka! I mean, Ulrika." The roving finger stopped, mid-air, indicating a slim, pint-size waif talking to a man who looked like Stewart Granger.

19.

Wait a minute. That was *my* Stewart Granger, the rude hotel guest! The woman was gazing up at him with large, liquid eyes. The minx! With her straight dark hair, parted in the middle and falling in her face, she was a throwback to the sixties. At that moment I wished the wispy little thing a long, lingering death à la *Love Story.* Lawrence smiled, before concluding, "Six Little Indians. Seven, if you include Wilhelmina Wooley, the Voice of the Mother."

I managed a half-hearted laugh. "Let me see. You're implying we're going to die, one by one, as in the Agatha Christie novel? There will have to be figurines for the murderer to push off the mantle every time he makes a kill. Swans maybe. Don't they sing one last song before death, kind of like Antonia in our opera?"

"Pure poppycock," Sven said. "That is, the idea that a swan keeps its trumpeting to a minimum in life then bursts into one last song before dying. The story originated with the mute swan, a bird that wasn't mute at all. It just didn't make any sound that resembled singing. And it didn't sing before it died, either."

"Whatever," Lawrence said. "Leave it to Sven to leach the poetry out of everything. Sven, the Antidote to Romance."

"Hell hath no fury ..." Sven didn't bother to finish the phrase.

"Speaking of our Antonia," Lawrence said. "Her name is Ulrika Mannschliesser." Antonia was Hoffmann's third-act love. (At least the third act of our version. Different versions of this opera exist because Offenbach died before it was completed and there was a fire in the opera house and the original score was destroyed and ... Never mind. Just take my word for it.) Anyhow, Antonia is an opera singer with a mysterious heart ailment who has been warned that singing will be the death of her. Naturally she sings anyway. And dies. (Hell, it doesn't stop the rest of us!) Actually, the devil makes her do it. The devil, or a baritone in league with the devil, is in every act, conspiring to prevent Hoffmann from bonding with the woman of his dreams. I could have used an excuse like that to justify my complicated history with the opposite sex. How else to rationalize lusting after Stewart Granger, whose only known attributes to date were a knack for disrespecting underlings and a weakness for simpering, pint-sized sopranos?

"She looks sickly," I said with a tad too much relish.

"Maybe Ulrika has a heart condition in real life," Lawrence said. "Get a load of that pale skin and feverish glow!"

"She's simply blooming under the benevolent gaze of Reade Phillips," Sven said, pinching Lawrence's cheek. Lawrence slapped the offending hand—a hulking appendage.

"Is that his name?" I asked.

"What? Did he run over your pet dog?" Lawrence said. "You're not looking kindly upon our angel."

"Angel?"

Lawrence's look questioned my mental competency. "Don't you recognize the name? He's the general director! Who do you think started this rinky-dink company? The guy's loaded." He rubbed his fingers and thumb together in the universal gesture. "We're getting paid way above standard. Why else would we be slumming at a time usually spent resting up for the summer festival gigs? May isn't exactly the peak of the opera season. But Ville d'Aurore is Reade's playground, and we are his playthings. Whatever else you say about Reade Phillips, he loves opera, and that makes him A-OK in my book."

20.

"My, aren't we a fount of information," Sven said. "But then, you've always been THE source, haven't you?"

"Opera singers are notoriously loud and indiscreet, present company included," Lawrence said. "I can't help it if I pay attention."

"Where did he get his money?" I inquired, indicating Reade. I hoped to get us all back on friendlier footing.

"He's one of those high-tech execs," Lawrence said. "Retired and cashed in at the right time. The usual."

"Hardly the usual," Sven sniffed. "How many of them would finance an opera company? The majority are like Paul Allen. Sports and rock 'n' roll. Please!"

Ulrika was all over Reade. Or was he all over her? It was hard to tell. "Who is the understudy you referred to?" I asked, tired of looking at the two lovebirds.

"As I said, one for all but NOT all for one, unlike The Three Musketeers and their fourth member, D'Artagnan. Teresa is the general female understudy."

"Is she up to it? There can't be many on this earth with the goods to do justice to Olympia, Antonia, and Giulietta."

Sven shrugged. "Joan Sutherland and Beverly Sills both did it."

"Well, yeah. But you have to admit, it's rare to find someone who can handle those coloratura hijinks and also project well in mid-range."

"Sure. If you're asking me, can she do it? I doubt it. I've only heard her sing Frasquita in Carmen. She's your understudy, too, by the way."

"Is she here?" I scoped out the room.

Lawrence indicated a slender blonde standing alone. "There she is. Come on, let's say hello. I say ..." he called out, as if acting in a Noel Coward play. "Teresa!" The girl smiled and waved. How could I have missed her? She looked like a child. There was not one speck of makeup on her pale lips, pristine complexion, and gold brows and lashes. She was a blank slate, begging to be colored in.

We all introduced ourselves. "Ah'm Teresa Belladonna," she told us. In response to my puzzled look, she added, "Mah fathuh was Eye-talian." Since I can't keep this up, just know that, despite her Italian father, her southern accent was creamier than pasta primavera sauce. Every other sentence was inflected like a question. "I'm from Lafitteville, Louisiana?" she said.

"Yes, I know it," I said, as if in answer.

"Where are y'all from?"

I looked expectantly at Lawrence and Sven. "She means you," Sven said. "The rest of us are well acquainted."

"I'm from Seattle," I said. "Sven, where are you all from?"

"I'm from Westport, Connecticut," Sven said. "More recently, Los Angeles. Lawrence is from Arabia."

"Now boys, be nice!" Teresa admonished, batting blond lashes at Lawrence.

"I'm from the Midwest. Chicago," Lawrence said.

Teresa, who had been staring at my chin all along, finally gave into temptation. "Honey, what did y'all do to yourself? That's a lulu!"

"Bike accident," Sven and Lawrence said in unison.

"Well, someone shoot that ol' contraption before it does more harm," she said.

"It's currently undergoing rehabilitation," I said. "And it wasn't the bike's fault. The tire went kaboom."

When I showed Teresa the offending jewelry fragment, her eyes widened. "Why, that looks familiar?" she said. "Can't say why. Maybe it'll come to me."

"So, missy," Sven said, "Debbie wants to know if you can really sing all those roles."

"Why yes?" she said brightly. "It's not a problem for me. But I probably won't get the chance to show y'all. I thought I was gonna be doing your part, honey," she told me. "I don't mind, though? I'll get my chance. Jesus will provide."

Normally Teresa's invoking the Lord's name would have put me off. However, I had already decided I liked her … as long as she didn't start praying publicly for my soul.

21.

Reade had apparently vacated the premises. I noted with satisfaction that his potential playmate, the wan but fetching Ulrika, was still among us, bonding with her fellow divas. From their body language, which involved considerable thrusting of bosoms, it must have been quite a conversation. A *my career is better than your career* lollapalooza.

"Come on, confess," Lawrence said to Teresa. "I've always wondered. What is your real name?"

Sven leapt to her defense. "Hey, don't be rude!"

"Emily Susan," Teresa replied, unfazed. "They called me Emmy

Sue? I changed it. The last name really is Belladonna, though. It means pretty lady."

"Yes it does," Lawrence said. "It's also a poisonous plant."

"Yassuh, I know," she said with a sigh. "Deadly nightshade. They use it in medicine. I guess I should change it. I'm learning the ropes here. It doesn't matter yet, because nobody knows who I am. They will, in time." She could afford to be patient, if she was as young as she looked. Not like me. I suppressed the urge to ask *how* young.

"Who's playing the evil baritones?" I said. "There's just one, right?"

"Just one," Sven confirmed. "An Italian pop singer, believe it or not."

"Yeah, and he's blind," Lawrence said. "They're bringing in Andrea Bocelli."

"Stop pulling Debbie's leg," Sven said. "Debbie knows Andrea is a tenor! The guy's name is Angelo Capellinerino. Although Reade Phillips could afford Andrea Bocelli."

"I hear you two charge the same rate," Lawrence said.

"Ha, ha," Sven said, with no pretense of amusement.

"Is Angelo here?" I asked, searching the room for a Vincent Price or Bela Lugosi type. Well, why not? Everyone else seemed to fit their part!

"Angelo doesn't arrive until tomorrow," Sven said. "He's flying in from Milan, supposedly in time for the sing-through."

"Well, well," Lawrence said, rubbing his hands together. "Our favorite Italian pop singer villain. Three bitchy, I mean bitchin', prima donnas. A last-minute Nicklausse, Gorgeous Gorsson and me, the best comprimario tenor in the biz. A local Spalanzani, older than the hills, and his tippling lover as Crespel. An illustrious conductor, Herr Hit-, I mean, Juergen Kopfschlager, who can't be bothered with social niceties. Oh yes, and our other lone wolf, the sleek and furtive dyke director extraordinaire, Corabelle Swift. This will be a kick in the pants, don't you think?"

22.

My grand total for the evening had been four glasses of wine. Three too many.

At 2:00 a.m. I woke up. I may have drifted off a few times after that, but for all intents and purposes I was awake. At around 7 I gave up and crunched my way along the filthy carpet to the shower stall, a coffin of pockmarked yellow plastic precariously plastered to the wall. My throat felt furry, and I was hollow-eyed and haggard, as though I had been serving time with Errol Flynn as a galley slave in *Captain Blood*. Except in that case, proximity to Errol might have provided enough pep to propel me through the day. Filled with foreboding, I abandoned my narrow monk's cell, laptop in hand, to the only pilgrimage for a sleepless eremite (at least in Ville d'Aurore), Starbucks. I decided that checking my e-mail might provide comfort by making me feel connected to the greater universe.

I was cheered, marginally, when I noticed that the bump on my chin had shrunk to half its record size. I already had what my mother once called a "lantern jaw," à la Fred Astaire. I certainly didn't need any extra.

Shoddy as my motel room was, you couldn't beat the location, two blocks north of Starbucks and, continuing on another quarter mile in the same direction, the historic Bragelonne Opera House, circa 1879. This boxy, three-story edifice had solid brick walls sixteen inches thick. The house, which accounted for two of the stories, accommodated roughly five hundred velvet seats in addition to six sets of private box seats. The ballroom, where the rehearsals would take place, was on the third floor.

Because Starbucks was the most convenient purveyor of caffeine, I shouldn't have been surprised to encounter fellow cast members, naturally those first on my list of People to Avoid before Morning Coffee. Primal instincts of self-preservation prompted me to lay low until they had finished making their purchases. I took a seat and erected a privacy barrier—my laptop. Good thing it was one of those big, cheap models.

Two of the divas, Camille and Ulrika, headed up a line that existed solely because of their shenanigans. Camille was ordering a Mocha Breve in a porcelain cup with a touch of foam ("No, that's too much!"), and Ulrika's order began with, "This is what I want. Now listen carefully." That's all I heard; the rest was uttered in hushed tones, as if what she had to relate was vital to the future of the entire Starbucks franchise. Camille was the grandstander, intimidating and proud of it. Ulrika was more like a small, querulous child, unconscious of how she came off. In this case, intense and downright rude. It was impossible not to overhear their conversation as they stood at the counter and waited with tapping pointy toes for the barista to complete their orders.

As usual my e-mail consisted mostly of spam. The "enlarge your pen$s!" ads and urgent missives to "dearest friend," from exiled Nigerian princesses ("I am sincerely needing your succor ...") found a way around the junk mail filters every time. The other urgent missive was from my mother, warning of yet another disastrous tarot reading. No wonder I hated checking my e-mail. Frankie was the only one I really wanted to hear from right now, and he preferred his cell phone. If Mom's readings got any more specific, she could jolly well call me, too.

I had just begun to research wound types on Wikipedia (my egg-like bruise was called a "contusion") when the dreaded female voices amplified. Camille and Ulrika had seated themselves a mere two tables away. If they so much as turned their heads, I was dead meat. I hoped they had lousy peripheral vision.

"Have you spoken with Juergen yet?" Camille asked.

"No," Ulrika said. "And when I do, I'll be brief. That shouldn't be difficult. He tends to keep to himself."

"Unless he's on the make," Camille said.

"With us around, he'll be on best behavior," Ulrika said. She smoothed back a long lock of silky hair, savoring its texture, while

Camille reapplied her lipstick. Two British Royals couldn't have acted more entitled. "Everyone here is on to him," Ulrika continued. "I'm surprised the orchestra didn't go on strike when they heard he was returning."

"Do you think he'll hit on Debbie?" Camille asked. I hadn't heard my name uttered with such mocking glee since middle school.

"She's a woman, isn't she?" Their shared laughter, unlike the tinkling twitters of the previous evening, emerged as a menacing and mirthless, heh, heh, heh. "Or so she claims! She has about as much shape as a baton. As to working female parts, we'll give her the benefit of the doubt. With most guys, all that's necessary is the correct anatomy. Even self-declared straight opera singers tend to be closet cases. The more androgynous the woman, the better! And you can bet Debbie has serviced her share of conductors—probably with disappointing results! I know a skank when I see one."

When they had stopped laughing, Ulrika said, "You have to hand it to Juergen, though. He's a perfectionist." Her expression was skeptical as she took her first sip of coffee, as if certain to find the order hopelessly botched. It must have passed muster, because despite her frown, she didn't leap to her feet in outrage.

"Conductors, phooey!" Camille exclaimed. "Anyone who can keep a beat and schmooze rich donors can conduct. If the orchestra tolerates you and it's halfway decent, you can't lose. That's where Juergen bites the big one. He's a real musician. There's no place for a real musician, except at the top. So here he is, reduced to leading community orchestras for rich eccentrics in haunted opera houses. If not for the piano lessons and coaching, he'd starve to death."

Ulrika nibbled, rodent-like, on her scone. "It probably didn't help that we both complained to management about him that time."

"Probably not," Camille said, her mouth stuffed with scone, efficiently dispatched in three bites. "Sexual harassment claims are taken seriously these days. I hope no one told him it was us."

"He doesn't have a clue," Ulrika scoffed. "There must be an unending stream of complaints. He's made his own bed, and, creep that he is, he'll lie in it alone! Orchestras screw up just to spite him. I'm surprised anyone hires him to do anything."

I heard a rattling behind me and turned to see two masculine hands gripping a raised newspaper. The man was either palsied or shaking with rage.

23.

As he lowered his newspaper and rose to his feet, the man's fierce eyes met mine. Had I done something to tick him off? I quickly reapplied myself to my Web search, but not before noting the details of his appearance. He was a big-city boy clad all in black, from his short-sleeved black T-shirt to his fitted black jeans and soft, black-leather shoes. Some Italian designer, judging from the quality. Since two of him would fit into one of Camille's costumes, I guessed that he hadn't chosen black for its slimming effect.

I soon realized that his rage had nothing to do with me. I wasn't even on his radar. It didn't take Miss Marple to deduce that this was the devil the ladies had been speaking of. Juergen Kopfschlager himself, our maestro.

Imagine the Little Dutch Boy after kicking a Heroin habit and becoming a beat poet, and—voilà!—you have a pretty good idea of Juergen. His seriously neglected chin-length hair was similar to mine, fine, straight, and dirty-blond (or was it just dirty?). The cautionary example of his hair more than justified the fortune I had spent preserving the exact honey-blond shade that had been the envy of my fourth grade class. Even distorted in rage, his features were handsome, if you like the Aryan type—thin lips, prominent cheekbones, and deep-set eyes.

The divas were oblivious. What to do? It was hardly the time to introduce myself. In the end we were spared further awkwardness on Juergen's account. When I looked again, the man had evaporated like steam wafting from the wand of an espresso machine.

I should have followed his example, but the aroma of coffee

held me in its thrall. My senses of smell and taste had again won out over common sense—something that frequently happened to me with men. Head lowered, I tiptoed to the main counter and whispered my order. At the pickup counter, I pored over a brochure that listed the calorie count of every Starbucks muffin and scone. I was temporarily distracted from my state of hyper-vigilance. Five hundred calories for a raspberry scone?!

All precautions were in vain. The women had spotted me. I willed my eyes to assume a serious, faraway look, as though weighing the risks and rewards of consuming a scone a day. Or perhaps they would buy the scenario that my brain, deprived of caffeine, had gone on idle, sort of like a computer screen saver. As if just now returning to full consciousness, I made a big show of registering their presence. *Oh, is that you?* I fluttered my fingers in a half-assed wave, claimed my triple-shot latte and scone, grabbed my laptop, and hightailed it out of there.

As I scampered away like a startled bunny, I thought about Mom's latest warning. As if my luck could get any worse!

24.

Never tempt the gods by wondering if your luck can get worse.

However, things seemed to be looking up. My voice, for instance, sounded relatively fresh, despite the wine and lack of sleep. The caffeine, sugar, and adrenaline-fueled breakfast, combined with a careful warm-up, had worked their magic. That is the beauty of good technique as well as the temperamental nature of the instrument. Sometimes you could flout the rules and still sound fine. At other times, you did everything right and wondered what could possibly have prompted your vocal cords (an astonishing one-half to one inch in length) to forsake you. Could it be allergies, acid reflux, an otherwise mild virus, neck or shoulder tension? Whatever the cause, you could usually work around it. But it wasn't fun. Imagine being a concert pianist who is asked to perform on a piano that is missing ivories or even keys, and you have a pretty good idea of what that is like.

A sing-through such as this one, preceding the blocking rehearsals and accompanied by full orchestra, was far from typical. Bringing in union musicians in advance of the actual run of an opera would have seriously strained the budget of most impresarios. A pianist usually stood in for the orchestra until the Sitzprobe (Sitting Rehearsal), which would take place just prior to the final dress rehearsals. Apparently Reade Phillips was not concerned about cost overruns.

In a letter enclosed with our schedule, Maestro Kopfschlager had explained that unforeseen events made it necessary for him to hear how our voices blended and carried over an orchestra. Clearly *I* was the only unforeseen event. Under normal circumstances, I never would have been hired without an audition. Even now, the company wasn't obligated to stand by its contract if I failed to please. Teresa was hovering like a vulture in dove's clothing, and no doubt half-a-dozen mezzos in the chorus were also figuratively if not literally capable of stepping into my nineteenth-century breeches.

In hopes of cultivating a Zen frame of mind, I took a detour along the gravel paths of Bragelonne Park and found a bench facing the opera house. From there I could monitor theater traffic. First to arrive was Teresa, delicate as a bouquet of Baby's Breath in her white-lace dress. The next one to strut in was Gorgeous Gorsson, Hercules unbound. I sighed. No use denying it. I was shaking in my boots. I tried to meditate by concentrating on the expanse of manicured green lawn. Next to a statue of a naked goddess, a sign read, *Warning: Bees. Keep off the grass.* That must indicate the presence of an apiary, as in the Jardin du Luxembourg in Paris, which posts similar warning signs. The bees roam during the day and return to their hives by night.

The traffic was now a steady stream of singers and musicians. 2:50 p.m. Time to face the music.

25.

As I crossed the lobby, I helped myself to a flyer entitled, "The White Lady of the Bragelonne Opera House":

During a 1901 production of Mozart's *Don Giovanni*, a young soprano named Victoria Le Moine made her debut as Donna Elvira.

Graydon "Gray Wolf" Grayson, in the title role of the infamous roué, was cast according to type, a situation that didn't bode well for his female colleagues. Miss Le Moine, too, shared an unfortunate trait with her character: mental instability. She, along with every other female in the cast, fell hard for "Gray Wolf" Grayson.

On opening night, a stage hand overheard Miss Le Moine informing Mr. Grayson that she was pregnant with his child. Although he already had a wife and two children in Milwaukee, Mr. Grayson vowed to leave his family and begin a new life with Miss Le Moine after the opera's final performance. Legend has it that this particular production achieved unusual dramatic authenticity.

After the final curtain, to no one's surprise other than Miss Le Moine's, Mr. Grayson skipped town. During the closing night party in the third-floor ballroom, Miss Le Moine kept vigil for her lover next to the picture window. At midnight, when everyone else had gone, Managing Director Harold Freeman entreated her to come away. Finally, at his wit's end, he went to summon help. Victoria Le Moine opened the window and plummeted to her death.

Ever since that evening, strange noises have been reported throughout the building, particularly in the ballroom, between the hours of 11:00 p.m. and 1:00 a.m. Windows open and shut, a woman weeps, and heels click on the oak floor.

> The next time a production of *Don Giovanni* was attempted in 1953, the opera had to be shut down after opening night. During the dress rehearsal, the bass baritone lead reported invisible hands tugging at his clothing as he stood in the wings. Then, at the end of the final scene, the trapdoor that was supposed to usher him into Hell malfunctioned, injuring his spine. Although he eventually recovered, he was not willing or able to continue the run. That very evening, his understudy died in a car accident. Management decided to cut its losses.
>
> Since that ill-fated 1953 production, Ville d'Aurore Opera has not staged another *Don Giovanni*.

"What did I tell you?" a voice said. I couldn't have been any more startled than if it had been the White Lady herself. However, it was only Lawrence. Wearing white trousers, it's true. "Sorry! Did I scare you?"

"I'm a bit skittish," I admitted. "Now I understand what you were talking about last night. The phantom, I mean. If we were in Europe, it would be business as usual. Every self-respecting old building has a White Lady."

"What other color would she be?" Lawrence remarked. "Idaho is not exactly a model of ethnic diversity. The Mormons are working overtime to contribute new souls to the population."

"You've sung here before," I said. "Ever experience anything odd?"

"Nope," he said, without a moment's reflection. "Bunch of hooey."

26.

"Hey, the chin-berg has retreated," Lawrence noted as we entered the stage door.

"The chin-berg?" I said. "Do you mean my contusion?"

"Are you experiencing confusion?" he said, peering closer. "You've got some interesting colors going, I see."

I hadn't taken a close look at my chin since morning. "Uh, Lawrence, I'll see you in there, okay?" I said, retreating to the bathroom.

The fluorescent lighting didn't help matters, but anyway you looked at it, I had a smaller but more colorful chin—purplish red, to be exact. Even if I had carried foundation in my purse, concealing this ruddy blotch would require serious theatrical greasepaint. With yet another profound sigh of frustration, I returned to the auditorium. Better your chin than your voice, I admonished myself. The *Wikipedia* article on wounds had reminded me that a contusion didn't vanish overnight. First it turned black and blue, then green and yellow. I might as well make my peace with it.

I mounted the stage to find my place in the professional pecking order. There were three semicircles of folding chairs: chorus in the back, secondary and minor roles in the center, principals up front.

I hadn't met any of my row-mates. Normally a comprimario tenor like Lawrence would be in my row, but the importance of his multiple roles had elevated him to the first tier. I pegged the guy on my left as an old Hell's Angel, with his long gray ponytail, potbelly, and flower child's Sunday best—a blue work shirt with a big striped tie, jeans without holes and a motorcycle jacket. The fresh-faced young man on my right would have made a dandy Mormon missionary, although those wide-set baby blues might actually get him in the door. Gray suit, white shirt. No tie, and you'd have to be Donny Osmond to afford the cut and quality of those duds. He shifted tensely toward me, as if drafting seldom-used muscles into action. This man kept himself on a tight leash. However, the smile he flashed was real.

"Who," he said.

"What?"

He shook his head. "Hugh," he said again, more distinctly, with a pronounced English accent. "H-u-g-h."

I consulted my contact list, which provided names and cell phone numbers. Hugh's last name was spelled, R-A-I-N-I-E-R. "Oh, like the mountain," I said, "*Raineer.*"

"No," the man said. "Not *Raineer. Rehnyay.*"

"Like Monaco's royal family," I said. He nodded solemnly. This comparison he would tolerate.

I amused myself by inventing an imaginary conversation between Easy Rider and Bonnie Prince Brigham Young:

"I say! That's a ripping motorcycle you have there!"

"Yep, that's my hawg!"

"Do you suppose I might try it sometime?"

"Get yer namby-pampy ass away from my Harley!"

"Might I interest you in the *Book of Mormon*?"

There was a commotion in the wings. The one word discernable in the cacophony was "bees!"

"What on earth?" Brigham, I mean Hugh, exclaimed.

"She must be talkin' about the bees," the old hippy drawled. "Reade just installed an apiary hereabouts. I guess she don't like 'em." He introduced himself as Bob Alter, the local slated to play Spalanzani, the mad inventor who tries to pass the doll Olympia off as his daughter. Funny to hear that distinctive opera-tenor resonance combined with a Texas twang.

"Or ELSE!" I heard Ulrika say before emerging from the wings. The languid, sultry siren had been transformed into a raging harpy. "It's those damn bees or me!" Peter, the shy college-kid stage manager, cowered before her, a blithering bundle of nerves. Poor Peter! With this menagerie, the company should have hired Nurse Ratchet from *One Flew over the Cuckoo's Nest* as stage manager. Not this poor innocent whose main social contacts to date had been the digitalized denizens of SimCity.

"She must be allergic," Hugh remarked.

27.

Picture an aging Italian screen star—Marcello Mastroianni at 65—over six feet tall, silver mane slicked back, complexion bronzed, aristocratic features slightly sunken like a jack-o'-lantern's the day after Halloween. That was Hubert Silvertone, the chairman of the company's board of directors and elusive host of the previous evening's party.

Hubert stood next to the piano, cleared his throat, and made a downward sweeping motion that caused the volume to lower. "Good afternoon, ladies and gentlemen," he began. "Thank you all for joining us in our ongoing quest to put Ville d'Aurore Opera on the International map. As you know, this production started off on a tragic note when we lost our original Nicklausse to an automobile accident. Fortunately Deborah de Lille was available on short notice to step up to the plate." A derisive snort or two penetrated the scattered applause, enthusiastically led by Sven and my two friendly neighbors. I smiled weakly.

"First, I think you have all met our new stage manager, Peter Haas." Peter gave a tense nod. "Peter and Ulrika Mannschliesser have been discussing Ulrika's concern over the newly established apiary in Bragelonne Park," Hubert continued. "I will pursue this matter with Reade Philips. In the meantime, if you are allergic to bees, please use the rear entrance." Sven caught my eye and waggled his eyebrows lasciviously. Honestly, the man was a case of arrested development.

Hubert paused. For a panicked instant I thought he had sensed that Sven was making fun of him. But no, he was whispering to Peter and pointing to an empty seat in our row. "We have a missing cast member," he said.

After consulting his list, Peter finally said, "It appears to be Wilhelmina Wooley." Someone stifled a laugh. Well it *was* a silly name.

Hubert cast a sharp look among the assembly. Although the source of the inappropriate laughter escaped Hubert's notice, it hadn't escaped mine. The man seated to the left of Bob Alter reeked of malted beverage. He didn't look like a jolly afternoon tippler. In his dark suit and skinny black tie, he might have been a hip funeral director. Noticing my interest and taking advantage of the temporary confusion, the man reached in front of Bob to give my hand a hearty shake.

"I'm Jim Sod," he whispered, wafting forth another gust of beer breath. "Nice to see a fresh face in this vaudeville show!" I sneaked a peek at the cast list. "Crespel," he said. "See, there … Jim Sod. That's me." He tapped the list, then his chest. Crespel was Antonia's father.

Hubert Silvertone reclaimed the floor. "Willy, uh, Mrs. Wooley, is the Voice of the Mother," he explained. "Fortunately her services are not required immediately. Just a reminder ... we will not meet again on this stage until the preliminary run-through, a week from tomorrow. Rehearsals will take place in the third floor ballroom." He paused, as if waiting to be challenged, then added, "Many of you are familiar with this facility. Please reassure your new colleagues that, despite the flyers in the lobby, the theater is not haunted." He paused to chuckle at what he clearly considered a joke. "And now, on with the show!"

"If any theater has a ghost," Hugh whispered, "it's this one!"

A rapid-fire exchange between Hubert and Peter sent the poor boy flying into the wings, clutching his cell phone.

Like Nicklausse, the Voice of the Mother is a small though significant role. In Act II, Dr. Miracle, another of those pesky Satan-worshipers, shows up unbidden to treat Antonia's illness. The evil doctor conjures up a nasty spirit to masquerade as the ghost of Antonia's mother, a singer who also died of a heart condition. The false spirit urges Antonia to sing, thus sealing her fate.

When my own mother, Lillian de Lille, becomes a ghost, would she urge me on to my own destruction? It was conceivable. She would do it with the best intentions.

28.

In the falderal over the bees and the unexplained absence of Willy Wooley, I had missed the entrance of the Evil Baritone. I soon spotted him, seated between Camille, the aging Snow White/courtesan Giulietta, and Sven, the larger-than-life tenor. Sven caught my eye and signed a thumbs-up. While ostensibly smiling in response, I was really observing Angelo Capellinerino.

I don't know what I had been expecting, other than the embodiment of evil. In that respect Angelo was a major disappointment. Once upon a time he might have been the Tom Jones of Pisa. Tom Jones was much older but far trimmer. This guy was in his mid-fifties. He wore a silk scarf and a fitted sports jacket that fit snugly over generous love-handles visible on either side of the folding chair. His black hair had the freshly combed, overly-dense look of an expensive toupee. His features appeared strong and regular in profile, aside from a pouch under his cleft chin. As if sensing my scrutiny, the baritone craned his neck and met my gaze with wide, puppy-dog eyes. I pretended to be staring abstractedly, only by chance in his direction.

Juergen Kopfschlager greeted us next. "Wilkommen and benvenuto," he began pretentiously, but then, we were a highfalutin' group. His English grammar was flawless, but his accent was so thick I wondered if he were purposely exaggerating it to add to the fear factor. I had never heard him speak until now, so who knew? "I trust we will all have an excellent time today, in that we are—so many of us—old friends. So, all of you, *my friends*, relax and sing your little hearts out. And, if you don't have hearts," (here he paused for the expected, though uncomfortable, laughter) "we hope you will apply all your other organs. I, in particular, hope to hear evidence of fully engaged brains and lungs."

I wondered whether Ulrika and Camille detected the underlying menace in Juergen's pep talk. But then, they didn't realize they had been overheard, at least not by Juergen.

And so we began. The singers in the prologue, including me, moved to the front, where we stood with our scores propped open on music stands to record the conductor's suggestions. The scene takes place in a bar, where the poet Hoffmann is holding court with a group of students while he waits for his latest girlfriend, an opera singer named Stella, to finish the night's engagement. (Even nineteenth-century straight men in operas resist going to the opera!) The students beg Hoffmann to regale them with his stories of past romantic adventures, while the evil bass-baritone Lindorf conspires to steal Stella.

"Why not stand next to me?" Sven suggested. I shrugged helplessly, implying, *Sorry, no room!* I was intimidated enough without his stentorian voice blasting full force in my ear. Nevertheless I soon found myself wedged between him and the Valkyrian living-doll Lisette, who moved aside with unexpected grace. She even winked and smiled. As for Ulrika and Camille, you'd think I had just claimed the largest private dressing room.

Before I knew it, the prologue was over. That's what stage fright can do to you—make it almost impossible to remain present. You are physically present, and somehow your mouth and vocal cords do their thing, but your panicked consciousness is cowering in a corner, whining, *tell me when it's over!*

29.

The biggest surprise was Angelo, the bass-baritone pop singer. With those pipes, he could have been singing opera his entire career. And Sven lived up to his magnificent rep. He was polished, confident, and flawless. A future star in the making.

The best part about being a minor character that appears in every act is that the others don't much care what you do as long as you don't derail them. And if you do screw up, there's time to redeem yourself. In my case, it helped that the conductor's attention was elsewhere. Juergen had an unpleasant way of silencing singers mid-phrase to consult with the young man seated to his right. As the two whispered back and forth, Hugh identified the mystery sidekick as Ludovic Vogel—the répétiteur, or rehearsal pianist. No wonder he looked so grumpy, I thought. His only reason for being here was to listen to Juergen complain. Because, from their expressions, I didn't buy that they were discussing tempi or phrasing.

Ludovic was small, dark, and handsome, if you liked the brooding gypsy type. After Juergen announced one of his heart-stopping timeouts following my little aria—when Nicklausse tries to warn Hoffmann that his new love is suspiciously mechanized—I feared the worst. However, his only comment upon turning his attention back to me was, "Good." I decided, for once, not to work myself into a lather of paranoid regret. It was perhaps not my best effort, but there would be other chances to prove myself. Unless ... If I were wretched enough, would they give my part to Teresa? Hadn't Sven mentioned that she was my understudy, too?

Just as I was gearing up for a full-blown panic attack, Jim Sod poked me from behind. "Not bad!" he whispered. I vowed then and there to put the lovely gentleman in my will.

Juergen was eerily subdued during the Prologue and most of the first act—the one with Olympia the Doll and my arioso. But his calm was deceptive. Olympia the Doll's part consists of one bravura aria with a lot of rapidly sung, extremely high notes. Other than that, she sings nothing but scattered words and phrases. Lisette made it look easy, even eliciting laughter with her doll gestures.

Until she croaked on the ultimate high E.

30.

In a definitive signal for silence, Juergen whipped his baton through the air with such force that it hissed like a whip. Then, giving Lisette the gimlet eye, he goaded her on to another attempt.

Again, her voice cracked. She shrugged.

"Are you capable of singing this note?" he demanded, as if accusing her of lying on her résumé.

"Of course," she sniffed. "I'm still recovering from jet lag." Lisette was one tough cookie. If I had blown that high note, I'd have blurted out a slobbering stream of mea culpas. The incident provoked more fevered whispering between Juergen and Ludovic, the least pleasant team since Hitler and Goering.

Now, to my knowledge, Lisette had done nothing to rile the Maestro. Maybe there was some weird history between them, too? Because really, his reaction was uncalled for! If he was going to be so hard on her, I shuddered to think what he had in store for the two divas who had publically humiliated him that very morning.

It was Camille's turn. In Act II, Giulietta the courtesan tries to steal Hoffmann's soul. The act opens with Giulietta and Nicklausse's famous duet, the Barcarolle. Camille had sung only one phrase before Juergen rapped his baton loudly on his music stand. "Madame," he said, voice grave with disappointment. "You are under pitch." Ludovic nodded in agreement. Mystified by this patently false claim, I looked around to see how the others were reacting. Eyebrows raised and eyeballs rolled. Jim and Bob seemed to be sharing a secret joke. Hmm, were they a couple? Later I'd hear them referred to as Jim & Bob. Heckle & Jeckle, Laurel & Hardy, Jim & Bob. Not that I'm implying anything about those others. Jim & Bob were definitely an item.

We began again. When the chorus joined in, Juergen actually whistled like a traffic cop to stop them. "No, no!" he said, his baton flying from his hand. It landed harmlessly in the empty seats of the audience, where Peter ran to retrieve it. "You are still under pitch, *Madame*," Juergen accused. "AND you are allowing Mademoiselle de Lille to drown you out. Would you like me to ask Mademoiselle de Lille to lower the volume?" This was absurd. I was in the deep end of my voice, and there was no way I was drowning out the honking mezzo soprano of Camille Parquet. The faces around me concurred.

Astoundingly, Camille proved unflappable. Juergen's jabs and jibes pricked their target as harmlessly as Lilliputian arrows on Gulliver. She went on to phonate her way flawlessly through Giulietta's punishing tessitura, never faltering as the duet with Hoffmann flowed in to the septet and the finale. Juergen interrupted with more insults about her intonation, but they lacked conviction. Camille had won this round. If Juergen wanted revenge, he was going to have to search harder for Camille's kryptonite.

Lisette/Olympia had to be counting her blessings. By now that tempest in an E-pot was a distant memory.

It was time for the third diva to take her medicine. Act III opens with Antonia's plaintive aria, "Elle a fui, la tourterelle" (She has Flown, the Turtledove). Ulrika was not my favorite person. She had mocked me in front of God and Starbucks, captivated my Stewart Granger, and invoked a death-sentence on the benign, hard-working bees—already stressed to the limit by Colony Collapse Disorder. She had admitted to tattling on our conductor, who was surely no worse a masher than ex-President Clinton (only with less charisma). However, try as I might, I couldn't detect any flaws in her vocal technique or interpretation.

Maestro Kopfschlager nevertheless bore down on Ulrika like the Red Baron, savoring every sally.

"Fraülein Mannschliesser," he said, teeth bared. "Would you do us the favor of singing in tune? And while you're at it, I would appreciate it if you didn't mark." His implication, that she hadn't been singing full voice, was met with a collective gasp. Ulrika turned, if possible, a shade paler. Slowly, her cheeks began to redden, then her face and neck—a bit like a developing Polaroid.

The maestro smiled savagely, nodded at his henchman Ludovic, and raised his baton to continue. Ulrika sang through the aria again, remarkably well under the circumstances. However, unlike the unflappable Camille, she was rattled. Her pitch and volume suffered. Most of her high notes were sharp and hollow, which is what happens when all your muscles tense up at once. Her shoulders almost touched her ears.

The orchestra was silenced with such speed and vehemence that it left musical skid marks, a trail of false notes that sputtered on for several seconds. Juergen lifted long-suffering eyes to Heaven. "I trust you will do whatever it takes to prevent this disaster from reoccurring?" he said. Although she held her tongue, Ulrika had the mottled look of a grenade missing its pin. And to think that I alone understood the true reason for Juergen's vendetta!

Despite our conductor's shenanigans, I enjoyed listening to my new colleagues. Jim Sod's singing did not suffer from the pitcher of beer he had knocked back that morning at the pub (according to Lawrence). He sang the part of Antonia's father with strength and conviction. Formidable acting skill was required to demonstrate convincing paternal love for this polecat masquerading as a show-cat.

It was time for the famous trio that ends the act, and Wilhelmina Wooley's chair remained empty. In this number Dr. Miracle and the demon possessing the portrait of Antonia's mother egg Antonia on until the poor girl sings herself to death.

"Miss de Lille?" Jurgen called out, as if expecting to find me absent. I held my breath. And here I had concluded the better part of my ordeal was over!

31.

"Would you be willing," Juergen said, "just for today you understand, to sing the part of the Mother?" And I had assumed he was going to let me have it! Criticize me, I mean, not assign me another role.

"Of course," I said, trying to sound like a helpful, flexible colleague instead of an overly ambitious singer, eager and willing to benefit from the flakiness or misfortune of another.

"B-But," rose a plaintive wail. "I'm the general female understudy!" It was Teresa, squarely within her rights. Darn.

"Thank you, Teresa," Juergen said, with unwonted kindness. "If this were opening night, you would be my choice. But you are, technically, a soprano, and your voice doesn't have enough carrying power in the lower range to be heard over the others. Besides, Debbie's quality is more matronly."

So much for my pumped-up ego! Talk about a back-handed compliment.

Teresa didn't press her suit. This is how I ended up singing a trio with Ulrika and ex-pop singer Angelo, a thrill for a motherly, second-string type like me. I hoped I hadn't permanently pissed off Teresa. I already had enough female nemeses in this company.

As my star rose in the heavens, Ulrika's continued on its downward trajectory. She was subjected to further criticism of her intonation and lack of carrying power. "Even the mezzo is drowning you out!" Juergen complained. "Sopranos always carry over mezzos. Where is the ping in your sound that we have known and loved?" Somehow she contained her fury.

I was beginning to feel magical, like Wart when he first discovers his powers in *The Sword in the Stone*. Admittedly, under the circumstances, I could have sung like a heavy metal rock star in the final days of a six-month tour and not have deflected our Maestro from his campaign of terror against the divas.

Then, at last, it was over. Although I suspected that my performance had not been quite the slam-dunk I had been led to believe, I still allowed the praise to wash over me like the waters of Lourdes. Since no actual healing waters were at my disposal, I could have used an ibuprofen. My head felt as if Juergen had been striking it repeatedly with his baton, which in a sense he had.

Thank God I was only five minutes from my crash pad. If only a sunken Jacuzzi awaited me! Alas, I would find nothing there but a moldering, jerry-built, decrepit coffin of a shower.

Jim, Bob, Lawrence, and Hugh invited me to join them for dinner. Although they were the nicest of the lot, I had endured enough for one day—enough proving myself and enough watching my back.

"Debbie," a voice called out as I cleared the exit of the theater. It was Reade, my multi-millionaire dream boy.

32.

The real Stewart Granger (according to his ex-wife, actress Jean Simmons) had been no picnic to live with. Well, even if Reade proved more macho and egotistical than Stewart, I wasn't thinking about living with him at this moment, only spending a little quality time. His niceness quotient was of zero interest to my libido.

Because I hadn't considered the possibility of Reade acknowledging my existence, I was stopped in my tracks. You might say I had turned to stone, gold, or a pillar of salt, but this isn't a fairy tale, myth, or Bible story. If you think the day's triumphs should have bolstered my ego, don't underestimate the depth of my insecurity. "Well done!" Reade remarked, clapping his hands. All that was missing was a hearty slap on the back. I was nothing but a hardworking sheepdog, singled out for a pat on the head by Farmer Reade.

"Thank you," said I, humble and lovable Shoeshine Boy (Underdog's alter ego, if you never watched Saturday morning cartoons). After an awkward pause longer than some waltzes, I turned to walk away.

"Uh," he persisted, "Would you care to—"

"Reade!" a voice trilled behind him. Camille. My fingers involuntarily curled and clenched into fists. Oh, for a chance to constrict that muscular throat! "Are we on for that drink you mentioned?"

"You told me you never drink on the evenings before you sing," Reade said.

"I don't have to sing tomorrow, do I?" she said brightly. "They're blocking the Prologue. Debbie does, doesn't she?" She might have been referring to the janitor.

"All right," Reade said. Did I imagine the disappointment in his voice? "Thanks," he said again to me. "You were great today."

"Yes, wasn't she?" Camille had developed a sudden case of

lockjaw.

They moseyed on, but I wasn't out of the deep dark woods yet. The next voice to invoke my name was Juergen's. I hesitated again. Smile frozen, eyes blank, I was the closest human equivalent to a happy face symbol.

Juergen smiled too, a toothy display better suited to a Doberman pinscher. "Peter spoke with Mrs. Wooley just now," he said. "Wilhelmina has gone home to Kansas. A family emergency. Would you be interested in performing the Voice of the Mother?"

33.

On my way back to my hovel, I wasted no time in phoning Frankie.

"Debbieeeee!" he responded. Dear Frankie. When he sang out my name, I felt like the most special person on earth. I suspected all his friends and clients felt that way. "Wassup, girl? How was the run-through? Did they run you through?"

"Not at all!" I crowed, infinitely grateful for this one-man fan club. In fact, your commission just went up."

"Naw … seriously? Don't tell me. Giulietta was crushed by a meteor, and you graciously stepped in."

"Uh … I don't really know what happened to her, but Wilhelmina Wooley, the Voice of the Mother, went home. So you are looking at—well, listening to, actually—the Voice of the Mother!"

"Yay!" he said. "You see, motherhood is still possible after all."

"Especially the kind where I'm actually a demon ghost."

"Aren't most mothers, when you get right down to it?"

"Mine isn't. But she's been doing a pretty good impression of one lately. She keeps doing tarot card readings for me that warn of death and destruction. It's getting so I dread checking my e-mail."

"Kind of like Carmen. You know, " 'Toujours la mort!' " It came out more like "two-jewer-la-morter," but I knew what he was saying. Just before Carmen's jilted lover stabs her through the heart, Carmen (who is a gypsy) does a card reading that warns of nothing but death.

"Hasn't your mom cried uncle before?"

"Cried wolf? Actually, no. That's what scares me."

"So, ignore her e-mails. Does your place have a wireless network?"

"Are you kidding?! The Pine-sol Inn?"

"Does that mean it smells clean?" he said.

"No," I said. "It means it smells like disinfectant. At least that's the top note. There are middle and base notes of mold and stale cigarette smoke."

Frankie groaned. "I know, sweetie. I am working on that, I promise. So, where do you get Internet?"

"Starbucks, so far. I may have to find a new place." It was then that the floodgates opened, and I poured forth my tale of woe, starring Ulrika and Camille.

When I had finished, Frankie whistled loudly enough that I had to hold the phone at arm's length. By now I was sitting on a bench by the lake watching the birds. I dreaded going home. After the whistle faded, Frankie was silent. "Frankie?" I said, worried. Only an aneurysm could account for this sudden silence.

"Still here," he said, clearing using the speaker phone. "I'm Googling." Click, click, click. "There! I'm reading about your two new buddies. They're both managed by the same fancy-schmancy agent, Harold Worthington from Columbia Artists, and they both have got credits out the wazoo. Ulrika did two seasons with Berlin Opera then moved on to the Metropolitan Opera's Young Artists Program. Camille was an apprentice at Houston and Santa Gay, I mean, Fe. They come by their bitchiness honestly."

"Wow," I said, deflated. "I'm glad I didn't know any of that going in."

"Reade can afford the best," Frankie said. "They're both veterans of the Ville d'Aurore Opera. That last production wasn't exactly smooth sailing, I hear. However, it was mostly a critical success. I guess Reade thought, *why spoil a winning formula?* Unless he runs the company ostrich style, he must have a clue about what goes on when the music stops."

"They take a chair away," I said, "and everyone throws their butts around so they won't be the only one left standing."

"Huh? Oh yeah, Musical Chairs. They still play that? I always thought it was a good way to teach kids to be mean."

"I wish I hadn't overheard them at Starbucks," I moaned.

"Well, it looks like you're going to have to lay it on the law," he said.

I had to think about that one for a minute. Had he meant, lay it on the line or lay down the law? "Do you mean I have to confront them?" I asked.

"Yeah. If they keep buggin' you. Why not? Show 'em who's hoss."

"Boss?"

"No, hoss, as in badass. You need to get with the pogrom, sweetie." It was fairly obvious that Frankie meant program, not pogrom—as in riots targeting the Jews—so I didn't bother to correct him. On the other hand, maybe he really had meant pogrom. Or had I only heard pogrom because I sensed really bad things were about to happen?

34.

You'd think that the discovery of rats congregating in her hole-in-the-wall would motivate the mouse to seek shelter elsewhere. But no. The next morning, caffeine-addict that I am, I scurried back into Starbucks.

It looked as if I was going to have my chance to follow Frankie's advice and show 'em who's hoss. There sat Ulrika, in the company of Lisette this time. From the look she gave me, I was in league with Osama bin Laden, or at the very least, Michael Bolton (who put out a very bad aria album several years back which, if there is any justice in the world, is out of print). "Well, hello there," she said, considering with cat-like satisfaction the silly rodent flailing a few paw's breadths away.

"Hello there," I parroted, my response laced with a soupcon of scorn. Moving right along, I placed my order and quickly provided exact change, willing the barista to sense the urgency of my plight.

"Did you know that Debbie is going to sing the Voice of the Mother?" Ulrika said to Lisette. "I wonder how she and Juergen bonded so quickly? Could it be that she shared some tidbit she had overheard?"

I snapped, morphing suddenly into *The Mouse that Roared* (a not-bad Peter Sellers' movie). "So you think I ratted on you?" I said in a deceptively low, hopefully menacing, voice. "Well, think again! It's a pity that you didn't check to see if the coast was clear before mouthing off. If you had, you'd have noticed Juergen sitting at the table behind me, agitated as an old percolator." Blessed Providence! My order came up at that precise moment. I strode out the door, proud of my courage, if not my metaphors. Had these women even seen a coffee percolator? Not unless they had a mom as cheap as mine! I hoped Ulrika didn't have homicidal tendencies, because the shade of red infusing her complexion when I fled the scene matched the color of those Devil Duckies they sell at Archie McPhee.

At the park, I found Lawrence squatting on my bench. "Do you mind if I join you?" I asked, trying not to sound territorial.

"Not at all," he said, flashing his best eight-by-ten-glossy smile. I hadn't fooled him. "Beautiful day," he added. He patted the spot next to him. "All warmed up and waiting for you." Good working weather for bees, apparently. Ulrika would have been in a panic. As I sat, he applauded. "Nice work yesterday. It must be tough proving your chops in this nest of vipers." Lawrence really was a snappy dresser. He had the casually cool urbanite look down. Fitted slacks, linen jacket, Italian loafers. Hair just so.

I laid out the contents of my paper bag. "Thanks!" I said. "That means a lot, coming from you. Did you hear that Mrs. Wooley jumped ship yesterday?"

"The question is, did she jump ship, or has our second swan taken a dive?" Don't think this hadn't occurred to me. After a moment of silence, he added, "Nice for you, disappointing for Teresa."

"I hope she isn't angry."

"She plays her cards close to the chest, so who really knows? But in my experience, Teresa's cool."

The caffeine had started to kick in. I sighed. "At least the men in this cast don't have axes to grind."

Lawrence had been basking in the sun, eyes closed. Now he opened one of them to peer at me. "You are such a tenderfoot," he said. "I don't mean that unkindly."

"What do you mean?"

"You've just scratched the surface."

35.

A bee landed on Lawrence's crisp linen jacket. He shook the fabric to gently dislodge it.

"Sven is nice," I said.

"Ha! Just don't rub him the wrong way. Or the right way, uninvited. It's tricky, no matter how you look at it."

"That sounds personal," I said. "He certainly lives up to his rep."

"Which is—?"

"Gorgeous Gorsson."

"Oh that. Been there, done *him*."

This gave me pause. So they *had* been involved. "Is that awkward?" I said.

"What do you think?" he said sarcastically. "With an ego like that? He has a short attention span, but he hates to lose a fan. He'll keep you on the line, if possible."

Too bad. However, it didn't have to affect my relationship with Sven. I had girlfriends in New York who were femmes-fatales I wouldn't wish on my own brother. (That's just an expression. It would do Roland good to meet his match. I'll revise that to say, not on my best male friend.) As a woman, and therefore not a potential victim, I saw no need to watch my step. "What about the other guys? Any other snakes in the grass?"

"Let me see … Not Hugh Rainier. He's a dish. Wouldn't be surprised if Sven goes for some of that. Don't know much about Reade Philips, except that he's a star-fucker. As for Ulrika and Camille, you don't want to cross them."

"Ooh, too late." I told him about my run-ins.

"Ulrika accused you of using sex to get ahead?" he said when I finished. "There aren't many avenues *she* hasn't explored. Besides, as the saying goes, you can only sleep your way to the middle." He spread his arms to encompass our little universe. "Voilà!"

"I can see why the women should watch their backs, but you're implying that our leading ladies are dangerous to everyone."

"I didn't say I was afraid, although I watch my step in their presence. I believe Sven's efforts to break his contract were mostly on account of them. He likes Reade and Ville d'Aurore."

"Was there a particular incident you know of?"

He folded his arms behind his neck and screwed up his face in concentration. "This is a small world. I've dealt with those two Praying Mantises before, in the inaugural production of Ville d'Aurore Opera, *Carmen*. Sven was Don Jose and Camille was Carmen. Lisette was the original Micaela, but she lost her voice and had to bow out, so Ulrika was Micaela. Angelo was Escamillo. The rest of us were Carmen's sidekicks, the gypsies from the Quintet. I was Le Remendando, Teresa was Frasquita, and Juanita (the former Nicklausse) was Mercedes. Jim Sod played Zuniga.

Juergen conducted. He's possibly the only heterosexual colleague Camille has ever rejected as a sex partner. Nothing to be gained by sleeping with him. He has too much artistic genius and not enough bootlicker in him to make it in this business." He threw back his head and laughed—not a joyous sound. "That's when Camille really burned her bridges with Juergen. Another conductor had originally been booked for this production. It must have been a rude surprise for her to find him once again presiding over us all like Richard the Lionheart reclaiming his throne from Bad Prince John.

"I have no objection to Juergen, mind you," he went on. "He is super easy to follow and whips the orchestra into shape, kicking and screaming all the way."

"So, what about Camille and Sven?"

"She fell for him, hard. Not surprising. His appeal is universal. All you have to do is hear him sing. Then you see him and well ... you'd have to be a panda not to rise to the occasion."

"So what? He's gay, isn't he?"

Lawrence made an impatient gesture. "He's a narcissist. If he's flattered by the attention, he responds. Men, women ... sheep, for all I know. Rumor has it he screwed Camille at least once. Ulrika, too, maybe both together. All I know is, each seems to have been blown away by the experience."

"He told you that?"

"He didn't tell me anything. Only, they're obviously obsessed with him. Enough to scheme for an encore."

"Huh?"

"One, or both, has something on him. I'd bet my eyeteeth. Well, not those. No career without them. I'd bet my molars." His attention shifted. "Hey. Isn't that Reade Phillips?"

36.

Reade approached, casually debonair in jeans and a plain black T-shirt. A star-fucker, Lawrence had called him. That counted me out.

"Enjoying the park?" he asked, baring a flawless smile that was worth whatever sum he must have spent on it.

"Sure," I said, "who can resist a miniature Jardin du Luxembourg?"

"You noticed," he said, taken aback.

"I'm more Daisy Miller than Daisy Mae," I said, instantly regretting my cheekiness. I had to learn to put a lid on that stupid loud-shy thing.

"Daisy who?" Lawrence said with a grimace.

"Daisy Miller was a Henry James character—a nouveau-riche American girl in Paris—and Daisy Mae was a resident of Dogpatch. Is that what you meant?" he said, disarmingly blasé. "So you've been to Paris?"

"Sure …" I cut myself off. No need to explain about the high school field trip.

He knelt down suddenly, disarmingly close. With dread, I realized he was focusing on my chin. "Maybe you should give the bike a rest until the opera's over," he said.

Instinctively I covered the spot, now blue-black like a symptom of the bubonic plague. "I'm not a klutz," I protested. "I can assure you that that is the first time I've fallen. I ride constantly." I spread my arms. "Everywhere. All over Seattle."

"Okay, okay," he said, raising his palms in surrender. "I get it. You're preparing to join the U.S. Women's Cycling Team in your spare time. Just be careful."

"Uh, Reade," Lawrence said, I think to get me off the hook. "Are you going to banish the bees?" Reade had his back to the sun, which made both Lawrence and me shield our eyes as we talked. I suppressed a giggle. Reade was the Sun King! Maybe that's why he had tried to copy the Jardin du Luxembourg. Had Louis XIV been the king who had built the palace and gardens—the original ones in Paris?

"I might relocate the bees for the run of the opera, if my attorney advises it. It's not as if these are Africanized bees. Unless you go out of your way to provoke them, they'll leave you be."

"Leave you bee ... Good one," Lawrence said, applauding.

Reade looked temporarily flummoxed. "Oh," he finally said. "Sorry. That was … unintentional. Don't you two have a rehearsal?"

Lawrence was checking the time on his cell. I said, "One more thing before we go. Do you know if Louis XIV was the one to oversee the creation of the Jardin du Luxembourg?"

"Louis XIII," Reade said, waiting for the punch line. I suppose it was an odd question. I could hardly explain that gazing at him blazing in the sun had brought to mind one of the grandest monarchs in French history.

"Well then," said Lawrence, slapping his thighs. "We should be easin' on down the road."

"I'll see you around," Reade said. Saluting us, he turned tail and strode in the direction of the theater.

Lawrence returned the salute with mocking accuracy, but not until Reade had left the scene. Watching the retreating form with naked appreciation, he said, "Reade is kind of a tight-ass in all senses of the word. But he sure is cute. And rich!" He gave me a brotherly nudge. "That Cupid's arrow was for you, baby."

I shook my head. "I think I would know if he was flirting with me," I said. "That wasn't flirting. That was proprietary disapproval. Besides, you said he was a star fucker. I am not now, nor am ever likely to be, a star. Besides, last night he went out with Camille."

Lawrence blew a hearty raspberry. "Camille. That ball-buster! I repeat, *beware*. And while you're at it, give Juergen and Corabelle a wide berth. Fortunately we all get a break from Juergen. He's left town until Corabelle finishes the blocking."

That was good news! "Are you telling me Corabelle is hard to work with?"

"No, she's a brick. And a fabulous director."

"Why worry, then?"

"She's a temptress, honey." He winked. "Hard to resist."

"No harder for me than for you," I said. "I have my areas of insecurity, but sexual orientation isn't one of them."

"We will see, my Doubting Thomasina," he said.

37.

For the blocking rehearsals we ascended to the ballroom, a grand old hall on the top floor of the opera house with stenciled walls and Venetian glass chandeliers. The festivities began at 1:00 p.m. with a large cocktail of Corabelle—a potent concoction, cocky though cockless. I could see Lawrence's point about her. She could have passed as the newest pop sensation. Justin Timberlake, not Britney Spears. And yet she was close to me in age. Boyish hair and girlish coloring, no makeup required. Full pink lips, suggestive eyes, killer body. Not a whiff of self doubt.

The first order of the day was an overview of Corabelle's directorial concept, a phrase that strikes fear and loathing in the hearts of many an opera singer and patron. Most of us wished the director would stick to the appropriate period. Wasn't the late nineteenth century kinky enough? During that time bourgeois society, caught in a vise of respectability, indulged liberally in drugs, sex, and profiteroles. But no, this was going to be another modern dress production.

In keeping with her macho image, Corabelle straddled a chair and illustrated her words with gestures large enough to read on the main stage. "My *Tales of Hoffmann* begins in the present," she explained. "The Hoffmann of the Prologue is in his early 60s, well-established as a literary celebrity and ladies' man, yet painfully aware that his legendary prowess requires a pharmaceutical boost. Think Jack Nicholson, only slimmer and with more hair. No, can that. Think Sean Connery in *The Hunt for Red October.*

"Act I takes place in the 80s. Olympia is Madonna in her earliest incarnation, the Boy Toy. After all, what was Madonna in the beginning but a blow-up doll in the flesh? The setting is a New York disco, and Spalanzani is a dead ringer for Andy Warhol. The party guests will have big hair and wear spandex and suspenders. You get my drift. Hoffmann is 32.

"Act II: the 90s. Corporate greed in the fin de siècle. Hoffmann is 42. Think *Eyes Wide Shut*. Lots of Italian Carnevale masks and—"

"I am not performing naked!" Camille burst in. "It's not in my contract." Everyone laughed, but she was deathly serious. There was a lot of murmuring. Rebellion was in the air.

"Did I say naked?" Corabelle said, hands on hips. "Believe me, Camille. No one wants to see you naked." She paused, clearly regretting her choice of words, as a few twitters escaped the chorus. "Uh … of course we would all like to see you naked," she back-pedaled. "However, life is full of disappointments. In this role you will be wearing the most beautiful lingerie of your life."

"We had better be talking negligees," Camille said. "Floor-length negligees."

"In your case, naturally," Corabelle replied. "With your understudy, however, all bets are off." I stole a look at Teresa, who could indeed carry off any state of undress, as long as her religion allowed it. Was there the tiniest hint of smugness in the girl's carefully blank expression?

38.

"Can I continue?" our director asked. "Okay, then! Schlemil has Bill Gates' bad hair, glasses, and rumpled chinos." She scanned the crowd until she found Hugh. "Sorry, Babe! This is going to be a stretch for you.

"Pittichinaccio ... Where are you, Lawrence?" Lawrence raised his hand tentatively, not happy to be called on. "Making you grotesque will be a challenge. Angelo … The villainous Dappertutto will resemble an aging Tony Bennett, including the monkey suit." Angelo's crumpled child's face drooped some more. Tact was not Corabelle's strong suit.

"Act III," she went on. "Ten years later. AIDS, of course. Antonia's mother died fifteen years earlier, infected in the 80s by her gay husband Crespel, who is HIV positive without having contracted full-blown AIDS himself. Antonia's mother passed it on to her daughter at birth, along with the fabulous voice. Antonia dresses Goth (picture Kate Beckinsale in the Underworld series), because she's obsessed with death. Hoffmann is 52."

"Kate Beckinsale's character was a vampire, not a Goth," Ulrika protested.

"Don't get technical on me. She dresses in head-to-toe black leather. You'll look great."

By now, most of the group had that slumping, slack-jawed look of stunned defeat. Like me, they must have been hoping for a traditional production. "As for Nicklausse," Corabelle said, her benevolent gaze fixed on me, "You don't age, honey. Your clothing changes, but you're Hoffmann's muse, an immortal. At the end, Stella (you, Teresa) enters the bar. Her costume identifies her as a conglomerate of the three women. Olympia's bustier, Giulietta's wild red wig and stilettos, and Antonia's black leather pants."

In the opera world, Corabelle was being hailed as a female Peter Sellars. (The opera director. The deceased actor's name is spelled differently). So if anyone could carry this bizarre concept off, it was she. I hadn't worked with a lot of ace directors. Directors of community theater and small-time touring companies tend to fly by the seat of their pants. They hire actors with good stage instincts then pray for spur-of-the-moment inspiration. Most of the time, I basically directed myself. However, as any good litigation attorney can tell you, hand-picking your jury is instrumental to winning the case.

After a short break, the blocking began. Corabelle, true to her detailed vision, was precise and no-nonsense in her instructions. She didn't consult notes or make arbitrary changes once she had seen how the action played out. We broke for dinner at 4:00 p.m., commenced Round II at 6:00 p.m. and disbanded promptly at nine. The Met couldn't be more efficient.

With Corabelle at the helm, Ville d'Aurore, which, for me at least, had begun to resemble the oppressive Pottersville, once again acquired the magic glow of Bedford Falls. And although we knew that the evil Mr. Potter, a.k.a. Juergen, was bound to return and murder sleep with his baton, it was nice to have a breather. Ludovic, minus his master, was an irritable but harmless presence at his piano. Like ammonia and bleach, Juergen and he wreaked havoc only in combination.

As Hoffmann's sidekick, I never strayed far from Sven's side. Fortunately his personal hygiene was excellent. I can attest to the potency of his animal attraction. My head just cleared his armpit, and he kept rearranging me, as if to correct my faulty understanding of the blocking. If he had been heterosexual, I might have assumed he was looking for excuses to touch me. Maybe he saw me as a new toy, a Nicklausse Action Figure. After all, in our imaginary universe, I was a boy.

In the prologue, the bass-baritone (aging-heartthrob Angelo) plays the first of Hoffmann's nemeses, Councillor Lindorf. He convinces the servant Andres (Lawrence) to allow him to intercept Stella's note to Hoffmann, so that our hero won't know his lady has invited him up to her place after the opera. As I mentioned earlier, Hoffmann retires to the bar to wait out his girlfriend's performance. Once there, he drinks too much and thrills the students with stories of his fabulous past exploits.

Speaking of thrills and chills, with a voice like his, Sven could have been singing the fine print on our contracts and still left us panting for more. The actual words he sings make about as much sense. The aria concerns a grotesque dwarf named Kleinzach, whose bones go click-clack. Fortunately for the audience, Hoffmann is distracted, mid-aria, by thoughts of Stella and starts singing about her instead. He already knows that Lindorf is bad news but not that he is the devil's spawn.

Sven … What is the allure of egomaniacs like him? Does their power make them sexy or their sexiness make them powerful? If Reade had expressed any interest in me, I might have been immune to Sven's charms. Forget about Reade. He was either showing Camille the town or his etchings.

I had a sympathizer in Lawrence. Every time our eyes met, he would shake his head and wag a forefinger.

39.

You go, Angelo! No question as to his sexual orientation. By lunch, the baritone had assembled a small entourage of chorus girls with father complexes or plans to make him their stepladder to stardom. He was in hog heaven, despite one obvious rebuff.

"Hey," Sven said while Corabelle was working with the chorus. "Lawrence told me about your run-ins with Camille and Ulrika. I hope you're planning to stay out of their hair as much as possible."

"This town needs another coffee shop," I said.

"The Lodge has pretty good coffee," he said. "Come dine with us."

I frowned. "Too expensive."

"More than Starbuck's? I don't think so!"

"Sven, do you think Camille and Reade are involved?"

"Ha, ha, HA!" he boomed, earning a dirty look from Corabelle. "Don't listen to Lawrence! Give Reade some credit. He's smarter than that. Although it's a mystery why he would welcome those two back. I shudder to think how much worse it would be if Juanita were here, too. Either Reade's a slow learner, or he was, shall we say, strong-armed. I wouldn't put anything past Camille and Ulrika."

"You sound as if you empathize."

Sven's narrow-eyed look said, *What does she know?* Then he changed the subject. "What do you think of Corabelle?" he asked, leading me in an impromptu swing dance.

I let him twirl me twice before I replied. "Seems like a good director."

"That she is. Good at other things, too, I hear, and strangely compelling, to everyone." He waggled his eyebrows.

"Do I have to guess what you're implying, or are you going to spell it out for me?" I said, mesmerized by his dancing auburn brows, impressively tidy and free of strays.

"You're no fun," he pouted. "Let's put it this way. Camille and Ulrika have eclectic taste when it comes to playmates."

"Aren't they both married—to men?"

"Camille's on Hubby No. 3. What difference does that make? Out of sight, out of mind."

"Point taken. I can understand forgetting your spouse. Not your sexual orientation."

"Can't you now?"

"Hey!" Corabelle yelled. "A little professionalism, if you please. If I want dancing, I'll bring in a choreographer."

It took some fancy moves, but I avoided dancing cheek-to-cheek with Sven for the rest of the day. Two weeks of rehearsals to go. Surely he would settle down. If Sven had been my first charismatic leading man, I'd have been a goner. Short-lived and painful affairs with too many like him (less attractive and talented, it's true) had left me with a degree of immunity. Enough to conclude his type was too rich for my blood. Guys like Sven are always on the lookout for someone new to dazzle—Hugh, for instance, or one of the cuter chorus boys.

As for Corabelle, she'd stop trying to catch my eye once she realized I didn't swing—as Frankie might say—in her neck of the woods. There is truth in what Sven had implied that first night. Lesbians tend to gravitate toward trouser roles, just as most countertenors are gay men drawn to the art of singing falsetto. As the one probable lesbian among the leads, I was the most likely candidate for Corabelle's companion of the moment. If she chose a chorister for a playmate, she could end up being accused of sexual harassment or favoritism.

When Peter announced dinner break, I hung back to let the others leave first. I killed a minute or two leaning out the window and observing the courtyard below. A few of the Ponderosa Pines were tall enough to clear the roof. Flower beds teeming with a variety of blooms marked the joint of the ell of park benches at every corner of the square. Each bed was overseen by a naked statue of a Greek god or goddess (I thought I recognized Diana the Huntress, with her bow and arrow, and Mercury, with his winged hat). The rest was bordered with a variety of red and green-leaved deciduous trees pruned into torturous, abstract shapes. The grass at the center was crisscrossed with cobblestone paths. Several feet below the window, a long pole displayed an American flag fluttering in the breeze. Was Reade a Republican? Weren't most rich men? The ballroom being on the top floor, it was a long drop to the walkway. Forty feet at least. Enough to produce a wave of vertigo.

"That's how she died?" a soft southern voice offered.

40.

"Ouch!" I cried. In retracting my head too quickly, I had banged my cheek against the window sill. Great. Now I would have a bruise there, too, if not another contusion. "That's how who died?" I said, touching my cheek to test for signs of tenderness.

The soft voice belonged to Teresa. "Victoria Le Moine? You know, the White Lady. The ghost?" As the general female understudy, Teresa attended every rehearsal, so inconspicuous and silent she might have been a phantom herself.

"She threw herself out this very window after Gray Wolf jilted her." After I backed away from the window as a precaution against siren calls to destruction, Teresa stepped into my place.

"Ever see her?" I asked.

"I believe so, yes. I feel her pain during performances? She wishes she hadn't done it. She wants to be on stage again. That's why she yanks at our costumes. Now she understands that art is worth dyin' for. Not a man."

I shivered. "Sorry, I don't buy that." I was aware that lots of people thought otherwise, or movies like *The Red Shoes* wouldn't be so popular.

"Well ..." Teresa sighed. "That's how I see it right now. I want this career real bad."

"If you're as good as they say you are, you'll get it. You have time."

Another sigh, close to a groan. "I know that!" She leaned out the window. As I prepared to grab her skirt, she backed up and closed the window. "Bye!" she called out as she walked away. "Enjoy your dinner!"

After the encounter with Teresa, I finally had time to retrieve my bike, good as new. (If only my chin would heal as quickly!) I spent most of my break biking aimlessly around town, trying to burn off a little pent-up, misdirected sexual energy. Finally I stopped at a deli, ordered a sandwich, and wolfed it down in a few bites. No wonder I was losing weight. I wasn't taking the time to savor any meals other than breakfast, and I was constantly in motion, fueled by nerves and too much caffeine. At night my anxiety kept me skating on the surface of sleep, banned from still waters by a thick layer of icy fear. If I kept this up, I was going to get a virus. It would be just my luck to lose my voice, and with it, my big break. I popped a chewable Vitamin C. No way was I going to give Teresa a crack at my roles.

When the exhausting day came to a close, I staggered home to my shoddy refuge, where I blocked out the neurotic warbling of the chorus with earplugs. A detective novel waited for me on the bed stand, one of Lawrence Block's "burglar" series. Ultimate escapism. And golly, did I need to escape.

Alas. The Moving Finger had written other plans for me. Escape, not escapism, would be the order of the night.

41.

At midnight my heart was still beating like a metronome set to presto and my eyelids refused to turn leaden. For the third time, I rolled reluctantly out of bed to visit the bathroom. The deafening flush was trumped by a CRASH! So loud it had to be ... my window? What the hell was that smell?

A plume of smoke rose next to my bed. I stood, frozen, waiting for ... what? The Wicked Witch of the West to materialize? I started to cough. Acrid fumes, by God, all over the place. I snatched my bath towel, covered my nose and mouth, and groped for the doorknob. The smoke bored into my eyes, which streamed for mercy. No time for robes.

Once liberated, I did the hundred-yard dash down the street, naked, a towel pressed to my face. Not one of those luxury bath-towels, either. By the time the fire truck arrived, I was doubled over, hacking my vocal cords to shreds. A hospital gown would have preserved my modesty better than the hand towel I had grabbed. My eyes watered and stung as if cauterized. That was how Reade found me.

"Uh, hi," I rasped, between coughs. Goddamn it, the smoke had done a number on my voice.

A crowd was forming down the block. Unless one of them was hiding in the bushes, the choristers had all found time to make themselves decent before evacuating their motel rooms. Well, good for them! They were more level-headed, or at least less on edge and panic-prone, than I. Reade looked at the smoking building, then back at me. "There are no flames," he said.

"No," I said, "I was wondering about that."

"Wait here," he commanded.

"I thought I'd go for a cup of coffee," I said. "Can I get you something?" He stared at me. "Just kidding. There is probably a dress code. Besides, I don't think Starbucks stays open this late."

After pausing briefly to drape his leather jacket over my bare shoulders, Reade tore off in the direction of the smoking building. I took advantage of the alone time to rearrange my ensemble, zipping up the jacket and trying to fashion the towel into a garment that might serve as a fig leaf. Hmm, too much material for a loin cloth, but not enough for a skirt. I ended up ripping the fabric into three strips and tying them together. The primitive diaper-like garment resembled a sumo wrestler's mawashi, a style unlikely to catch on in opera circles.

When Reade finally returned, I was huddled against a tree, teeth chattering. It gets damn cold in Northern Idaho in the middle of the night in May, and his jacket could have used a lining. Men! They're always too hot.

"How are you?" he said.

"Cold," I croaked. The poor chorus kids! Tomorrow all they would be good for was "The Song of the Volga Boatmen." "I didn't see any flames," I said. "They must have put out that fire lickety-split."

"No fire," he said. "Nothing but smoke."

"Where there's smoke—"

"There are smoke bombs," Reade finished the sentence for me, not quite as expected.

42.

"Smoke bombs?!" I repeated.

"A prank. Only one of them landed in a room. Yours, as it happens. Three other bombs never made it past the sidewalk. All of them had notes attached: Enemies of Elitist Entertainment, EEE for short. Probably kids from the community college, mad that I wouldn't supply state-of-the-art sound equipment for their original rock musical. What do they want? I sank over $10,000 into that fiasco."

"Ten thousand dollars seems more than generous."

"I thought so. But as far as everyone in this community is concerned, I'm Mr. Bottomless Pockets."

"Let's see." To lighten the mood, I reached experimentally into the pocket of his leather jacket and drew out a package of condoms. I thrust it back in, cursing my need to be clever.

It was too dark to make out his expression, but when he spoke, it was as if my gaffe had never happened. Come to think of it, why should he be embarrassed? "Whenever they need anything," he said, "I'm the one they come to." Even condoms? I thought. He added, "That's the drag of having money."

"Yep, it's a drag," I agreed without conviction. My voice was deep and crackling. It would have been a good time to audition for *The Sopranos*, which, in case you missed it, was about the mafia, not a reality show about dueling divas. I rose, carefully, to my feet. "I hope you're not going to need your coat right away," I said.

"Keep it as long as you like," he said. "Hell, keep it, period."

I ran my fingers along the buttery leather. "If it were less humongous, I'd take you up on that offer."

He laughed. "It would fit most opera singers just fine."

"You hired a relatively svelte group."

"What can I say? I'm shallow. Dramatic verisimilitude is important to me."

"Yeah, and it's nice when singers look their parts."

"That's what I said."

"I know." Either he didn't respond well to being teased, or he didn't have much of a sense of humor. I suppose the situation wasn't all that amusing. I had narrowly escaped being smoked like a salmon, and who knew what the fallout would be for my voice? We stared into the thick haze hanging in the air for what felt like the length of an intermission.

He was trying hard not to dwell on my lower half. "Aren't you feeling a bit … naked?" he finally said.

"Yes, now that you mention it," I said. "But I'm not, you know. I've invented a towel thong. It's quite chic! Wait until *Vogue* hears about it! Now, can we please get out of here? This place is a good setting for a low-budget horror film."

"Yes," Reade said, "not for anything else, however. I'm going to check you into the Ville d'Aurore Lodge." With this, he took off his flannel shirt and handed it to me. It was extra large. Gratefully, I tied the arms around my waist and buttoned the last four buttons. Now I was the one trying not to stare. Reade's broad shoulders and chest were naked under his shirt. Busy as he was, he clearly set aside time to work out.

After my heart finished skipping beats, Reade's words finally sank in. The Ville d'Aurore Lodge! I thought. That meant a bathtub, even a Jacuzzi. But then what? "What about my stuff?"

"Don't worry. Someone on my staff will collect it. It will all need to be washed or dry-cleaned."

"I'm not crazy about the idea of people pawing through my things."

"It beats bringing that odor along into your hotel room. Come on. Let the valets take care of it. In the meantime, the hotel provides bathrobes."

I sighed happily, anticipating the caress of plush terrycloth. "What about the chorus? Are they okay?"

"Better than you, I imagine, although I don't think many of them will be singing full voice tomorrow."

"Will they be joining me at the Lodge?" I asked, feigning indifference.

He laughed. "I'll find another motel for them. It'll be an improvement over that dump. You won't be lonely at the Lodge."

"What do you mean?"

"The principals are staying there already."

43.

It was 2:00 a.m. by the time Reade deposited me in the lap of luxury. My lungs had an ominously saturated feeling and my teeth were chattering—a delayed reaction brought on by exposure to cold, shock, and Reade. His coat wasn't the most calming of garments, laden as it was with his pheromones.

Davy Jones (the wandering phantom of the sea, not the Monkee) would have been almost at home in my bathtub. It may not have been four fathoms deep, but it was the largest I'd had the privilege of using. I filled that porcelain monster as full as I dared and turned on the jets. As I blissfully sank into its swirling depths, I felt all the clenched muscles whose existence I normally ignored begin to loosen their grip. At around 3 in the morning I stumbled, semi-conscious, toward the bed, large enough to accommodate a Latter-Day-Saints love quadrangle, and drifted into a deep sleep.

When I awoke, I thought I had died and gone to Club Med. Sunlight was streaming in the bay window. Damn it, the clock read 11:00 a.m.! I told myself not to panic. Rehearsal didn't start until one in the afternoon. And what was I supposed to do, anyway, attend in a bathrobe? A message light blinked on the phone. I followed the directions to retrieve it. Reade, of course:

"Sleep as long as you like, Debbie," he said in an official tone devoid of any intimacy I might have imagined in the night. "I hope you're feeling better. When you're up, call me on extension three-four-nine. Your clean clothes will be delivered as soon as you give the front desk the go-ahead. Simply dial zero."

An hour later I was clad in fresh jeans and a T-shirt, eating brunch with Reade in the main restaurant overlooking the lake. Things weren't so bad. My lungs were congested, and I could have narrated the *Three Billy Goats Gruff* without disguising my voice, but I probably could have sung in a pinch. Not that it was advisable to sing with swollen cords. I reported this to Reade.

"Glad to hear it," he said. "No need to attend rehearsals today. Teresa is standing in for you and will take notes." My face must have given me away, because he added, "Don't worry. I doubt she has any designs on your part."

"Because it's so small?" I rasped.

"Because she's a nice kid, and Nicklausse doesn't show her off to best advantage. I've known her since she was ten. She's a good Christian girl."

"This may come as a shock, but there are many instances in history of devout people behaving badly."

"Amen!" he said, raising his water glass to me as I finished off my second latte. "I've taken the liberty of making an appointment for you with an ear-nose-and-throat doctor for 2:00 p.m. I don't want you risking permanent damage to your lungs or voice. Best to err on the side of safety."

"Thanks, Dr. Dan."

"*Dr. Dan, the Bandage Man.* A slim volume from my father's collection of Little Golden Books. I don't want you to think I'm a country yokel who doesn't understand your literary references."

"Since when is a software magnate a country yokel?" I savored another delectable morsel of, ironically, smoked salmon.

"Since when am I a software magnate?" he said indignantly, as if I had accused him of working for the IRS.

"I thought—"

"I won the lottery," he interrupted. "In actuality. Sorry to disenchant you. I'm surprised you didn't Google me. Everyone else does."

"I don't even Google myself."

"You should. It's very interesting."

44.

Did Reade mean that he had Googled me or that, in a general sense, Googling oneself was advisable? Fortunately he interpreted my silence correctly. I would have to work on my Poker face. "Of course I Googled you," he said. "Your agent was trying to convince me you could hold your own in my opera company. I had never heard of you, so I wasn't going to take his word for it. You have nothing to be ashamed of. The customers on Amazon.com are crazy about your CD. Four stars."

"I think that's Frankie assuming various noms de plume," I said.

"You're being modest. I didn't disagree with any of those reviews. The cover is a little ... daring."

"You mean tasteless. That's Frankie's doing, too. I loathe the cover art."

"I like it. It's a side of you I wouldn't have suspected."

"Do you remember my telling you that I'm more Daisy Miller than Daisy Mae? Well, I've got some Daisy Mae in me, too. I would roll in the hay a lot more often if I weren't allergic." Great, now I was implying that I was promiscuous. Nothing ever came out the way it was intended when I was with Reade. Still, he was smiling, an expression that didn't come easily to him.

I surveyed my plush surroundings, admiring the high ceilings draped with white lights, the rugged chandeliers composed of wooden antlers, and the billboard-sized reproductions of the Cloisters' unicorn tapestries. "How long can I stay here?" I asked.

"For the run of the opera."

My gasp of delight led directly to a coughing fit. When I had recovered, I asked, "How does that fit into the budget?"

He shrugged. "To begin with, I am pretty damn rich. If you Google me, which I fully expect you to do, you'll find that I invested my lottery winnings wisely. Also, I own this hotel. I'm embarrassed that my penny-pinching accountant stashed you in that depressing hole-in-the-wall along with the chorus, especially since Juanita's death left her room unoccupied. We're fully booked this time of year. So, without consulting me, the incompetent desk clerk gave the room away to someone on the waiting list. Needless to say, that kid is finding a new job for the summer. Mrs. Wooley's untimely departure gave me the chance to put things right. That's why you caught me being, uh, uncharacteristically impatient the afternoon you arrived."

"You knew who I was?"

"I recognized you from your headshot. Surprised like that, in the middle of chewing that kid out, I couldn't get my bearings in time to greet you properly. Please accept my apology."

"Of course," I said. "Actually, that explains a lot."

He paused, cleared his throat. "I have a question." This was followed by an awkward pause, then, "Another latte?"

I relaxed. "That's easy. I better not."

"That's not my question." He summoned the waitress and pointed to my empty mug. "Decaf this time," he told her. To me he said, "What I want to know is, how come you aren't in worse shape? That smoke bomb landed right next to your bed."

"I wasn't in bed."

"Where were you, then?"

"If you must know, I was in the bathroom."

"Did you switch the light on first?"

"You're not some kind of pervert, are you?"

He blew out his cheeks in exasperation. "Just answer the question."

"No. I installed my own personal nightlight in the bathroom. It's very cool, an illuminated representation of Van Gogh's *Starry Night*. Don't tell me ... you own the original."

"You're kind of cynical. Anyone ever tell you that?"

"My mother. All the time."

"I'm just trying to establish whether the person who threw that bomb believed you were in bed." I wasn't sure what he was getting at, but his implication, along with the ill-advised second latte, was giving me the jitters. "Because if you had been in bed," he continued, "you would have been toast."

45.

"I don't mean it would have killed you," Reade continued, "not unless you had been drugged, but it would have spelled the end of this particular singing engagement and maybe a few to come."

I let this sink in. There were no pending engagements, other than the usual Seattle small-potatoes gigs I managed to dig up, but I didn't care to reveal that fact. Anyway, he probably knew it already from all the Googling. "What are you implying?" I finally asked.

"I'm merely connecting dots. First Juanita, our Nicklausse, dies. Willy, Antonia's Mother, drops out, offering no satisfactory explanation. Now this. I don't buy that it is a random act of cultural hostility. The bomb landed too conveniently in your room. Any chance that it's personal?"

"I have no prior history with these people. So, no. Not unless you're wrong about Teresa. Who else would benefit? Who would be so hostile that he or she would risk everything to put a few chorus kids out of commission for the sole purpose of zapping a minor character like me?"

He tapped his fork absently on the table. "Among those chorus kids is also the second-string cast. Did you think Teresa is the only understudy? "

"Now that you mention it," I said, "where did you get a student chorus this time of year?"

"They're from the North Dakota Academy of Music. I arranged for the voice majors to be dismissed early so they could get practical experience in exchange for room and board."

"Never heard of it," I said.

"My niece is a flute performance major there. The school has attracted enough talent to give you hotshots a run for your money."

I looked around the room. "Are you talkin' to me?" I said in my best Bronx accent, jabbing my thumb in my chest like De Niro. "I don't see any hotshots here, especially with money."

He flashed that stingy little smile again, the one where he stretched his thin lips and crinkled his eyes. "You don't think I'm paying enough? Don't answer that. Anyhow, there's some weird shit going on."

"I should have listened to my mother." He looked prepared to roll his eyes. My shtick was already becoming predictable. "She reads tarot cards. Nothing but bad news, I'm afraid. Except—"

"What?"

He didn't need to hear the part about the handsome stranger. "Do you believe in that stuff?" I asked.

"If this keeps up, I might start."

"By the way," I said, avoiding his eyes. "If you get a chance, could you retrieve my Van Gogh nightlight?" I knew I was blushing. This was silly. I wasn't asking for my Teddy Bear!

He reached into his satchel, pulled out the nightlight, and handed it over. "Never underestimate me," he said.

46.

The doctor assured me that if I could keep quiet for a few days, I'd soon be "right as rain." He did prescribe a cortisone dose pack to help things along. "I know you singer types," the jolly ENT chuckled. "You don't want to take any chances!"

Yes, he knew us well, particularly what we wanted. Singers are notorious for abusing cortisone, because even a tiny spot of swelling can prevent your vocal cords from coming together properly. Sing on that spot before it heals, and it can become a nodule. Scrape off the "node" and you've got scar tissue. Scrape off the scar tissue and you've got more scar tissue. You get the idea.

One measly block beyond the clinic, I gave in to the urge to test my voice. A series of pitiful squeaks emerged. Have faith, I told myself. Do as he says and shut up! Then, to torture myself further, I went to rehearsal to languish on the sidelines like a wall-flower at a high school dance.

At 7:00 p.m. they had just begun a run-through of the prologue and the first part of Act I, including my aria. I'm sorry to report that Teresa was the total package—convincing actress, accomplished singer, and sensitive musician. And now I could see that Sven's antics weren't customized for my benefit. Teresa got the same treatment. Sven poked and prodded her with familiar schoolboy relentlessness. The girl wasn't having any, however, and once or twice slapped his fingers away with transparent annoyance. Sven's Nordic god appeal was lost on Teresa, who treated him like Dennis the Menace.

At the end of the run-through, everyone flocked to me for a firsthand report. Sven, Lawrence, and Bob Alter crowded to the forefront, while Angelo, Lisette, and Teresa hovered a few steps behind. "Enemies of Elitist Entertainment?" Sven thundered. "You have got to be kidding! Anti-opera terrorists? It's like poachers openly protesting the Wildlife Federation. Don't they know we're an endangered species? Our habitat keeps getting overtaken by rock festival producers and real estate developers."

Lawrence, the last to drift away, whispered, "Smells to high heaven, don't you think?"

"What? The smoke bombs?"

"Figuratively speaking, you imp. You know, that something like this should happen after your clashes with the Titanias. Camille and Ulrika. I'd bet my sweet bippy they were involved."

"Oh, come on," I said. "Even they wouldn't stoop so low. It's too dangerous for vocal health to be anywhere near smoke bombs, not to mention the risk of discovery."

"They could have arranged the attack."

"What, with the Ville d'Aurore mafia?"

"Then why, Miss Smarty Pants, would this group target the chorus? And you, of course. Why not the principals?"

I shrugged. "Beats me. I guess I was in the wrong place at the wrong time."

Lawrence snorted in disgust. "If they *are* anti-opera terrorists, I hope they got the resentment out of their systems. Rock superstars make millions. In our elitist little corner, unless you're one of The Three Tenors, half-a-million is shooting the moon. Sixty thousand a year net income—after you've written off the cost of voice teachers, coaches, sheet music, recordings, and publicity—is a fabulous career. Unless you're Sven. Then, someday, you might make as much as a third-rate attorney." He looked at his watch. "Ooh, it's late! Gotta run." He kissed his fingertips and danced away. Such a buoyant exit had to mean a rendezvous with Hugh.

"Hey girl!" Lisette called out. I looked over my shoulder to see whom she might be addressing. We had hardly exchanged two words, so I was instantly on guard. "Sorry to hear about your ordeal," she said. "Come on, I'll walk you back to the hotel. We'll take a detour through the park. I don't know about you, but it takes more than a few bees to scare me! Besides, they're all in their little bee bunks by now." She picked up a flyer and rattled it as we cleared the lobby. "Have you read about our White Lady?"

"Yes. Lawrence says there's nothing to it." Silence stretched between us as we approached the pond. One of the automated streetlights chose that precise moment to click on, startling me.

Lisette laughed. "I can see you're not convinced. Don't take Lawrence's word for it. No self-respecting ghost would bother with a dyed-in-the-wool cynic like him. Personally, I can't write her off out of hand. When we were rehearsing *Carmen*, I got spooked more than once."

"Lawrence said you lost your voice." I cleared my own throat, wishing the healing process would speed up. "That must have been a tough break for you."

"I had to bow out during rehearsals," she said. "No biggie. That goody-two-shoes Micaela is hardly my dream part. Que sera, sera."

It was hard to believe Lisette could be so blasé, but, unlike me, she was probably booked ahead for the next five years. What was one missed opportunity? After all, here she was again, in a much juicier role. "Why didn't Ulrika protest the bees during *Carmen*?" I asked.

"The hives are newly established. How was Reade to know one of his singers would be allergic?"

"So, what was your experience with the White Lady?"

"Just a feeling, I suppose. Icy bursts of air in stuffy rooms, props gone missing. Several of us felt tugging at our costumes while we waited for our entrances."

We were standing at the door of my room, so I invited her in. "Another time," she said. "I need to make a phone call, and you need to rest your voice."

47.

On my bed stand I found an extravagant bouquet of red roses with a typeset note reading *Get Well Soon*. At least Reade had bothered to sign it. With leading ladies to woo and hotels and theater lobbies to decorate, he had to purchase flower arrangements by the truckload. Or was he afraid of being sued?

I checked the progress of my contusion. It was finally healing nicely. Not gone, but faded enough that it no longer called attention to itself. I hoped the next disaster would at least wait until my voice had recovered. Next disaster? What was this, the Seven Plagues of the Bible's Revelations? I had endured the painful sore and the sea of smoke, which meant that next I would be dealing with bloody streams and springs.

I was in for another restless night. I had drunk so much water and herb tea that I had to pee every few hours. Each time I woke, I tested my voice. Considering how phlegm accumulates while you're sleeping, this was more likely to cause needless panic than provide reassurance.

The next day, Saturday, was a continuation of Act I blocking. Once again Teresa sang the hell out of my little aria. Damn, was I edgy! I blamed the cortisone the doctor had prescribed for inflammation.

"She's not bad, don't you think?" Sven remarked during a break.

"Fabulous," I snarled.

He gave my arm an ostensibly comforting squeeze. What was he up to? "Aw, come on!" he said. "Teresa doesn't have your *je ne sais quoi*. And her voice is the wrong timbre. She was meant to be warbling above the staff along with the birdies. Nothing earthly about her."

"Except her ambition."

Sven put a dollar in the vending machine and retrieved a bottle of water. "What? I must be missing something."

"Think about it," I said. "If one of the three divas doesn't drop out, what hope does Teresa have of singing? I might be her best bet."

"Why not target Lisette, Ulrika, or Camille?" He gestured broadly in their direction. Fortunately no one was paying us any heed.

"They were all tucked away in the Lodge. My place was an

easier target." I knew I was being unreasonable, but I couldn't help myself. I was too jealous.

"If Teresa had wanted to guarantee your absence, she could do better than smoke bombs. Why not real ones?"

"She's not a complete monster."

"She's not a monster at all. Bet you anything."

"Bet your life? What about my life?"

He crossed himself dramatically and gave my cheek a playful pat. "I'm not that dumb!" Just as I was starting to heed the voice of reason, he added, "Why tempt fate when fate is so obviously champing at the bit?"

48.

The next morning I managed to warble a few scales that passed muster, although my voice remained thin. This meant another two days minimum of watching Teresa show me how it's done. I was in a horrid mood. To give my spirits a lift, I put on a pleated skirt, feminine white blouse, and low-heeled Mary Jane style shoes. No need to dress like a man today. Reade had encouraged me to walk through the blocking while Teresa sang, but I told him I'd rather watch and take notes. I couldn't very well change my mind now. Today I'd inform Teresa that tomorrow I would resume my rightful place in the blocking. Everyone was marking, anyway.

Steeped in self-pity, I ignored the glaring divas at Starbucks, ordered takeout, and headed for the haven of my favorite park bench.

Lawrence had gotten there first. I was veering off to the right to search for unoccupied territory, when he summoned me over. I couldn't very well snub him, so I reluctantly complied.

He whistled. "Why if it isn't Pollyanna herself!" he said. "Nice knee."

I sat beside him and ran my fingers over the solid, quarter-sized scab. "It's like being ten again," I said. "I was always skinning my knees."

He gave my face a frank appraisal before saying, "At least your 'contusion' is almost a bad memory. You must be a fast healer."

"I wish my vocal cords would hurry up and follow suit. I'm starting to understand how the Little Mermaid felt."

"Don't worry," he said, sprawling comfortably in the warmth of the sun. "The prince knows how you sound already."

The more he sprawled, the straighter I sat. "Prince, schmince," I said primly. "What kind of an idiot trades her voice for legs, anyway?"

"She also got a soul."

"I still think it was a bad deal."

"You're in quite a mood today."

I slumped. "Sorry. So, distract me. What's happening outside my world of woe?"

"I think Ulrika's has set her sights on Hubert Silvertone," he said. "I saw them talking outside the Boulevard Bistro. He was kind of leaning in, like so." He leaned in and gave me a hilariously lecherous look. I couldn't help but laugh.

"Oh good, you're starting to thaw," he said.

"Are you serious?" I said.

"Yep," he said. "And she wasn't pulling away."

"Hmm, isn't it a tricky business to cavort with the married chairman of the board?"

"Well, if you think about it," Lawrence said, sinking back into a comfortable reclining position with both arms stretched along the back of the bench, "there is this elaborate pecking order in opera companies, see? Choristers, lowliest of the low. Rarely do they get to be understudies or take on bit parts, as they can in a company of this size. So they are pretty much stuck with each other.

"Next come the comprimario roles, several rungs above the covetous chorus and just insecure enough not to want to be tainted by association with their underlings. That's us, of course. Like choristers, we spend a lot of time discussing the failings of the leads and speculating about their bed-partners, often erroneously, but in truth, panting for an invitation to be included in their exalted ranks.

"The principals, from their own prior experience slumming in the lower echelons, know the score and so aren't particularly eager to wriggle around in the same field as these snakes in the grass. They tend to keep to themselves, and, when loneliness strikes, hook up with their co-stars or find a non-singer associated with the company, such as Hubert Silvertone. Depending on the degree of their insecurity, they gravitate toward whomever threatens them most or least, or simply those they tolerate best. The über-confident, like Sven, hang out with whoever they please, including the conductor or the stage director."

"What about Reade?" I said.

"What about him?" Lawrence teased. "Oh. You mean, is he seeing anyone?

49.

"Maybe Camille," Lawrence said. "Lisette says she saw Camille sitting with Reade in his Jaguar. That is one beautiful piece of machinery. I mean Reade himself, of course."

"Were they doing anything?"

"What, like necking in the back seat?" He paused dramatically while I stared him down. He clearly enjoyed playing with my head. "Probably not."

I sighed with relief. I regretted judging Lawrence so harshly. His conversation was doing wonders for my mood.

"Angelo appears to be making progress with the chorus," Lawrence went on. "I heard him invite two girls back to his room. They said they would think about it, so I don't know if he scored. His English is a little iffy, so I'm not sure he was really aiming for seduction. I think he said, 'You come drink with me in my room? We have a party.'" His accent was so dead-on that I was soon helpless with laughter again. "I don't know," he continued. "Maybe the word 'party' isn't quite so suggestive in Italian. Maybe he was going to have balloons, hors d'oeuvres, and a piñata!"

"Lawrence, you're killing me!" I said, unable to stop laughing. "Angelo and the chorus girls don't fit in with your theories of non-fraternization. You said the chorus is stuck with each other."

"Oh, that!" Lawrence said, with a wave of dismissal. "After you factor in sex, the entire hierarchy falls to pieces. Anything goes. Principals sleep with choristers, directors with supernumeraries. All fraternizing is frowned upon, but no action is taken, not like in a normal workplace. You'd think that in an opera company, where the epitome of high art is practiced, a loftier morality would prevail." He paused. "Of course, compared to last time, the cast seems to have taken a collective vow of celibacy. Very disappointing. I'm counting on you, Debbie."

"For what?" I was still wiping my eyes.

"To breathe some life into this mausoleum. So far you're doing fine."

"No thanks!" I said. "Please, let someone else step forward. Every time I catch my breath, some new disaster occurs."

"At least you have new digs." He gave me a wicked smile.

"Amen!" I said. "I don't pine for the crusty floors and moldering shower stall of the Pine Tree Inn, I can tell you. Speaking of excitement, are you having any luck with Hugh?"

"That depends on how you define 'luck.' We're getting to know each other. *Getting to know you*," he suddenly sang out, "*getting to feel free and easy!* After 'getting to know you,' can 'free and easy' be far behind? Speaking of free and easy, Jim & Bob tried to hone in on my action. According to Hugh, they invited him to take part in a threesome."

"Yuck," I said. "I could do without that mental image."

"Tell me about it!" he said. He checked his cell phone. "Oops! We better skedaddle. Time's a wastin'."

"Just a second," I said, leaning forward to slip my shoes back on. Then I sat back again to retrieve my lip gloss from my purse. "Okay then—OW! Shit, shit, shit!" I leapt to my feet and frantically batted at my skirt.

"What is it?" Lawrence said in a panic. "What happened? Have you been shot?"

"Shot?!" I said. "No. But there's a goddamn bee drilling me in the butt. Get away, you little bastard!" I screamed at the bee.

"Here," Lawrence said, "allow me." I gladly let him take over. "Well, he's toast," Lawrence said. "I hope you're not allergic."

"A little bit," I admitted. "Stings, bites, they all swell up on me."

"Do you mind if I have look?"

"Knock yourself out," I said, wishing I hadn't worn the thong underwear.

He lifted up my skirt. "You're in for one supersized buttock," he said, letting it fall again. "He got you squarely on the cheek. Too bad that skirt is such flimsy material. Jeans might have given you some protection."

"Man!" I moaned. "The only reason I wore a skirt was because I didn't have to dress like a guy for the rehearsal."

"It sure is cute!" Lawrence offered. "At least it's not tight. With those pleats, no one will guess a thing."

"Unless you tell them," I said, giving him a stern look. "Lawrence, I'm serious. You can't tell anyone. It will just give Ulrika more ammunition against the bees."

"Uh, Debbie? How are you going to keep from scratching that thing? It's going to itch like crazy!"

"I'm still a spectator, right? I'll go buy one of those gel packs and sit on it. No one will be the wiser."

50.

The gel pack solution worked for almost an hour, until my butt warmed it up. Then, as Lawrence predicted, the itching commenced with a vengeance. I started sneaking in vigorous bouts of scratching when I thought no one was looking.

During a break, Sven approached, singing in falsetto: "*I have an itch to scratch; I need assistance!*"

Damn that Lawrence. "*Rocky Horror Picture Show*," I said wryly, "one of my favorites."

"You are the most accident prone person I have ever met, hands down," Sven said, admiration in his voice. "And don't blame Lawrence. I forced it out of him."

As long as he knew, I surrendered to the irresistible urge to scratch. "Does everyone know?" I said.

"Well, they know you're scratching your ass, if that's what you mean."

"Great. Just don't tell them about the bee sting. Say it's a rash."

"*That* will make you popular!" he said.

"NOT crabs or anything disgusting like that!" I said, exasperated. "Tell them I ran into some poison ivy."

"Where?"

"I don't know. Isn't there poison ivy or oak or something like that growing around here? I'll say it happened during a bike ride."

"Reade's going to take that bike away once and for all. Mark my words!"

"Okay, then, no bike. I was taking a stroll and—"

"What?" said Reade, who had approached with the stealth of a ninja. "You were taking a stroll, and … a bee stung you."

Sven shrugged. "See, no more need for subterfuge!"

I gave him a reproachful look. "Goddamn it, Sven!" I said.

"Don't blame him," Reade said. "I saw you and Lawrence in the park. Your movements and, er, vocalizing, gave you away."

I thought about Reade spying on us while Lawrence checked out my bare buttock. Any hope of earning Reade's respect had been quashed, once and for all. "Can I go get another gel pack now?" I said with a sigh.

51.

Before my quarters had been turned into a smokehouse, I had already concluded that Sven, with his wide repertoire of misbehavior, was as tiresome as a little boy on a family car trip. At every opportunity, he had touched me casually, on the shoulder, at the waist. He tested to see if I were ticklish. If I had been wearing a skirt, he probably would have declared it "Dress up day!" As I watched how skillfully Teresa fended him off, I had to admire the girl. She was a lot tougher than she looked!

These antics earned stern looks from Corabelle, nothing more. Directing Sven had to be like staging court productions starring England's madcap monarch of the Restoration, Charles II. What did you say? Your highness, stop messing with your mistress and pay attention?

One of Sven's favorite activities was crooning obscene versions of our lines in my ear. For instance, he enjoyed tweaking Nicklausse's little aria, the one where he attempts to warn Hoffmann that his true love is a mechanical doll. Our translation went like this:

A doll, there was, with eyes of glass,
Fluttered her fan with such panache,
So like a colorful young peahen,
A pretty little peahen!

This was Sven's version:

A boy, there was, with bedroom eyes
What lay between those shapely thighs?
Perhaps he hid a precious organ,
A pretty little organ!

My initial nervous laughter made it tough to apply the brakes later on. Don't get me wrong. I enjoy dirty doggerel as much as the next person. I just didn't want Corabelle to write me off as the class cut-up. Sven should have understood the awkward position he had put me in. He was king of the hill, and I was an ant. If there were going to be repercussions from his antics, the load of dung was going to bury me.

Opera singers are every bit as bawdy as other theater performers. Inhibited types tend to get over it quickly or find another profession. Teresa, however, was a rarity: an Amish farmer at a car show. She was so green that her skin took on that shade whenever Sven treated her to one of his ditties.

In the afternoon Corabelle blocked the second half of the doll scene. Hoffmann is trying to woo the doll, whose only response (because of a limited vocabulary) is "Yes!" A male fantasy, if ever there was one. Our translation went like this:

Is this not a dream, conjured up from a fever?
I thought I heard a sigh escape those lips I long for.

Sven's take contained extra syllables but had the advantage of rhyming:

I tire of wet dreams, oh how you give me fever!
Alas you have no orifices, not e'en a warm, wet beaver.

"That's disgustin'?" Teresa commented, during a break (not a question, just her way). "That boy needs to learn a thing or two about appropriate behavior."

I agreed, but since my beef was with his teasing ways, not his adolescent sense of humor, I responded, "I wish he'd stop trying to crack us up and focus on the staging."

"Well, I don't think it's funny?" she said. "This is the strangest group of classical singers. I don't know why Reade hired them back. They're not serious about their art! Those two ladies, Ulrika and Camille? They are not nice."

I could certainly agree. "What makes you say that?" I asked.

"They think it's amusin' that your dwellin' was attacked by anti-opera terrorists. And Ulrika is cheatin' on her husband. That poor fellah left her a message, which I tried to deliver. When I knocked on her door at ten p.m., I heard a man in there."

"Do you know who it was?" I said.

"I have no idea. They were laughin' and stuff? Too bad those anti-opera terrorists didn't teach *her* a lesson? I don't mean to be nasty. I jus' don't like her, and I feel bad about it! I certainly won't throw the first stone. Although behavior like that is against my beliefs."

Teresa pointed at Corabelle, who was sharing a private joke with Sven. "Now that one. She's nice! She's a perverted fornicator, but I can't help liking her! Know what I mean?" I nodded. "She likes you," Teresa said, clicking her tongue. "Oo-ee!"

I had wondered if anyone else had figured out why Sven's teasing hadn't earned me a slap on the wrist. I wasn't used to being ogled by a female director. In fact, this was the first time I had been aware of any woman's attraction to me. I was flattered. Corabelle was a genius, with a knack for charming snakes of the human and reptilian variety. Her post-adolescent male features and adorable mop of hair would have been perfect for Peter Pan. Lose the breasts, and you could easily forget she was a woman.

When the rehearsal ended at 9:00 p.m., Sven and Corabelle invited me to join them for a drink. "Tomorrow's the Lord's Day," Sven said, "when we sinners are expected to beg forgiveness for our sins. I have some catching up to do, if I'm going to commit my quota for the week. And as far as sins go, Debbie, you must be way under par."

"How would you know that?" I said, holding the door for them.

The three of us ambled down the sidewalk in the direction of the hotel. Sven continued: "Do you think anything escapes Lawrence's attention? If there were the slightest whiff of scandal associated with you, he would tell me. Come with us?"

Curious as I was to experience Corabelle and Sven after hours, I had already been talking too much. "Thanks for asking," I said, touching my throat. "I don't dare."

"Of course," Corabelle said quickly, "didn't mean to tempt you." Her smile said otherwise.

52.

On Sunday I saw neither hide nor hair of Reade. Not even Lawrence surfaced to tell lurid tales of all the action I was missing in my wing of Rapunzel's castle. I wished someone princely would come around and ask me to let down my hair.

The female leads were due at the theater dressing rooms for a fitting at 4:00 p.m. The prospect of a Clash of the Titanias (Lawrence's phrase), without referees to keep all these fairy queens from beating each other to death with their wings, made it difficult to relax. I watched *The Red Shoes* on PBS, although I had seen it often enough to recite many of the lines from memory. Not so long ago, it had been the must-see movie for aspiring dancers, a story of a beautiful ballerina torn between love and her career.

Ruthless Impresario: Why do you want to dance?
Ballerina: Why do you want to live?
Ruthless Impresario: Because I must?
Ballerina: That is my answer, too.

Except that she doesn't get to live. The red shoes dance her to death. Not exactly escapist entertainment, under the circumstances. Those lines summed it up for us crazy artistic types. The classic bit of advice given to performers in all professional training programs: If there's anything else you can do with your life and still be happy, go for it. Too late, many of us come to realize we really wanted the fantasy, not the nitty-gritty reality.

Just as I was pulling myself together to leave for the fitting, my cell phone rang, the opening bars of Carmen's aria, the Habanera. "Frankieeeee!" I said. I didn't have time to talk but couldn't resist a chance to chat with my best buddy.

"Debbieeeee ..." he trilled. "Why didn't you tell me about the near-fatal encounter with the birds and the bees?"

"Just the bees, thanks. The birds and I are on excellent terms."

"That's what you get for wearing a skirt. Impersonating the adolescent male is your destiny, Babe. Get used to it."

"Who did you talk to?" I said, annoyed that he knew every detail. "Sven? You're very well informed."

"Don't try to skirt the issue," Frankie said sternly, a chuckle in his voice.

"Enough humor at my expense," I said. "It's a good thing I'm not deathly allergic. The sting still itches like an SOB, though." The mere mention of it got me scratching furiously again.

"I can just picture it," Frankie said. "Don't let anything more serious happen, okay? You're already skirtin' the edge."

"Are you done?" I said. "Because I have a costume fitting."

"Yeah," he said, "almost. Just be sure that you're …" He paused to catch his breath before breaking into song, the tune barely recognizable: "*I'm through with skirtin'. It's you that I'm thinkin' of. Ain't misbehavin'…*"

"Flirtin'. The words are, I'm through with flirtin'," I said.

"Glad to hear it," he said. "Flirtin' is even more dangerous than skirtin'. And Babe?"

"Yeah?"

"Watch out for that terrorist group. What do they call themselves? Enemies of Elitist Entertainment? What a load of crock. I worry about you, Babe. This time you really are a babe in the woodshed."

"Uh, I guess the woodshed is even more dangerous than the woods."

He paused. "You bet it is!" he finally said.

"Reade thinks the smoke bomb incident was just a prank," I said.

"Reade, is it?" he said in a wheedling falsetto voice. "You on good terms with him? Sven says he's a stage-door John."

"Don't you mean, Stage-door Johnny?"

"I call 'em like I see 'em. Sven says he's almost as rich as Bill Gates."

"No one knows how rich he is, OR who he's screwing," I said, too quickly.

"Relax, Babe. If he really is Mr. Wham-Bam, he'll get around to you eventually, and you got enough problems. Like the song says, *Smoke gets in your lungs*."

"Eyes."

"Huh?"

"Smoke gets in your eyes." I crooned the chorus of the Jerome Kern tune: "*When a lovely flame dies, smoke gets in your eyes.*"

"How about this? *When the smoke bombs are flung, smoke gets in your lungs!* Or this one: *Ashes, ashes, we all go down.* So, step carefully and avoid the fires. Frying pans, too, while you're at it."

"Reade's only interest in me is making sure that I don't sue him."

"*Sue me, sue me*," Frankie sang, then, still approximating the tune from *Guys & Dolls*, he improvised, "*Why won't you screw me? I love you!*"

As he sang on, I tried to interrupt: "Frankie, I'm really late. I gotta run!" He was still singing when I ended the call, grabbed a sweater, and raced out the door and through the hotel lobby, nearly knocking over a startled bellhop in the process.

53.

As usual, the conversation with Frankie had both cheered me up and made me late. Fortunately Reade had arranged for me to keep my bike in the room behind the main desk along with the bikes belonging to his employees, meaning that I didn't have to go to the trouble of unlocking it. There was a cold rain pounding down outside, so I arrived at the theater looking like I had gone for a dip in Lake Ville d'Aurore. I was chilled to the bone and feeling like an idiot for not planning ahead.

As I entered, Ulrika's angry voice resounded throughout the theater. It was as if the building itself had found a means to express its outrage over a hundred-plus years of violation. "You expect me to wear this?!" it cried. "I look like death!"

"That's the point," replied a long-suffering female voice I didn't recognize. "Better get used to it. The makeup will heighten the effect."

"Are you saying I'm sallow?" Ulrika raged.

"Of course not!" the woman pleaded. "With the right foundation—"

"And this leather bodice! I look flat as that nosy little Deb—"

"Deborah!" The woman hailed me with frenetic good cheer. "Is that you? Goodness, dear, you're going to catch your death."

"Sorry I'm late." I shook her hand. "You must be Mrs. Perlmutter."

"Call me Mary Jo," she said, smiling. It could have been my recent viewing of *The Red Shoes*, but I saw her as a retired ballet mistress, scary slim, with her hair bound in the kind of bun that gives you a natural facelift. She had the perpetually hungry eyes of someone who had restricted their calories for too many years. I guessed her age to be late fifties, from the permanently furrowed brow and the startling stripes of white hair contrasting with black, à la Cruella de Ville. She handed me a towel while turning her attention back to the overwrought Ulrika.

"I'm warning you! There is no way that I'm going to wear this … this … *wig*," Ulrika persisted, tongue-tied by the injustice of it all. "It's a terrible color for me!"

"I told you. It will look fine when you adjust your makeup," Mary Jo explained with superhuman patience. "It has to be black to fit Corabelle's concept. Raise your objections with her! Olympia's a blonde, like Madonna, Giulietta's a redhead, like Nicole Kidman, and Antonia has black hair—"

"Like Alice Cooper's," I said, or rather blurted. Damn it. That was the problem with getting so little sleep. I was too punchy to censor myself.

Ulrika hurled the wig at the mirror, where it landed at an odd angle. The well-groomed road kill of some unidentifiable, abused creature.

Mary Jo came to the rescue, rearranging the wig lovingly on its Styrofoam stand. “I'll discuss the matter with Corabelle,” she said. “Your own hair would almost work, but you need about four times the volume for the stage. As for the costume, don't worry. We'll get you a super push-up bra and lace up the back like a corset.” She inserted a few strategic pins. “Better?” She smiled blandly.

“*Whatever!*” Ulrika said, furiously unbuttoning the bodice and slinging it over the ironing board. “This had better all be fixed by next time.” And with a toss of her own long, straight brown hair, she was gone.

Unheeded, I located the section of the rack marked Nicklausse and stripped down to my T-shirt and panties, my only dry garments. The first item I tried on was a pair of slacks, fawn-colored with suspenders. Those pants would have made a stick figure look pudgy. It was a good thing I wasn't heavily invested in cutting a dapper figure on stage. My mother was going to be disappointed if she expected me to fuel anyone's fantasies.

Mary Jo clicked her tongue. “That won't do,” she said, pursing her lips. “Those trousers add ten pounds to your derriere. I'll fix them, don't you worry.”

“What about *this* horror?” Camille demanded, calling attention to her skin-tight negligee. It was full-length but slit up the sides, revealing her generous thighs. The décolletage barely covered her nipples. “I'm falling out!” Indeed, her breasts were bursting forth like rising soufflés.

Mary Jo whipped out her measuring tape and spanned Camille's bust. “Your bust is four inches bigger than you told us. You're lucky the fabric has some give in it.” She stepped back to assess the situation. The outfit was too tight overall. Instead of showing off Camille's hourglass figure, it accentuated her figure flaws. The effect was more over-the-hill streetwalker than comely courtesan. “I need to consult Corabelle,” Mary Jo finally said. “This can't be what she wanted. Here, let me unzip you.”

Camille's brow furrowed. That was the last glimpse I got of her before she turned around to allow Mary Jo to help her out of the dress. Something had set the wheels in motion. What was it? *I should have gone easy on the scones? That breast development cream really works!* Or, *when was my last menstrual period?*

54.

Camille was gone by the time I finished putting on my own wig, and for this I was truly thankful. I didn't need any hostile witnesses to my sad transmogrification.

The severe cut and blue-black color had clearly been chosen to enhance the looks of a Hispanic hottie, not a golden-skinned Gaul. I almost sympathized with Ulrika. I looked like a jaundiced kid whose mom had given him a bowl cut. Making this wig work was going to require *a lot* of stage makeup.

I gulped and resolved not to make a fuss. Who cared if Nicklausse appeared to be a terminal case? What did it matter if the whole point—that as Hoffmann's muse he was eternally healthy and possibly immortal—would be lost?

"That makes you look bad," a flat male voice commented. At least that's what I thought he said. His lips quivered when he spoke, otherwise the mouth barely moved. All that was needed was a ventriloquist's dummy, a part he himself could have carried off successfully. How long had he been standing there, this wizened leprechaun in the olive-green jumpsuit?

"I was thinking the same thing," I said.

"Mary Jo," the man said. "The lady needs a better wig."

"You have a good eye, Rudolf," Mary Jo said. "I'll see what I can do." This turn of phrase made me aware that even if the man did have a good eye, the other had problems. It was either blind or wandering. Was that what was meant by wall-eyed? Whatever it was, his eyes were not in sync.

"Thank you," I said. "I'm Debbie de Lille."

"Rudolf Tieflander," the man said. One tooth protruded

through tight, upturned lips. The pains the man took to hide what must be a truly unfortunate set of choppers piqued my curiosity. I found myself watching his mouth in fascination lest he let down his guard for an instant.

"Rudolf," Mary Jo said sternly, "What are you doing here? This is a costume fitting. You might have walked in on a naked woman!"

Bingo! I thought, noticing the way his good eye darted about in guilty confusion. "Sorry," he said. "I do most of my cleaning Sundays. Usually no one is here."

He made a special effort to lift the corners of his lips for Teresa, who had been hanging back from the rest of us. When the distracted girl registered his presence, she waved and smiled. With an atypical lack of animation, she said, "Oh, hi there, Rudy?"

"Come on, sweetie," Mary Jo coaxed. "Since Lisette still hasn't shown up, we'll do a fitting for you."

"Okay," she said softly. "You know I'm happy to wear any ol' thing."

"That's the beauty of you," Mary Jo said. "You look wonderful in any ol' thing." They exchanged a spontaneous hug.

"You all seem well-acquainted," I remarked, picking up on that infectious Southern accent.

"We go way back," Teresa said.

Mary Jo patted me on the back. "Don't worry, Debbie," she said. "I'll get you another wig. That one is better suited to Juanita's coloring and little heart-shaped face. The pants would have been infinitely worse on her. They've got to go, too. I just need to get Corabelle to focus. And I'm still working on your 'Voice of the Mother' costume." She rummaged in the rack and pulled out what looked like a size 16, chiffon mother-of-the-bride dress. "There's no point in trying it on, because Corabelle's going to need to rethink the whole outfit now that you're stepping in. Not to mention that it's a bit large—"

"Hey there," Lisette said as she burst into the room. "Sorry I'm late!"

55.

Like me, Lisette was dripping wet, and also like me, she had ridden to the theater on her bicycle. She had spared no expense in outfitting herself in professional-quality gear—the highest-end helmet, race shoes, sport tights, and jacket. Lisette was firmer and more muscular than you'd expect from seeing her in her usual loose but low-cut clothing. She could definitely carry off the early-Madonna thing before the pop singer discovered personal trainers and yoga. Mary Jo tossed her a towel. "Please wipe off the sweat," she ordered, as if Lisette had ushered in an army of ravenous moths. "It's murder on costumes. I'll be with you momentarily."

"It's raining buckets out there, if you hadn't noticed," Lisette said. I had to wonder why Mary Jo was being so much harder on her. Maybe it was all the gear. Come to think of it, I wasn't dressed like a cyclist, nor had I worn a helmet. Mary Jo must have assumed I came on foot and simply got stuck without an umbrella.

"Lots of good biking around here," Lisette said as she dabbed herself with the towel. "We should go for a ride together, Debbie. After this I was planning to explore the hills on the other side of the college. Come with?"

"In the rain? I'm hardly dressed for it." Aside from the fact that it was colder than 60 degrees outside and windy. I wasn't that hardcore. Apparently Lisette was! "If it stops raining, I could—"

I broke off in mid-sentence. Teresa, too modest to change in front of us even if Rudolf hadn't been lurking about, emerged from behind the screen. The costume was a tribute to what the right color palate and tailoring could do. We stood, clumped together and gaping, in that tiny dressing room, like a huddle at a zombie football game. Granted, Teresa had the slim shape and complexion to carry off just about anything. On her lithe body, Corabelle's concept was exonerated. Giulietta's auburn wig complemented her poreless skin, Antonia's black leather pants clung to legs Kate Beckinsale would envy, and Olympia's Madonna-style bustier had never looked less trashy. I understood that Stella was an amalgam of Hoffmann's women; however, she was also supposed to be a contemporary opera singer post-show. In that respect, the costume failed. Rock star? Yes. Opera diva? Nope!

Teresa appeared as ill-at-ease as those little boys in photos from the twenties whose mothers got their kicks from dressing them as girls. I didn't think her discomfort stemmed from baring too much skin. Perhaps she was imagining the possibly homicidal envy of Camille and Ulrika when they saw her. Lisette, on the other hand, pensively stroked her chin as if recalling a pleasant memory.

Unluckily for me, the rain had stopped by the time we were finished. I struggled to keep up with Lisette as we pedaled laboriously up the hillside. Between gasps and grunts, I told her how terrific she looked in her Olympia costume. I meant it, but her sidelong look was skeptical.

"I've been busting my butt to get into shape for this," she finally said. "Corabelle's famous for her burlesque costumes and cockamamie concepts, as if opera singers who don't starve themselves into anemic husks deserve to be exposed for the fat slobs they are. By the time you hit thirty-five, even crash diets don't do the trick. You starve yourself down to nothing, but instead of appearing sleek and slim, you look like a three-day old helium balloon. Teresa's how old, 22?"

This kind of talk made me acutely self-conscious. Although Teresa had nicer curves, we were about the same weight. As if reading my thoughts, Lisette stood up on the pedals and increased her pace. I kept up, though by now I was weary to the point of nausea. Before shooting far ahead of me and out of earshot, she called out, barely winded, "It will be interesting to see how that southern-fried ninny holds up after another fifteen years of this lifestyle—if she makes it that long."

56.

While waiting at the local Chinese eatery for my order of pork-fried rice, I mulled over the day's events. Was Camille pregnant? If so, she wasn't happy about it. That might mean it wasn't her husband's or that a baby would present too long a detour in her career path. What was the connection between Teresa, Mary Jo, and Rudolf—the beauty, the ballet mistress, and the village idiot? Were Ulrika, Camille, and Lisette really friends or simply united in spleen?

I headed back to the hotel. Lonely I may be, but living in the Taj Mahal of the Wild West did much to console me. Besides my colossal bathtub, my accommodations included a balcony with a hot tub, which I planned to use as soon as I dashed off a note to my parents. Their generation still believes that nothing shows you care like a hand-written epistle. I used a free postcard of the Ville d'Aurore Lodge, picked up in the lobby. My Mom, a fan of thrift, would approve.

Dear Mom and Dad,

This is a photo of the place where I'm staying, believe it or not! The general director is fabulously rich and wants his singers to have the very best treatment possible. I like to ride my bicycle around the area, which has the feel of a spiffed-up frontier town. This is a nice group. I'm becoming friends with Sven (the fabulous tenor lead), Lisette (one of the principal sopranos), and Lawrence (the main character tenor). Great news—they've given me another part, the Voice of the Mother! Her portrait comes to life, and Mom, I actually get to wear a nice dress and look pretty!!

Admittedly, this was the Hallmark Channel version of my life in Ville d'Aurore so far. I could hardly let Mom think her tarot predictions were coming true, could I? My bike accident, the smoke bomb attack, the bee sting … these were all just bumps in the road. From now on I would surely find freshly poured blacktop and green lights all the way. Wasn't I planning to take back my roles tomorrow?

That last bit of news in particular would make Mom's day. Her daughter, looking feminine and pretty on stage! I left the postcard on the massive roll-top desk, turned on my ancient cassette player, and eased ecstatically into the churning, steaming water of the hot tub. At home I managed my stress with yoga. If only there was time for a class here and there! On my own I usually became distracted after a few sun salutations. Oh well, two weeks would not be enough to undo the last three years of conditioning.

This was the last week of blocking, so I was busy memorizing the Voice of the Mother's music. I had been listening to the recording a lot using the tape player and my iPod, mouthing the words and humming the tune until it became part of my tongue's muscle memory. That way, even if my brain blanked, the tip of my tongue would soldier on. Because sleep deprivation threatened to make me stupid, I would need to know this part in the marrow of my bones.

The words weren't particularly complicated:

My voice is calling as in times long past.
Oh! Keep singing, my daughter! Sing!
My voice is calling! Sing! Keep singing.
My voice is calling, is calling you home.
Never stop singing!
Oh dear child, hear me calling.
Oh dear child, hear me calling as in the past.
Ah, my spirit is calling, is calling.
Hear what I say! Obey my voice.

You get the idea. Lest you conclude the translation is weak, know that the French is basically word-for-word the same. No poetry is lost.

You may recall that this apparition isn't Antonia's actual mother. It's an evil spirit taking her form. The blocking would be a no-brainer because the portrait stays in the frame when it comes to life.

I simmered for a good half-hour in the hot tub under a spectacularly starlit sky before climbing into bed, the Voice of the Mother's words and melody looping endlessly through my brain. I began to despair of ever dropping off.

Wait a minute! I had to be asleep, because I was hearing that melody in an all-too-real sense: distant strains, as though wafting in the still night air from an orchestra playing on a boat in the middle of Lake Ville d'Aurore. My eyes were open, yet the music played on. Was it an aural hallucination?

"Deborah," said a low, breathy voice. "De-bo-rah!"

57.

"De-bo-rah!" The ghostly summons was followed by otherworldly moaning. It was impossible to tell if it belonged to a male or female.

I sat bolt upright. This was real! I leapt out of bed, threw open the door, and dashed out into the hallway. Naked. Not even a towel this time. The door slammed behind me. I tried to turn the knob. Locked out. Not that it mattered. There was someone or something in that room, taunting me, and I wasn't going to brave it for the sake of public decency. Only, NOW WHAT? I sank into a corner and hugged my knees, shivering.

I passed several anxious minutes like this. "Uh, Debbie?" Goddamn it, it was Reade. "Are you all right? I heard a door slam." Averting his eyes, he draped the familiar leather jacket over my huddled form. "I hope you don't mind," he said. "You look, um, cold."

"There's a ghost in my room," I said, my voice muffled by the jacket.

"A what?"

"A ghost!" I wailed.

"All right," he said, preternaturally calm. "I'll see what I can do about it."

"I'm not talking about a mouse," I said, put off by his tepid response. "It was moaning and calling my name!"

"I'll fetch a robe and another keycard while I'm at it. Are you okay on your own for a minute?"

"Sure," I lied. I wanted to throw up.

As soon as Reade was out of sight, Sven appeared, wearing a robe a few sizes too small. One of the three bears had raided Goldilocks' closet. The robe gaped to his waist, revealing a thatch of flaming-red chest hair. "What's up?" he asked, reasonably. "Why are you trussed up in leather like a bundle left out for room service?" His eyes fixed on my bare feet and ankles. "Hmm. Are you naked under that?" He stepped forward, as if intending to find out for himself.

"Sven!" I remonstrated.

He retreated and threw up his hands. "What?" The robe flew open. "Oops!" He pulled it back together, not before I got an eyeful. Let's just say his equipment was proportionate to the rest of him. "I keep meaning to ask for a bigger robe." He had the grace to look embarrassed.

Reade rounded the corner and placed a robe in the hand that I managed to snake out from beneath the leather encasement. I drew the robe in and disappeared within the bulky fortress like a turtle retreating into its shell. "What are you doing awake?" I heard Reade say to Sven. "We have those in all sizes, you know."

"I heard voices," Sven replied, "and music. The third-act trio. I dreamed I had missed my entrance."

"See?" I gasped, winded by my struggle to wriggle into the robe. I felt like Houdini trying to put a straitjacket on underwater. I tried not to think of how ridiculous I must look. It wasn't as if I could sink any lower in Reade's estimation. After that last fiasco with the bee sting, he was used to seeing me make an ass of myself.

Finally, my efforts rewarded, I rose to my feet and tied the sash in a double-knot. "I'm not crazy," I declared.

"No one said you were crazy," Reade assured me. "For your sake, I hope the weather stays cool at night. If I stop wearing a jacket, the next time this happens, you're going to be plum out of luck."

"The next time," Sven repeated. "How intriguing! Debbie, are you in the habit of cavorting around in the buff?"

"Only when attacked by anti-opera terrorists or evil spirits," I said.

"Don't get your panties in a twist," Sven said. "Oh, I forgot! You're not wearing any! Come on, let's go to your room and play *Ghostbusters.*"

A door opened, and Corabelle stepped out into the hallway, a young Kate Hepburn in her red silk pajamas. "What's going on?" she said, squinting painfully into the light.

"How are you with evil spirits?" Reade asked, opening my door and switching on the light. "We're going to perform an exorcism in Debbie's room."

"Huh? Oh, okay." She wandered after them, half-asleep.

I waited, leaning against the wall, trying to remember the term for driving ghosts out of places. Could you exorcise a room?

"The door to your balcony was unlocked," Reade said.

"I don't usually lock it."

"Better start. No one's there now. My guess is that someone is trying to scare you silly."

"Why don't you stay in my room tonight?" Corabelle offered.

"Or mine," said Sven.

"You don't live here, do you?" I asked Reade.

"You'd rather stay with him?" Sven said, hands on hips. The robe gaped again.

"Cover yourself, you big stud!" Corabelle commanded, pointing an accusatory finger. "That thing is scarier than any ghost."

"I wasn't asking Reade—" I stopped, reddening. "I only

wondered what he was doing here at … uh, what time is it?"

"One in the morning," Reade said. "I was playing Poker. The boys have a weekly Sunday night game. If it goes too late, I sleep over. Lucky for you the others left already. Or the entire Ville d'Aurore police force might be offering you their jackets."

58.

In the end, returning to my own room seemed the lesser of the evils, not that an offer from Reade wouldn't have been tempting. It was dawn by the time I fell into a light, troubled sleep. In my dream I was stuck in the back seat of a car with the radio blasting the third-act trio. "Turn off that damned music!" I yelled, before realizing that there was no driver. I woke up just as the car sailed into a canyon, *Thelma and Louise* style.

Naturally it took a while to shake this off. Eventually, aided by my new best friends Advil and Benedryl, I drifted off once more, this time into blessed nothingness. If Sven hadn't pounded on my door at half past noon, who knows how long I might have slept?

Before I left for rehearsal, I searched in vain for the postcard to my parents. I had left it on the desk, but in all the commotion, it had probably been swept underneath or behind the furniture. None of the heavy pieces would budge. No biggie! I'd pick up another card in the lobby. The note was easily duplicated.

Today we were blocking Act II, which featured the high-class courtesan, Giulietta, played by Camille. Giulietta's soul belongs to the evil sorcerer Dapertutto, our Italian Elvis, Angelo. With the aid of an enchanted diamond, Dapertutto hypnotizes her into stealing the souls of her lovers by collecting first their reflections, then their shadows. Don't ask me to explain the difference, although one seems more irrevocable than the other. Hoffmann loses his reflection, but at Nicklausse's urging escapes with his shadow (that is, his soul). So what does the reflection stand for? His free will, his sense of self? Among Giulietta's admirers are Schlemil (Hugh

Rainier), and a hunchbacked dwarf named Pittichinaccio, played by Lawrence. The act opens with the Barcarolle, the famous duet between Nicklausse and Giulietta.

Camille and I stood in spitting distance, the figurative wall of ice a foot thick. Whenever she looked my way, her eyes fired off splinters. I had to wonder if someone other than Ulrika had been actively chilling the air between us. Otherwise, how could I be enough of a threat or irritant to be worth so much negative energy?

Lawrence was getting on swimmingly with Hugh, dashing as ever in a Polo shirt and tan trousers that would have been perfect for a game of croquet at *The Great Gatsby's* garden party. Their body language prompted Corabelle to comment, "Hey. You two are rivals, remember?"

"Don't worry," Hugh said. "Once I see him in his dwarf costume, I'll be sufficiently disgusted." Lawrence frowned.

Sven and his oversized, uh, ego, were on best behavior. He spared me the usual teasing, as though aware that one more affliction, no matter how minor, might cause me to fill my jacket pockets with enchanted diamonds and walk slowly into Lake Ville d'Aurore. I overheard Camille asking him about my spirit visitation the night before. Who had told her? Stupid question. If Sven had mentioned it to Lawrence, it would find fertile ground in the manner of dandelion seeds on a stiff breeze.

"She didn't make it up," Sven insisted, "I heard the music, too."

"Okay, so she left her tape player on and dreamed the rest," Camille declared loudly, for the benefit of the entire cast. "She likes the attention. Probably set off those smoke bombs herself, too."

"Sure," Sven said. "After exploding the one in her room, she ran down the street, naked, scattering bombs like breadcrumbs to make a trail." He winked at me as he strolled to the water cooler to refill his bottle.

Act II features a hell of a lot of standing around and singing, despite the enthusiastic antics of a chorus of prostitutes and their johns. I had given up trying to befriend the chorus. My move to the

Lodge hadn't helped matters. They didn't exactly snub me, more like treat me as if I wasn't worth the effort. There was a complete alternate cast among them, and I had overheard enough to suspect that some of the girls, especially my understudy, were miffed because their credentials were as good as or better than mine. Maybe so. I still didn't consider them suspects. If harming me was the goal, why not find a method that wouldn't pollute your own quarters with noxious smoke?

Act II climaxes with a sword fight where Hoffmann kills Schlemil. The way things had been going, I worried that the swords had been tampered with. No worries! Sven and Lawrence, who had already perfected their choreography with the fight director, attacked each other like old fencing pros, rather than former lovers with a bone to pick. Interesting, how the men didn't seem at risk. I don't know why I was surprised. Being a talented man in the performing arts is like being a female math/science wiz in the age of affirmative action. Ninety percent of the roles are male, and a similar percentage of the talent pool is female. Even I could do the math. With plenty of work to go around, why resort to homicide?

Had this vendetta turned personal? Why was this person targeting the supporting women? First the original Nicklausse, then the Voice of the Mother. Hmm ... What was the deal with Wilhelmina Wooley?

59.

In the middle of the night, my cell phone burst into tinny song. Half-asleep, I answered. A familiar eerie voice whispered, *De-bor-ah* ... The caller ID said pay phone. Prank callers had to take extra precautions these days to remain untraceable.

So much for a decent night's sleep. I switched on the light. How to relax? Using the hot tub would mean exposing myself on the violated second floor balcony. How had the intruder avoided detection? The least complicated route, for a circus performer, would be from the room above mine. Impossible to picture the plump and possibly pregnant Camille dangling cat-burglar-style. And there couldn't be much strength in Ulrika's matchstick arms.

I took another deep-sea bath instead, even though that indulgence seemed like an unfortunate waste of water. At the moment Ville d'Aurore had plenty of that element. If the three mountain lakes within easy biking distance weren't enough, then there was the rain that had been pelting us continually for two days straight.

When I made my bleary way down to breakfast at 10:00 a.m., the first person to greet me was Lawrence. "Hey girl!" he called out. "I'm meeting Hugh."

"Good for you, good for Hugh," I said, inanely.

I didn't expect confidences from Lawrence regarding his love life. I had already pegged him as the type who was only indiscreet with other people's secrets. "Nice dark circles," he said. "No rest for the wicked, eh?"

"The wicked are resting just fine. That's the problem. They have boundless energy for pranks, any time of day or night."

"Something new? You have got to be kidding." His attention was wandering toward the host's desk, where Hugh was making a grand entrance. The path to our table might have been a runway at a fashion show sponsored by *Men's Vogue*.

"For a small-time opera singer, Hugh has a nifty wardrobe," I said. "Rich parents?"

"I dress well," Lawrence snapped, "and I'm not rich."

"You look great, Lawrence, but even I, who don't know diddly-squat about men's clothing, can see no expense has been spared on his. Rich boyfriend?"

"Maybe."

"Beware, Lawrence," I cautioned, as Hugh arrived.

"Beware of what?" Hugh said.

"Beware of the cinnamon rolls," I said. "Really large. A zillion trillion calories."

Hugh and Lawrence kissed each other's cheeks three times,

Continental style. "Debbie was just bringing me up to date on the latest threats to her life." Hugh looked politely expectant, as though only mildly interested.

"It's hardly worth repeating," I told Hugh. To the waitress, I said, "Two eggs and a bran muffin, please. A tall latte, two shots." After the others ordered, I continued, "The ghost, denied physical, or metaphysical, access, contacted me via cell phone."

"Go on," Lawrence said, as Hugh stifled a yawn. "What did it say?"

"Just the same old name-calling."

"Bitch, whore?" Hugh suggested helpfully.

"No, just De-bo-rah." I imitated the scary voice, creeping myself out all over again.

"Why did you leave it on?" Sven said from behind my chair.

"Leave what on?" I twisted my neck so abruptly it made an audible crack. When had Sven crept into hearing distance? Either he was a master of stealth, or we were all too preoccupied to notice, me by my story, the guys by each other. Sven laid a hand on Hugh's back, a vaguely proprietary gesture. Uh-oh. A triangle was forming, one that wouldn't jingle harmoniously.

"Her cell phone is possessed," Lawrence explained.

"Didn't you tell me your mom's a psychic?" Sven said, pulling up a chair between Lawrence and Hugh. "She should hold a séance and talk some sense into these ghosts."

"No self-respecting ghost is going to stick around while my mom natters on," I said. "I'd have better luck if the culprit *were* a ghost. This particular phantom hasn't done anything that couldn't be accomplished by earthly means."

"Hmm. If I were you, I'd worry about how far he, or she, is willing to go," Hugh said, stroking his smooth chin.

"Now you're scaring me," I said. "As in, will they try to hurt me or—"

Lawrence silenced me with a raised hand. "Perish the thought," he said. "Oops, sorry. Poor choice of words." To Sven, he said, "What do you think, Ulrika or Camille?"

Sven twiddled his thumbs for a few seconds before finally shaking his head. “Neither. When your tongue is already a lethal weapon, why bother with elaborate stunts? The smoke bomb thing and the late-night visitation both involved careful planning and considerable risk of discovery. As for the prank phone call, anyone can do that.”

“I wonder what really happened to the first Nicklausse,” Hugh said. The table was silent as the waitress served our food.

“Terrible accident,” I said, repeating the stock answer, although no longer believing in accidents. In fact, I experienced a sudden urge to take out my cell phone and call Mrs. Wooley, the departed (I hoped not dearly) Voice of the Mother. Where had I stashed that contact sheet?

“Nicklausse is such a minor part,” Sven said, “No offense intended, Debbie. It doesn’t make sense.” I looked at my watch. It was 11:00 a.m. Two hours remained until rehearsal, enough time to dig up the contact list and go on the Internet. Besides, I wasn’t eager to hang around and moderate an unequal, unacknowledged sparring match between the Three Tenors. This particular type of rivalry had not been a problem for the original tenor trio, the notoriously heterosexual Domingo, Pavarotti, and Carreras.

60.

Lisette intercepted me at the door to my room. She was geared up for another marathon bike ride, in her ongoing quest to do justice to that Madonna costume. “I heard you had a couple of rough nights,” she said.

A couple? Had Lawrence phoned her from the breakfast table? “Last night was a prank call,” I said. “No big deal. The night before, I think my room was broken into.”

“From where? Not the hallway, surely.”

“I don’t know. I need to find out who’s in the room above mine.”

"I think I am."

"Really? Did you hear anything the night before last?"

She shrugged. "I wasn't there."

"Where were you?" I blurted. God, who did I think I was, her mother? "I'm sorry," I backpedaled. "It's none of my business."

She waved me to silence. "Don't apologize. It makes perfect sense. Let me explain. My keycard disappeared from my purse. I assumed it was misplaced, but it must have been stolen. When I came in yesterday morning, I had the desk re-key me. It appears someone took advantage of my absence."

My brain was racing. Where had Lisette been? And how had the intruder known she wouldn't turn up suddenly to interrupt his activities? Not much risk, it's true. The entire episode lasted five minutes, max.

Lisette looked over her shoulder to see if anyone was in earshot. "I was with Hubert Silvertone," she whispered. "Don't tell anyone. I'm not proud of it. Hell, I'm divorced, and everyone knows his marriage is a sham. I'm sorry if my fooling around put you in danger."

"I guess I'm not surprised he's looking for greener pastures," I said. "I met his wife at the get-acquainted party. I call her Aunt Vee. She looks like Andy Griffith's Aunt Bee, but she's a pit viper in disguise. I was feeling fragile that night anyway because of that giant lump on my chin. After she finished whittling me down to size, there was little left of me but that lump."

"Aunt Vee! That's a good one. Hubert will enjoy that. Not to defend her, Debbie, but this business requires that you grow a snakeskin of your own and a venomous tongue to match. Aunt Vee had no power over you! You should have given her a taste of her own medicine."

"But she's the wife of the chairman of the board!"

"So what? Oh well, you couldn't know that the only weight she has to throw around is her considerable girth. Not that I should talk."

"You're looking great," I insisted. "Have fun on your bike ride.

I wish I could join you."

"Why can't you? It would be fun!"

"I'm tempted!" I lied. "But I better not. I have to check my e-mail and catch up on phone calls. In our little microcosm, it's so easy to forget there's a great big world out there."

"Tell me about it!" Lisette said. "Well, see you later. I have way too much time on my hands, with only the one act. I'm going to lose another ten pounds if it kills me!"

As I watched her head off down the stairs, I considered what I had just learned. Lawrence had paired Ulrika with Hubert Silvertone. The man got around!

61.

Back in my room, I retrieved the contact sheet from between the pages of my Hoffmann score and phoned Mrs. Wooley's cell. As I waited for an answer, I thought of my ancient car, languishing on the street since my arrival. If I didn't move it soon, they might assume it was abandoned and haul it off to the junkyard. Finally I heard, "Hello?"

"Is this Mrs. Wooley?"

"Uh, yes," came the cautious answer.

"Well, thank goodness," I said. "I'm Debbie de Lille. Nicklausse from the *Tales of Hoffmann* cast?"

"Yes?"

"I know this is nosy of me, Mrs. Wooley, but there's been some funny business here, and I wondered if you'd be willing to tell me why you left. I mean, if there's a reason other than the one you gave. Um ... if it's really family trouble, I don't want or need to know." This was not going well.

She came to my rescue. "It was the note."

"What kind of note?"

"A threatening one." The timbre of her voice changed. Her larynx was tightening, raising the pitch. In other words, she was upset. "Juergen and I are old friends, or I never would have accepted the job in the first place," she said. "We don't need the money, and my husband wasn't happy about my going off again." An audible sigh, then, "I suppose you'd like to know what it said. Something like, if you value your life, you'll leave town by tonight. I'm sure there's nothing to it, but, under the circumstances, why take the risk?"

I thanked her and ended the call. Just the excuse I needed to contact Reade! Or, alternatively, I could tear off all my clothes and streak through the lobby. So far that had proved a reliable method of contacting him.

After I checked my e-mail (nothing, this time, not even a dire warning from Mom), I typed "Reade Phillips Ville d'Aurore" on to the search bar. His name scored a multitude of hits. The richest source was an interview published four months earlier during rehearsals for the company's inaugural production of Bizet's *Carmen*.

Poll any random group of middle class Americans, and *Carmen* and Puccini's *La Bohème* would be the two operas they *might* have heard of. Music from *Carmen* had been plundered for TV commercials, *Gilligan's Island*, Muzak, etc., so the highlights were instantly recognizable. Thanks to catchy tunes and universal themes of sexual betrayal, tragic love, and untimely death, *Carmen* and *La Bohème* are the easiest sells in the opera repertoire.

On to Reade ... Ten years ago, at the age of thirty, he had won the Idaho State Lottery, invested in biotech stocks, turned a large fortune into a gigantic one, and now owned the better part of Ville d'Aurore. Until his life-altering windfall, he had been a police detective. That explained the fraternizing with the local boys in blue. It also made any interest he had shown in me look like professional curiosity, darn it all.

A former police detective willing to blow a fortune on opera! Wow. Not a type you ran across every day, outside of Europe.

I scanned the *Ville d'Aurore Herald's* review of *Carmen*. "Juanita Macaree-Smith, filling in for an indisposed Camille

Parquet, lights up the stage like a sparkler during a blackout as the wild child Carmen." Funny, Lisette hadn't mentioned anything about Juanita taking over for Camille. Carmen is one of those rare parts that—with a few note alterations—mezzos or sopranos with strong middle ranges can take on.

A rave for Sven, naturally, and Angelo: "What a pleasant surprise to hear a pop singer who can cross-over successfully to the opera stage. A vocal powerhouse with charisma to match." No wonder Reade had asked Angelo back.

"Another last-minute replacement, Ulrika Mannschliesser, did not disappoint. Her exquisitely voiced Micaela, approached with unusual dramatic sensitivity, elevated that milquetoast into the realm of high tragedy." Ouch. Poor Lisette! She claimed not to care that illness had robbed her of the chance to sing Micaela, but seeing someone else run away with your role had to hurt. Clearly she had the maturity to put things into perspective.

A blurb in *Opera News* and larger article in *Classical Singer Magazine* concentrated on Sven and his prospects for future glory. That was it. Nothing for Camille or Lisette to quote in their press releases from that experience!

Reade had played it safe by presenting an opera he could sell out, not one that would interest reviewers from trade journals such as the Met's *Opera News* or London's *Opera Magazine*. These reviewers didn't bother with houses of this size unless unusual fare was being offered. Corabelle had done her best to shock by changing the setting to present-day Cuba, but as the one reviewer pointed out, Cuba is so backward that the setting was almost conventional.

This production of *Hoffmann* had more potential for attracting wider attention. Juanita's sensational demise, Corabelle's daring staging, and Sven's rising-star status (thanks to the Corelli Competition) might spur magazines and Internet sites into sending reviewers.

I was surprised to find recent items about Ville d'Aurore Opera. On *OperaChatter.Com*, I found the following mention:

"Word is, Wilhelmina 'Willy' Wooley fled the latest Ville d'Aurore production of *Tales of Hoffmann* because of a threat on her life. Has the White Lady who haunts the opera house returned to harass the living? A little songbird tells me a fresh curse has descended on Ville d'Aurore Opera. First a death by automobile, next a terrorist attack with smoke bombs. What next?"

Good question, I thought. They didn't know the half of it! Could the genome of my persecution be found in the DNA of this company? Because torture wasn't an option, nothing would be gained by questioning Camille or Ulrika. Rudolf and Mary Jo weren't in the thick of things, but janitors and costumers sometimes heard more than people realized. Lawrence might have a few more stories to tell, but he tended to avoid revealing anything that put him in a bad light. Reade and Lisette were valid sources, not to mention the likes of Jim & Bob, Corabelle, Teresa, and Juergen. I would need to keep my eyes and ears open for opportunities to hear their sides of the story.

62.

The pas-de-trois going on between Sven, Lawrence, and Hugh was becoming less graceful. Because I couldn't catch most of the dialog, the story played out before me in pantomime. This afternoon's rehearsal was a run-through of Act II. Sven would approach Hugh. If Sven caught Lawrence watching, he would retreat. One minute Lawrence and Hugh would interact in character (meaning as rivals for Giulietta's hand), the next as potential lovers. Hugh would flirt with first one, then the other. Was Sven genuinely interested in Hugh or just bored? This could not end well.

Then there was Camille, determined to attract Sven's attention. She had it, in the context of the story. Hoffmann was so infatuated with Giulietta that his soul was on the line. Then I'd see her whisper in his ear, and he'd glower, an expression that was pure Sven. What did she have on him, and why bother? She was married. He was gay.

Well, technically, bi.

I ate dinner alone in my hotel room. Again I thought about re-parking, or at least checking up on, my car. Then time ran out and I had to rush back to rehearsal.

During the dead space in which Corabelle blocked the villain's aria and the love duet and inserted the fight sequence, I kept to myself. Once I caught our director looking in my direction, uncharacteristically subdued.

When, as Nicklausse, I pulled at Sven's coat, coaxing him to escape with me, he snapped, "Watch the jacket! It's Armani."

Corabelle put her hands on her hips. "What is this? Should I give you a special rehearsal coat from the costume shop in hopes that you just might permit yourself to stay in character?" They glared at each other.

After Corabelle stormed away, he said, "I'm sorry, Debbie."

"No problem," I said. "I can see that you're … under strain."

He grimaced. "To put it mildly," he said.

I had trouble picturing Camille as Carmen. Cold-blooded courtesan, yes, hot-blooded Spanish cigarette girl/smuggler/serial seductress? No. Small wonder it was Juanita who blew the critics away. In the opera, Carmen jilts her mamma's boy lover for a lusty matador. Here, Camille was the picador, the one who prepares the way for the matador, infuriating the bull by driving spikes into its back. Her bull? Sven, of course. Sven was already snorting and pawing the ground. How much more could he take?

According to Lawrence, Ulrika had her own agenda with Sven. In one respect at least, she and Camille were rivals. Would she, too, choose to wave her red cape in Sven's face, unaware that he had already been primed by a picador?

63.

The next morning I set out to check on my car. No matter that only a week had passed. I had a bad feeling.

There was a chill in the clear morning air. Shivering with foreboding more than cold, I rode my bike down Arrowhead Avenue to the spot where I had parked the car, next to a row of ornamental plum trees. At the time I had noticed how the red leaves contrasted with the sky-blue paint of my Civic. There was no Civic to be found, only a white Volvo. This had to be the place—at the end of a dead-end block, by the entrance to the pocket park. In the unlikely event that my memory was playing tricks on me, I pedaled up, down, and around the area, unsteady and dispirited. No bird with a broken wing could have appeared more pitiful. My strength failed me. It was as if the weight of my bicycle had increased tenfold. Finally, after a quarter of an hour, I abandoned hope.

The few rundown pre-fab ramblers in the area were recessed and tucked snugly behind barriers of hedges and dense clumps of rhododendrons. The perfect spot for a car thief to operate unobserved. Old as the car was, it was a Honda, prized for its parts. Chances are, my faithful friend had been vivisected, and its few salable assets were giving new life to vehicles down in Mexico.

Blinded by tears, I must have been quite an object of pity at Starbucks, as I ordered my raspberry scone and double latte. The whole cast might have been congregating there, for all I noticed or cared. I sought out my usual park bench, hoping for once that Lawrence might be there to comfort me.

After a morning of poking me with its fickle fingers, fate had decided to take pity. There on the bench, as if provided by the gods to boost my sagging morale, sat Reade. He glanced up distractedly from his newspaper, unaware of his divine mission.

"Hi there, Debbie!" he said. "Have a seat."

I sat, my tears temporarily dried. "Would you like some?" I offered, breaking my scone into pieces.

"No thanks," he said, slapping his six-pack abs. "I have to be careful at my age."

He couldn't have been much more than 40 and looked ten years younger. "If you say so," I said, sipping my coffee. "By the way, I'm afraid my car is history." As blithely as this remark was uttered, it was followed by a torrent of tears.

Reade reacted with typical male helplessness, murmuring, "There, there" and patting me gingerly on the back, the way one might comfort an aged neighbor who smelled bad. After about ten minutes of this, I regained my composure. We both sat silently as I continued to sniff. I had used up all the Kleenex in my mini-packet and now had them all wadded up in my fists. Not knowing what else to do, I stuffed them in my purse.

Finally Reade said, "Better?" Then he went back to flipping through his newspaper. I was about to be insulted, when he asked, "Have you seen today's *Ville d'Aurore Herald*?"

"No."

"Was … is your car by any chance a light blue Honda Civic LX?"

64.

I held out a shaky hand, and Reade passed me the newspaper. The brief news item read *Local Teenager Plunges into Lake, Drowns.*

> Lester Romaine, 19, drowned yesterday after driving into Lake Ookietamma. The divers who retrieved his body say the automobile is a 1992 light blue Honda Civic LX. According to the boy's parents, the vehicle did not belong to Lester. Police are investigating.

"They don't give the plate number," I said, clinging to a shred of hope.

He made a call on his cell. "Sally? Do you have the plate number of that car they fished out of Lake Ookietamma today? 113 OMG. Thanks." The waxy pallor of my cheeks was answer enough.

"My car has been claimed by pond scum!" I lamented, tears springing to my eyes afresh.

"Lake Ookietamma is amazingly clean," he said. "I'm sorry. Bad joke. Only, don't feel sad. This is really your lucky day. I'll buy you a new car. You'll like the new Honda Civics. You'll be amazed to discover how much cars have improved in the past fifteen years. They have air-bags, cup-holders, CD-players, all manner of modern conveniences."

"No need to be sarcastic," I sobbed. Damn it, I had thought I was done with tears! However, these were tears of happiness. A new car, Zowie! "I can't help it if I couldn't afford a new car," I said, feeling vaguely guilty about this new, false plea for sympathy. Now that I would soon be the proud owner of a new car, I was enjoying his pity. I was a helpless girl, entrapped in a web of evil. Why wasn't Reade using my despair as an excuse to enfold me in his arms? Instead, realizing that my supply of Kleenex was exhausted, he handed me a folded handkerchief.

"I'm sorry, Debbie," he said. "I joke when I'm uncomfortable. I hate to see a woman cry. What worries me is what the investigation will find."

"What do you mean?"

"You're accident prone. Suspiciously so. I doubt the Enemies of Elitist Entertainment is going to claim responsibility for this one. Not only that, it wouldn't surprise me to hear that your car was booby-trapped."

Suddenly I was dry-eyed. "Give me a break! This isn't Iraq."

"Come on, Debbie, I'll take you to the station. The guys will want a statement."

I consulted my watch. "I have a rehearsal in twenty minutes."

"They're blocking Act III today, right?" He made another call. "Corabelle? I have to take Debbie to the police station. No, she's okay. But her car's a goner. Some kid drove it into a lake." He listened. "Who knows? Probably joy riding." Another beat. "Sure, I'll tell her." He ended the call and said, "Corabelle says you can skip this afternoon's rehearsal. She'll work with you this evening. Damn it, now I wish we had reported the other incidents. When was the last time you drove your car, by the way?"

"A week ago. I haven't needed it."

Reade tapped the newspaper repeatedly with his forefinger. "How have you been getting around?"

"By foot or bicycle. I don't need to buy groceries because the hotel provides everything. Anything else I've needed has fit easily into my backpack."

Did I imagine the condescension in his smile? For a rich man, life had to be a lot more complicated. "If the car was tampered with, your frugal ways saved your bacon. This time at least."

65.

In Act III Nicklausse is basically an afterthought. Hoffmann woos his aspiring/expiring, singer/fiancée, Antonia. At the end of the act Nicklausse makes a last-minute entrance in time to stop Antonia's father Crespel from stabbing Hoffmann. It was as if the librettist had said, *Shoot, forgot about Nicklausse. Can't exclude Hoffmann's conscience!* The part of Antonia's mother, referred to as *the Voice* in the script, is more integral to the action. Because I would never leave the picture frame, my blocking would be elementary, a stunt to be worked out with the tech crew rather than the director.

Reade held my hand—figuratively at least—during the interview at the police station. He helped supply details of everything that had occurred to date, including the smoke bomb bombardment by the EEE and the 1:00 a.m. haunting accompanied by the Act III soundtrack. When I mentioned the threatening cell phone call, he made me swear to notify him immediately if anything the slightest bit suspicious happened, even if it was little more than an odd bubble pattern in the hot-tub.

"I'm sorry about your car," he said when he dropped me off at the hotel. "I can take you by the Honda dealership tomorrow morning, if you like."

"That's kind of you, but no," I said. "Let's wait until I'm about to leave Ville d'Aurore. No point in providing fresh targets for thieves or vandals."

"You're a smart girl, Miss de Lille," he said, then saluted me, a brave soldier in his opera corps. I was Viola in *Twelfth Night*, except that in this version, Duke Orsino knew I was a woman and couldn't care less. Who was Olivia in this story, Ulrika or Camille? How about Teresa? I hadn't seen Reade hit on Lisette, but why not? As for me, I was merely someone Reade needed to keep tabs on. At best I was his personal spy, at worst a lawsuit, should one of my *accidents* do me in.

Before I left Reade's protection, I told him about the phone call with Willy Wooley. "Do me a favor," he said when I finished the story, his voice tense. "No more detective work, okay? Let me handle things from here on out."

I had expected a slap on the back, not a slap on the wrist! Feeling badly put-upon, I bid him a curt farewell.

Word of my latest misfortune had spread by the time I rejoined the rehearsal. "You okay?" Corabelle asked, touching me lightly on the shoulder. "I hear you're going to get a new car. Go for something sleek in silver! Reade can afford it. You can call it Silver Lining. All right, you drama queen, enough of hogging the limelight. Let someone else have a little attention."

"Gladly," I said.

Corabelle introduced me to Jason Bell, the set designer, so he could help me acclimate to the mechanical frame where Antonia's mother would come to life. A no-nonsense, flamboyant man who hardly bothered to glance my way, Jason would have failed to pick me out of a lineup of three if called in to the police station two hours from now. He wasn't all that memorable himself. Tall and boney, with a disproportionately small, sneering face and stringy hair.

Jason spelled out every possible hitch—nothing within my control, by the way—as if explaining the workings of a landmine. From what I could tell, my job basically involved moving into place and finding my light. Okay, slightly more complicated. The portrait—there was a slight resemblance—was painted on a sheer canvas that would disappear when backlit, so I needed to memorize the figure's pose. Jason's simple message consumed a full half-hour. After I got the gist, I only half listened.

The scene unfolding between Sven and Ulrika competed for my attention.

66.

Sven and Ulrika had that stiff, breakable look of outrage that was unmistakable at twenty paces, despite their obvious efforts to keep the matter private. It was indefinably more disturbing than what I had witnessed earlier between Camille and Sven. Sven was definitely seeing red. It was merely a question of who would be gored.

Corabelle opened the rehearsal by running the trio, mechanical frame and all. As predicted, the portrait revolved smoothly into position, relieving me of the burden of having to stand in place for the first part of the act. "Okay, let's see the whole thing," Corabelle said, mostly for the benefit of a conspicuously bored Ludovic. "This is a quick change for you, Debbie, so Mary Jo will be waiting in the wings to help."

Antonia's death scene is brief, by opera standards, although you could argue that she spends the entire act dying. Afterwards Nicklausse enters with Hoffmann, utters two words, "Unhappy man!" and drags him to safety before Antonia's father, Crespel, can kill him. Naturally Crespel blames the lover instead of the real culprit, the doctor.

Corabelle congratulated me by snaking her arm around my waist and giving it a squeeze. "You've got a tiny little waist, for a man," she said. "In this act you're every boy's dream: his mother and his best friend, only he doesn't have to feel bad about lusting after you." At a loss for a suitably flippant response, I giggled inanely. I was fourteen again, and one of my father's handsomer postal employee friends was fondling my thigh under the dinner table. Disturbing, though not exactly unpleasant.

The entrance of Mary Jo rescued me from further regressions into adolescence. "There's a new wig waiting for you," she said. "On your next break, give it a try."

"Go ahead," Corabelle said, waving me on. "I'm going to run the first few scenes again. We won't get to the trio again tonight, so you can go back to your hotel room and fantasize …" (she paused wickedly) "about your dream car."

I descended the winding staircase to the basement, humming my part. This was my way of whistling in the dark, as if music, like bear bells, really had the power to hold scary things at bay. I didn't need to believe in ghosts to worry about my safety in this place. Under the circumstances, Reade wouldn't approve of my wandering down here alone, but what was the alternative? To drag one of the others along for company? After this I would run like hell to my room, dead-bolt the doors, and take a long, hot bath with Travis McGee and *The Deep Blue Goodbye.*

Bless Mary Jo's tight gray bun. The wig was a decided improvement, just the right shade of golden brown and a shaggier, softer cut to frame my long face.

"Nice," a man's voice said. I screamed. Not a very loud scream, kind of like the low moan that rises up in the throat, unbidden, at the sight of a mouse. I was about to improve upon it when I identified the intruder as Rudolf Lowlander, the janitor, staring at me cockeyed. One of Rudolf's eyes wandered off while the other stayed disconcertingly fixed on my face.

"Hi Rudolf," I said, trying to pretend that my pulse wasn't still revving up as my flight or fight response kicked in. "You startled me."

"I didn't mean to," he said, moving in closer. I repressed the urge to counter him with a backward step. "You're nice," he said, in a way that made me never want to hear the word again. "Those others, those sopranos, they're not. Teresa is nice. Those others, they treat me like dirt. I may work in dirt, but I'm not dirt."

"Of course you're not!" I said in my best guidance-counselor voice. “You’re a nice man yourself.” *Nice* in the icky way he said it, anyway. I turned back to the mirror and fooled with the wig, hoping to get the point across that I was a busy woman. No such luck.

“That other one died,” he said, his good eye meeting mine in the mirror.

“Uh, who—?”

“The one with your part. Juanita. She wasn’t nice.”

“You knew her?”

“She was in *Carmen*. She wasn’t supposed to be Carmen, but it worked out that way, didn’t it?” He smiled, the kind of expression Vincent Price mastered in his later films.

Thank God I was listed unequivocally in the *nice* category. I hoped Santa Claus was listening. “Uh, Rudolf, what are you talking about?” Knowing (and hoping) not to have this chance again, I resisted the urge to make a mad dash for the stairs in favor of continuing my interrogation.

“She was a sneaky one. She worked it out. She told that other one, the one playing the good girl, not to complain when she got sick. Those are the breaks! She said. She had a nerve.” He glowered at the memory. “Not nice.” So Lisette had complained, had she? Loud enough for Rudolf to hear. She was human after all. “I think she knew,” he said, after a pause you could drive a hearse through.

“Who knew, Rudolf? And what did they know?”

“The good girl. She knew what Juanita did.”

“What Juanita did? What did she do, and how do you know it?” I hoped I didn’t sound as exasperated as I felt. This was as annoying as that old *Who’s on First?* routine.

“She arranged it. I just know,” he said, thrusting out his lower lip. This psycho didn’t know anything. Time for my getaway. I removed the wig at a deliberately unhurried pace and brushed out my hair. “Well, Rudolf, it’s been nice, uh *good* talking to you.” He wandered to the stairwell, barring my exit. I was Joan Fontaine in the Hitchcock version of *Rebecca*, confronting the simpleminded fisherman down by the dock. She went in the sea ... Ugh. I supposed someone like Rudolf would be impossible to fire, with affirmative action and all. But Reade should be aware, if he wasn't already, what a creepy, possibly criminally-deranged employee he had.

"Excuse me!" I said as I pushed past him. My relief was short-lived. Once back at the hotel, I realized with a heavy heart that I had left my backpack at the theater.

67.

Damn it, I needed that backpack! Sure, I could get a new keycard for my room, but what about my money, ID, etc.? I girded my loins and sprinted back to the theater, breaking all personal records for speed. The rehearsal must have ended early. The lights were off, and no music emanated from the ballroom. And yet the lobby door was unlocked. Why hadn't I phoned Reade? Hadn't I promised not to do anything foolish? Removing my shoes, I tiptoed up the winding back staircase with exaggerated stealth in the manner of a Looney-Tunes American Indian.

I heard whispering, froze, and cowered. I could just make out the voices of Sven and Ulrika.

"Camille told me her little secret," Ulrika hissed. "And that's just one rip in your net of lies. All that's needed to unravel the whole thing is to put a bug in the ear of whoever organizes that competition."

"So what?" he shot back. "I'm booked into the next decade. Yes, they could withdraw the prize. But if they did, I wouldn't change my press releases. I won that competition fair and square. Who's going to care if I fudged my age?"

"Excuse me! I call five years more than fudging."

"I'm not going to discuss this with you anymore."

"Fine, then take the consequences."

"I could say the same to you," Sven said.

"Oh yeah?" she challenged.

"Isn't it interesting about Debbie's car? You know, your husband being a mechanic and all."

"I haven't touched that bitch's car."

"So you say. I might claim otherwise, with sufficient motive. I wouldn't put it past you. Don't you see how useless this is?" Sven was pleading now. "You're an attractive woman, but I'm not interested! I'm not into women! As a rule, I mean. What makes you think you're going to blackmail me into going for you again?"

Ulrika's tone changed abruptly from combative to wheedling, "You enjoyed it. You know you did!"

"Sure, in the moment. I was drunk and horny." A slap reverberated throughout the stairway. "Ouch! That's gonna show."

"Good. It's about time your actions had consequences! You haven't heard the last of this." Hmm, now I understood. Ulrika was unbalanced. Make that stark-raving mad. No woman in her right mind would consider blackmail an effective strategy to win over a man's affections. We were in *Fatal Attraction* territory. And what was Camille's little secret? Could she be pregnant with Sven's baby?

Ulrika's stomping footsteps gradually died away. I didn't allow myself to imagine what might have transpired if they hadn't both used the front staircase. Damn it. If only I could ask Sven to escort me home! But then he might realize what I had overheard ... To hell with it! I was too freaked out not to take my chances.

"Sveh-eh-ehn?" I called out after sneaking back down to the lobby. The tremolo of fear in my voice made me sound about 95.

68.

"Debbie?" Sven responded from the darkness.

I slipped my shoes back on. "I thought that was you!" I said with forced heartiness. "My backpack is around here somewhere, and I'm too freaked out to search for it on my own. Come with me?"

"Of course," he said. There was a tap on my shoulder.

"Eeeek!" I shrieked. I held my hand to my leaping heart. "I'm sorry, Sven, you startled me. I'm so glad you're still here. Uh ... why are you still here?" After all, I didn't want him to think I had been eavesdropping.

"I came back for my, um, backpack as well," he said. He hefted it over one shoulder for emphasis. "Where do you think you left yours?"

Unbelievably, considering the kind of day it had been, my bag lay in the corner, exactly where I left it. Everything appeared to be in order, keycard included. "That's a relief," I said. "What a day!"

"Yes," he said. "I'd suggest a drink, but I'm toasted already. Not in a good way."

"Oh?" I said. "Hoffmann is a killer role."

"You said it," he said, snaking a companionable arm along my shoulder and around my neck. When I flinched, he pulled away. "Sorry. I didn't mean anything."

"No, I'm sorry. I'm jumpy as hell. I had a run-in with Rudolf in the costume shop."

"Oh him. He's harmless."

"That may be. He sure doesn't seem harmless."

We were both silent as we walked past the park toward the Ville d'Aurore Lodge. "Nice night," Sven finally said. We stood on the lawn that overlooked the lake, illuminated softly by the lights of the marina. All was still, except for the lapping of water against the shore. "Sit with me for a minute?"

"All right." I kicked off my shoes and sat a few feet away from him, cross-legged on the damp grass. "It's a bit chilly," I commented.

His laugh was an unconvincing *heh heh heh*, a gutted version of his usual full-bodied guffaw. "I can't read you, Debbie," he said. "That sounded like a hint. I'd rub your shoulders, but I have been slapped around enough for one day." He probed his jaw experimentally.

"Yes," I said. "I'm a regular spitfire. And I've noticed how reluctant you are to take chances."

He unfolded his long body, leaning back on his elbows and stretching his legs. "You're relatively harmless, I guess, other than your sharp tongue."

I folded my legs in a lotus position. "Thank you, I think."

"Sarcasm is not unknown in my family," he said, gazing up at the stars. "One of the advantages of being estranged from my parents is that I'm spared my father's rapier wit."

"You're not in touch with them at all?"

He folded his arms behind his head. "It's not official. I call my mom every eon or so. At Christmas I went home for two whole days. I thought, once I had made it to this point in my career, that … I mean, everyone, uh, everything else falls into my lap. With my parents, it doesn't matter. They don't have a clue what goes into an opera career. While I was in high school, my father wanted me to play football. I became a cheerleader. Later he wanted me to become a surgeon, like him. I became an opera singer. He told me to grow up, so I grew tall. There's no pleasing some people."

"Yes," I said, nodding vigorously. "My parents are desperate to marry me off."

"Interesting," Sven said, reaching over to give my neck a squeeze. "I'd think some rich doctor would have snatched you up by now." My neck smarted from Sven's playful mauling. The man didn't know his own strength. Frankenstein's monster hadn't intended to kill that child, either.

"When it comes to romance, my timing isn't the best," I said. I stood, ostensibly to massage a cramp in my leg. Time for a touch of levity! "You know how the song goes," I said. "*For everything, turn, turn, turn, there is a season,*" I sang, in a free adaptation of the old Byrds' song. "*A time to wed doctors, a time to sing opera....* I never could get those seasons right! The time to marry doctors was college. The time to pursue the singing career was in my twenties. I took a few wrong turns in the opera rat race, and the only way I'm going to meet a doctor is if I end up in the hospital. Come to think of it, the odds are in my favor right now."

"Careful. You might overshoot your goal and end up in the morgue."

"Don't think it hasn't occurred to me."

"The thing I ask myself is, why *you*?" Sven mused. "Why would anyone be envious of *you*? Professionally, I mean." He blew out a breath of air. "That didn't come out right. Sorry!"

I waved away his apology. "I'm not offended. I ask myself the same thing."

"Did you overhear anything?" He was looking out at the marina.

"About what?"

"Don't play dumb. I assume you heard at least a part of my conversation with Ulrika. Otherwise you wouldn't have known it was me. Come on, Debbie, with everything that's happened to you, you'd think twice about asking for help without being damn certain whom you were addressing."

"The timbre of your voice is unmistakable," I said truthfully, then went on to lie, "I wasn't close enough to make out actual words. I realized you were arguing with a woman. After what I witnessed during rehearsal today, I assumed it was Ulrika."

He stood up, locked his fingers around one of my biceps, and looked me squarely in the eye. "Arguing," he said, mimicking my voice. "That's putting it mildly. Listen up, Debbie. Watch your back with the women in this cast. Don't let yourself be cornered, and don't piss them off." He released me then leaned over to kiss my abused arm. "I can't seem to keep my paws off you, darlin'. Forgive me." He held up his wrist and pushed a button to light up the face on his watch. "Time for bed," he concluded. "Thanks for keeping me company. Come on. I'll escort you to your room."

In the florescent hallway lights, Sven looked significantly older than his true age of thirty-four.

69.

The next morning, Reade was waiting for me in the park. I had stopped flattering myself that he was motivated by desire. "Here," I said, handing him a latte. "I thought I might run into you."

He had the grace to look embarrassed. "By the way," I added, "I finally did some Googling."

"Hmm. Learn anything interesting?"

I settled back on the bench, aiming for a Travis McGee-type air of cool indifference. "About you?" I smiled, as if recalling some delicious item. "Naturally. Mostly, though, I was learning more about my colleagues. Great *Carmen* review, by the way, although I can see why you don't post it."

Reade's lips twitched. He wasn't buying my act. "Yeah." He sprawled next to me on the bench. In his designer shades, he out-Travised me by a mile. "According to that review, it was the Sven, Juanita, and Ulrika show. With the attitude Juergen was giving all three of my leading ladies during the run-through, I didn't want to add insult to injury." He frowned. "I wish I could figure out what has gotten into him. His diplomacy skills have deteriorated since that first time around. Frankly, I'd replace him if I could. I'm worried about how this is going to play out when he returns tomorrow."

"What's Hell Week without the devil?"

"From what I hear," Reade said, "everyone is already hot under the collar."

"What did you hear?"

"You first."

I wrestled with my conscience. Repeating Ulrika's threats meant ratting on Sven. On the other hand, Reade wasn't likely to care if Sven had fibbed about his age and would have nothing to gain by exposing his star tenor. "Okay," I said with a sigh of resignation. "I overheard Ulrika taunting Sven about the Corelli Competition. He altered his birth certificate by five years in order to qualify."

Reade nodded. "What does she want him to do?"

"Huh?"

"I assume she's blackmailing him."

"I don't know. It's bizarre. I think all she wants is to have sex with him again."

Reade, who had been focused intently on the activities of a robin pecking at the ground, turned to look me in the eye. "Again? Isn't he gay?"

"Most of the time."

He turned his attention back on the bird. "I'll be damned."

"Camille is holding something over his head, too," I said. I thought about repeating my theory that she was pregnant with Sven's child. With no evidence other than her increased bra size, I decided not to start spreading wild rumors.

"Do you have any idea what that might be?" Reade asked.

"No," I said. "But I think I can enlighten you about Juergen. As far as Camille and Ulrika are concerned, anyway."

"Go on."

"I overheard them discussing his ineptitude with women. They found out that I had been listening, but they didn't notice Juergen."

"Goddamn harpies," Reade muttered. "Bunch of adolescents, including Juergen. He's bad at reading women, and I'm sure they messed with his head just to pass the time. Every one of them could use a lesson in professional conduct."

Surprising talk, considering the source. True, I had only Lawrence's word for it that Reade was a star-fucker. But then, I had seen him in action that first night. Even though I hadn't been privy to Reade and Ulrika's conversation, it didn't take an expert to interpret their body language.

"What was Juanita like?" I asked.

For a moment he seemed lost in thought. Finally he said, "Hmm … what can I say about Juanita? She was very talented, certainly. I'm amazed the reviewers didn't like her in *Der Rosenkavalier*. She was one hot tamale as Carmen. Of course the vocal demands are entirely different. The tessitura of Octavian is almost soprano, so yeah, I could see her straining on the high notes. And I suppose giving a male character sex appeal is harder for a woman like that than simply doing what comes—" He paused.

"Naturally?" I said, finishing his thought. Reade knew an awful lot about voices for a money man.

"Juanita was a Latina scorcher. I've always found that, when someone is truly graced with sex appeal, it registers with both sexes. Women might not like Juanita personally, but few could deny her animal magnetism."

"What made Camille miss the performance?"

"It was her own fault. She insisted on going for a drive, to calm her nerves, she said. Her car broke down. A leak in the radiator, I think it was. She was stranded on some back road where she couldn't get a signal on her cell. Because of her outfit—a tight skirt and stilettos—even the short hike to the nearest farm house to summon help took longer than it should have. There was no snow, but the temperature was below freezing. When Peter reported that she hadn't signed in, I told Juanita to suit up. Camille called at ten minutes to curtain to tell us she was on her way, but I made an executive decision to go with Juanita." He paused. "Anyhow, I should have cast Juanita to begin with."

"Weren't you suspicious?"

"Huh?"

"Sounds like a setup to me. I'll bet Camille thought she was meeting a man, someone she was incredibly hot for. Why else take a drive to nowhere dressed like that?"

"She always dresses like that."

"It's classic *All about Eve*."

"You think?"

"Have you seen the movie?"

"Of course," he said. "Bette Davis's car trouble allows her understudy Ann Baxter to go on in her place and become a star. In that instance Ann is smart enough not to do her own dirty work. She trusts the arrangements to Bette's best friend, who thinks Bette could use a lesson in humility."

"You know your classic movies," I said. "Anyone ever tell you that you look like Stewart Granger?"

"Constantly," he replied without hesitation. I cursed myself for gushing all over him. "I'm kidding," he added. "No one has ever told me that. Jeff Chandler, yes, but he wasn't half so classy. Thanks.

It's a nice compliment."

"What's a nice compliment?" Teresa asked. Where the hell had she come from? She was wearing a bright yellow sundress with little black flowers. That's when I suddenly realized there were no bees buzzing around us.

"Reade, where are the bees?" I asked.

"Oh," Reade groaned. "I had them rounded up and moved for the run of the opera. According to my legal counsel, it was the only solution."

"I could just shoot that Ulrika!" Teresa exclaimed, stamping her tiny foot. "Those poor little ol' bees!" She looked cuter than a honey bee herself, in her yellow and black finery. It occurred to me then that Reade might think so, too. Sure, she could have used a little mascara and lip gloss, but her figure was as close to perfection as it gets outside of New York or LA, and she was a good ten years my junior. Reade didn't have that glazed-over, reduced to Silly Putty look infatuated men get, but that didn't mean anything. At his age, you didn't wear your heart on your sleeve.

"Don't worry, Teresa," he said, enjoying her precious little tantrum. "The bees will be back as soon as Hoffmann closes. I can assure you that Ulrika will not."

"Well, so long guys!" I said, trying to sound chipper. They seemed to have forgotten that I was standing there. "I'll see you at the theater."

70.

Hell Week was nearly upon us. I didn't see how the atmosphere could get any less hospitable. We were already exhausted, pissed off, and interacting with glacial formality. I was holding up better than most, considering. My voice had recovered sooner than predicted.

Even the perpetually upbeat Corabelle was in a foul mood. I understood why after Sven showed me the article in the *Weekend*

Journal. It began as the usual pre-performance puff piece, providing a summary of the opera's plot and a paragraph of background on Jacques Offenbach, the composer. Offenbach's main body of work had been close to 100 satirical operettas written for the French stage. This, his one stab at grand opera, was completed by another composer after his death. If only the journalist had stopped there.

But no. There followed an account of the smoke bomb attack by the EEE, Enemies of Elitist Entertainment, and the tragic car accident of Juanita Macaree-Smith, beloved by Ville d'Aurore audiences who fondly remembered her brilliant Carmen.

The author proceeded to quote Corabelle, impressively articulate:

> In our version, Hoffmann is a world-weary celebrity author of our times, reminiscing with his fans about the misspent, final three decades of his life. Each of his three great loves is an icon of her decade and a female archetype. Hoffmann longs for a poetic ideal of a woman. No one, be she flesh and blood or man-made, can live up to that. The closest is the sexual obsession of his old age, the opera singer Stella. However, human weakness, age, and dissipation thwart him to the very end, and he is left with nothing but his art, embodied in his best friend, the sexually ambiguous Nicklausse. In other words, his ideal companion has been by his side all along. Like most of us, he is too blind to recognize true love when he finds it.

So far so good. But then came the clincher. In the last few paragraphs, the reviewer, obviously on the prowl for controversy, had interviewed Ulrika and Camille. Here was Ulrika's contribution:

> In this *update*, my character Antonia has AIDS, the legacy of her mother and father. In the original, of course, she suffers from a mysterious heart ailment. Personally I'm not a fan of

> updating. A heart condition isn't a sexual disease; AIDS is. What man in his right mind would want to marry a girl wasting away from AIDS? It's simply not plausible.

The topper was Camille's two cents worth:

> You're supposed to conclude that Hoffmann is a closeted homosexual; that, if he weren't so afraid to confront the truth, he'd recognize that Nicklausse is his soul mate. Corabelle is famous for her avant-garde concepts, so she must know what she's doing. Personally, I think that sexual politics have no place in opera.

Small wonder Corabelle was furious. These quotations were akin to mutiny. Summoned by Peter, the timid stage manager, Reade showed up at rehearsal to practice damage control. Whatever he said convinced Corabelle to keep a lid on her outrage. So instead of the real culprits being chastised, we all took the brunt of Corabelle's wrath.

Although he sang as brilliantly as ever, Sven looked strung out. It had to be exhausting being the company sex object. In Act III, which we would finish blocking this afternoon, Sven had minimal contact with Lawrence, who played the deaf old servant Frantz. There was no divisive human element in the form of Hugh to exacerbate the situation. Frantz's aria is the comic high point of the opera, if milked for all it's worth. Lawrence's comic chops were more than equal to the task.

> Night and day, without much pay, I work my fingers to the bone,
> While by myself I wail away, tho' I'm not known for my lovely tone.
> From Master's scorn, I have found relief,
> I sing my song ... now and then.
> I wish I could sing with greater ease!

Tra la la ... Opera fans are hard to please!
Tra la la ... I would bring them to their knees!
La la la (etc.)
No! No matter how I try, this song is too high!

A character tenor doesn't need the world's greatest voice. In fact, a reedy, nasal quality can enhance the comedy. Lawrence's instrument, while not as strong as Sven's, was almost as beautiful and easy, so in this aria, where Frantz is supposed to butcher the high notes, Lawrence had to fake the struggle. It's a high-wire act of knowing when to let the voice break, while winking at audience as if to say, *I could sing this in my sleep*. Lawrence was so funny that even Sven was moved to laugh the infectious Ha! Ha! HA! of more carefree times. Afterwards Sven approached Lawrence. Although I wasn't close enough to hear their words, the way they laughed and touched would have made Hugh jealous, no matter whom he was favoring.

Sven and Ulrika were as dour as the farmers in American Gothic, and their kiss was less convincing than the most wooden peck from some Hollywood B-movie filmed in the prudish post-Code forties. Corabelle kept communication to a minimum, moving us around as impersonally as pieces on a chess board. The edgy atmosphere would have oppressed Cindy Lou Who. I wasn't exempt, especially because I had taken to brooding over Reade and Teresa. What healthy man wouldn't respond to that fresh-faced Songbird of the South?

Lately I had been avoiding Lawrence. I wasn't anxious to hear him shine his unreliable spotlight on my miscreant colleagues unless it was to expose my persecutors. Still, when he invited me to join him and Hugh for dinner, I was down-in-the-mouth enough to accept.

"Great, Hon!" Lawrence said. "Wait a minute, will you? I'm going to the Little Boys' Room."

71.

While I loitered in the lobby, partially concealed by a larger-than-life statue of the Comte de Bragelonne, Angelo strolled by, looking as though he could use a pat on the back. "Hello, Angelo," I said in my primitive Italian, "You're looking nice tonight." He nearly jumped out of his Italian leather boots. We had never spoken, other than to introduce ourselves, so I guess my comment did come out of the blue. He looked stylish and sophisticated in his crisp white shirt and well-cut slacks, a navy blue jacket flung over one shoulder. The man should go easier on the cologne, I thought, as he moved in too close for comfort. "You sing beautifully, too," I continued in Italian, "Bravo! The diamond aria is magnificent."

He kissed my hand. "You speak Italian!" he said, also in that language.

"Poorly, I'm afraid," I demurred. Although, really, I meant it! Like most American classical singers, I had a working knowledge of Italian, French, and German. Although my accents in all three were deceptively authentic, I rarely attempted actual conversations. Simple phrases were another story.

"Why don't you join me for dinner?" he said, staring deep into my eyes. Uh-oh. And here I had assumed I was at least ten years too old and several cup sizes too small to interest him.

Suddenly I heard Camille's voice emanating from the backdoor of the theater. She was close enough to overhear but shielded from view. "Hi, Ulrika," she said, "Where would you like to go to dinner?" Angelo was distracted into silence.

"How about Chinese? The others haven't discovered Mr. Wong's."

"How did the rehearsal go?"

"Fine," Ulrika said. "I've got to hand it to Angelo, he sounds great as Dapertutto."

"Lucky for him that he can perform somewhere. I mean, outside of bed!"

They both laughed. "I hear he's attempted to fuck most of the chorus," Camille remarked.

"He knows better than to try his luck with us again," Ulrika said. "I hope he has a generous supply of Viagra. Everyone knows time has taken its toll on the leaning tower of Pisa!"

"Yes they do," Camille replied, "thanks to you." And they were gone. The conversation had been carried on in an undertone, for them. That's the trouble with opera-singer resonance. Even pianissimo phrases fill the theater.

"Angelo—" I began, wracking my brain for a breezy comment that might defuse the contrails of nastiness that hung in the air. With his soft brown eyes, I had never seen him look anything but cuddly and benign. At this moment, fists clenched, teeth set, and brown eyes blazing, he was the most convincing Dapertutto, ever.

"Please don't," he said, warding me off with the outstretched palm of his hand. "I'm sorry, I must go now." He fled the theater.

72.

Lawrence arrived just in time to see Angelo storm out. "Phew!" he said. "What's eating him?"

"Still in character, I guess," I said. I saw no need to compound Angelo's humiliation by informing the town crier. "Where are we meeting Hugh?"

"Mr. Wong's."

"Good Lord, no. Call Hugh and tell him anywhere but Mr. Wong's. I overheard Ulrika and Camille saying that's where they're headed."

We opted for the healthful Green Bar, where we ordered salads. Here I was treated to all the news unfit to print, even on *OperaChatter.Com*. Angelo and the chorus girls, of course. Camille and Reade? Lawrence's evidence, that they had been seen having drinks and engaged in intimate conversation, was unconvincing. What might have interested me was who Hugh was favoring this week, Sven or Lawrence. There was little chance I'd learn the answer tonight, if indeed the fickle Hugh had made up his mind.

"What about Lisette?" I asked suddenly, remembering what she had said about dallying with Hubert Silvertone during that first haunting. "I think she's carrying on with someone."

Lawrence wrinkled his nose. "I don't think so, honey!" he said. "If she had been catting around, someone would have heard that big tail going bump in the night." This got me thinking ... what about Mrs. Silvertone? How could Hubert get away for a whole night? Wouldn't it have been safer for him to come to Lisette's room? This was silly. It was too stupid a slip to be a lie. Mrs. Silvertone had probably been out of town, and Hubert didn't want to risk being seen at the Lodge.

"Anyone can keep a secret if the stakes are high enough," I said. *You, for instance*, I added silently.

His thin bottom lip jutted as he pondered the possibility. "Well maybe. She might be able to bully someone into sleeping with her. God knows, she's no Shrinking Violet. Dominatrix is her default career." We all laughed. "No, really! I read it on the Internet."

"You did not," Hugh said, giving him a playful slap.

"I could have," Lawrence said. "Maybe I'll send an anonymous tip to *OperaChatter.Com*."

"What about Reade and Teresa?" I proposed.

"Hmm, that's juicy! Nah … she's too naive for him. He's a complex man. You should get some of that, Debbie. He likes you."

"Along with everyone else," I sighed.

"So? Fight for him, baby."

"I don't fight for anything," I protested. "I wouldn't even be here, if it weren't for the dumbest of dumb luck, my agent Frankie, and Sven's desire to get out of his contract."

"Sure, but you're running with it, big time. Don't sell yourself short."

"That's right," Hugh agreed. "Think tall. Be the man we all

know you can be. Show us how it's done!"

"Frankie Donato's your agent?" Lawrence said, eyes bulging with disbelief. "You must be doing something right. He's prime cut, too."

"All I did right was to attend the same master's program. He took pity on me. He'll be here opening night. I'd be happy to introduce you." Both Lawrence and Hugh were thrilled at the prospect.

Back at the theater, damsel-in-distress Teresa was being comforted by Reade and Corabelle. Hysteria became her. She cried decorously, like a movie star, with a swollen mouth, glowing cheeks and a few photogenic tears, delicate rivulets unsullied by dissolving mascara.

"What happened, darlin'?" Lawrence said, kneeling at her feet to take her hand.

"They destroyed my costume!" she wailed. "My Stella costume."

"Who did?" Hugh asked, raising an eyebrow. "No, don't tell me. The Enemies of Elitist Entertainment, right?"

Reade narrowed his eyes at Hugh. "How did you guess?"

Hugh shrugged. "It's a damned convenient scapegoat, if you ask me. No need to tell you who detested that costume more than anyone." He directed his gaze to the headshots of the three divas, recently mounted in the lobby.

Lawrence blew out a breath. "Honey, it doesn't take Hercule Poirot!"

"Damn them," Reade said under his breath. "At least this is one act of vandalism I can easily repair, Teresa. Mary Jo has all week to replace that lovely costume. We'll keep the new one under lock and key."

The blocking of the Epilogue went on as scheduled, with Teresa making a brave appearance as the opera singer Stella at the end. After Stella, Hoffmann's ideal woman, finishes her evening performance, she goes to the bar in search of her lover. She finds him there, passed out, and leaves with his rival, Lindorf. The real winner is Nicklausse, a.k.a. Hoffmann's muse. His/her master will continue to create his stories without feminine distractions, at least until the next screwed-up babe comes along.

When it came to love, the fictional Stella liked to keep her options open. The same could surely not be said for her alter ego, Teresa.

73.

Juergen was back. Had he been slumbering deep in the black lagoon, like Godzilla, gathering strength for his last stand?

It was hard to say whether Juergen's return was responsible for the change in Camille and Ulrika. Although still snooty and superior, their bad behavior became less overt, as though they had finally cottoned to the fact that lack of discretion might negatively impact their careers.

Just as mysteriously, the attacks on my person stopped. The new target was Teresa.

The EEE had followed up on the destruction of her costume with a type-written note attached to a rock and tossed through her hotel room window. It read, *Homegrown girl turns traitorous!—THE EEE.* This cut Teresa to the quick. "How can they say such a thing?" she wailed. "I love this place! My heart is divided equally between Ville d'Aurore and Lafitteville. I've never been mean to anyone!"

"She's right about that," Lisette commented, upon witnessing Teresa's latest breakdown. We were sitting in the audience of the theater, waiting for the Sitzprobe to begin. Loosely translated, this means Sitting Rehearsal, a sing-through with orchestra, everyone sitting around in chairs. On stage, the new wood floor was in place, positioned at a gentle rake so you didn't have to worry about falling into the audience. Some stages were so steeply raked you felt like a mountain goat.

As usual, Lisette was an island of calm. She might have been waiting for the Zoo to open, rather than for Juergen to play Zeus, relishing his power to elevate or demote us according to his whims. "This EEE is in left field with its choice of targets," Lisette commented. "First you, who have no prior history with Ville d'Aurore, and now Teresa, who wouldn't hurt a flea and doesn't even have a decent role. Why not Reade? He's the one who makes the financial decisions. I'll tell you why! They're scared of him. It's easier to attack those who can't fight back. The EEE is sort of like an attack of hives. They're not really dangerous, just real irritating."

"You don't think there's a danger they'll go too far?" I said. "What about that hapless teenager who went joyriding in my car?"

"They didn't claim responsibility for that, did they?" Lisette asked. "Well, no matter. It seems like these people have never heard of the Law of Unintended Consequences. We'll assume for the moment they had nothing to do with booby-trapping your car. I don't see how smoke bombs and costume destruction are supposed to compel Reade to give more money to the less elitist arts. What if one of their protests goes awry? That rock could have conceivably hit Teresa on the head and killed her."

"Is your husband an attorney?" I asked.

"Ex-husband. A litigator. How did you guess?"

"For a minute, there, you were sounding a lot like my ex-boyfriend, Winston."

Lisette grimaced. "Attorneys make bad-news partners. The whole time they're compiling evidence against you, you don't even realize you've been indicted."

"Where is your ex now?"

She looked me straight in the eye and said, "Dead."

74.

My eyes widened. "Really?"

Lisette smiled. "Dead to me. Technically, my asshole of an ex is very much alive. And he's not really my ex. Not yet. The divorce isn't final."

Against all expectations, Juergen was surprisingly benign during the Sitzprobe. In fact, most of his criticisms were reasonable and directed at the orchestra. While Ulrika and Camille were singing, he assumed an air of sneering irony, as though he had plenty to say but had been muzzled. Reade's constant presence might have had something to do with that. I hoped he would attend all the remaining rehearsals. Apparently some of us were incapable of playing fair in the absence of a playground monitor.

Dinner was a deli sandwich, turkey and Muenster cheese, which I brought back to my room so I could eat while I returned my mother's call. The combination of food and Mom usually led to indigestion, but there was no help for it.

"Debbie!" my mother boomed, forcing me to hold the phone away from my ear. "We got your postcard. What a nice hotel! This wealthy general director, is he single?"

"Mom!" I scolded, only it sounded more like Maaaaaahm, having been stretched to convey a maximum degree of annoyance.

"Well, is he?"

"No," I lied, just to be contrary.

"Too bad." Well, good, I thought. I've heard the last of that one.

"How's Dad?" I said.

"Very much looking forward to the trip."

I choked on a bite of sandwich.

"Debbie, dear, are you still there?" I heard Mom call out as I dislodged the morsel with a glass of water. "Are you okay?"

"I'm fine, Mom," I said, when I had recovered enough to speak. "Some food went down the wrong pipe."

"You shouldn't eat so fast."

"You're not serious," I said. "You're really coming to opening night?"

"We wouldn't miss it! Roland will be there, too, with his girlfriend." I moaned. "What was that?" she said.

"Why is Roland coming?" I was whining. I couldn't help myself.

"He's your brother!"

"Duh!" What was I, ten years old again?

"Dear, you're not making sense."

"Mom, please put Dad on." I ordered myself to calm down.

"Honey?" Dad said warily, as if bracing for unpleasantness.

"Dad, please tell Mom you don't need to come. And whatever she said to blackmail Roland, she needs to take it back."

"I heard that!" It was my mother. "Roland is coming because he wants to, cross my heart."

I checked my watch. Damn it, time to go back to rehearsal. I had no choice but to surrender. "Fine, lovely. It will be *lovely* to see you all." A cyborg couldn't have missed the sarcasm in my voice.

"Good!" she said brightly. "According to the cards, Opening Night is going to be rough. You're going to need all your loved ones around you. Hugs and kisses!" Before I could react to this outrageous pronouncement, she had hung up.

75.

Saturday was the Piano-Tech rehearsal, a drawn-out, excruciating affair held mostly for the benefit of the Tech Crew. Tempers were short and would have been shorter still without Reade's oversight. For me, it was a mixed blessing. He treated me with friendly neutrality, same as Ulrika and Camille.

All of Reade's warmth seemed reserved for Teresa. After the rock crashed through her window, he had appointed himself as her bodyguard, and she was all over him like frosting on a cake. As Stella, Teresa did no actual singing and was only on stage briefly during the prologue and epilogue. The rest of the time she sat next to Reade in the tenth row of the audience, where they carried on a running whispered commentary, chummy as an old married couple watching home movies.

Sven, a silk scarf entwined around his throat, asked me to spread the word that everyone should keep their distance because he was fighting a cold. He did look uncharacteristically pale and wan. Lawrence and Hugh spoke only when absolutely necessary, so I assumed they had quarreled. Angelo had never been chatty, but now he was also standoffish, convinced that we were all against him. Even Corabelle and Lisette, who could normally be depended upon for a random sarcastic crack, were mysteriously preoccupied. Jim Sod and Bob Alter were the same as ever—friendly but distant. In other words, the rehearsal was not only a touchy affair, but agonizingly dull, depressing, and devoid of comic relief.

After the ordeal was finally over, everyone other than Jim & Bob evaporated into the ozone like runoff after a summer storm in Death Valley. Since I desperately wanted a drink, what better time to kick back with these two men, who might be able to provide the missing tiles to the Byzantine mosaic that had been assembling in my head ever since the smoke bomb incident? When it came to extracurricular drinking, you could count on Jim Sod.

"Great idea," Bob—the old Hell's Angel with the Texas twang—said in response to my proposal. "I'm frankly surprised we're the only ones with a hankerin' for strong spirits. That rehearsal was a trip, man! What's gotten into everybody?"

"If you don't know, I certainly can't tell you," I said as we entered Sammy's Joint, a hop, skip, and a jump away from the theater. This was a genuine neighborhood dive, the kind of place where everyone knows your name, like the song says, because it's tattooed on your lover's biceps. Everyone knew Jim 'n' Bob's names. That was for sure.

Jim, graying hair clipped short and slicked back, wore his signature black suit, white shirt, and skinny tie. Jim was the funeral director in the Clint Eastwood western. Bob belonged on another set—maybe a Mad Max movie—in his motorcycle jacket, cowboy boots and worn jeans. Slowly and steadily Jim downed one beer after another, while Bob nursed a glass of lemonade diluted with ice water. "I don't drink," he said, "anymore."

As far as alcoholics go, Jim was the functional kind. "I prefer the atmosphere of today's rehearsal over what we've experienced during the past week," he commented. Although he had quickly quaffed a pitcher of beer and a few shots of rum for good measure, he didn't break a sweat or slur a syllable. "This is not what I'd call a fun group. In fact, Bob and I are thinking about retiring. The only reason we perform anymore is for fun. This doesn't qualify. Right, Bob?"

"No way, José!" Bob said, sipping his lemonade.

"How long have you lived in Ville d'Aurore?" I asked.

"'Round 'bout twenty years, I guess," Jim said. "Good place. Before Reade started the company, I more or less stuck to musicals and operettas. Bob 'n' I are classically trained. We met in the opera program at Juilliard. It didn't take long to figure out that we're too laid back for this business. Reade convinced us to move here, said he'd introduce us to his contacts."

"*Reade* convinced you to move here?" I said, more confused than ever. "Was he at Juilliard, too?"

"Yep!" Jim said. "Then his sister got killed, and—I'm sure you know all this."

76.

"His sister got killed?" I was turning into a parrot.

"Reade was a fabulous baritone," Bob said. "But he went into law enforcement instead, to find his sister's killer. It was some ex-beau, a great-lookin' sociopath they both knew from grade school. Last person you'd suspect."

"Poor Reade," I said.

"Not so poor anymore," Jim replied, pouring from the second pitcher of beer. To the burly waiter, he said, "Plate of nachos, Sammy? Sammy's the owner. Sammy, this here's Debbie de Lille. Fine singer."

"Thanks," I said.

"Don't mention it. It's only the truth. Bob and I have family money to tide us over. We teach some at the local community college. And Bob directs there. It's a good life."

I asked about Rudolf. "He's been here a long time, long as us. He's an odd duck, harmless. Not quite all there, if you get my meaning. A few beats short of a measure."

I laughed, dutifully. "How long has Teresa lived here?"

"All her life."

"Not with that accent," I said. I sipped my wine and grimaced. It was my fault. No one ordered wine in a place like this. You ordered beer. I hated beer.

"The beer's better," Jim said, pouring himself another glass. "But you asked about Teresa. She goes back and forth. She was adopted. Then her adoptive parents divorced. Her mom lives in Louisiana, her dad here. Growing up, she spent the majority of the year in Louisiana, and that accent wins out every time. I pick it up just talkin' to her, don't you? It's catchier than Bob's."

"I'm from Texas," Bob volunteered. "Dallas. Not the place to be gay."

"What about Ville d'Aurore?" I said, assessing the other patrons. It was a safe bet they weren't big Sondheim fans. "Neo-Nazis and Mormons, right? Not the first haven you consider when fleeing social oppression."

"Heh, heh, heh!" Jim chortled, slapping his thigh. "Do you take everything at face value? The outskirts are another story, but Ville d'Aurore is true blue. Most of these guys are so open-minded, they might have been raised by wolves." His eyes followed one particularly well-muscled specimen. "Or apes. Like Tarzan. Before Jane, that is."

"How well do you know Reade?" I asked, before he got too side-tracked.

"Oh, it's Reade you're interested in, huh? Lawrence said you two were an item. I knew you'd cut to the chase sooner or later."

My cheeks flamed. I was never going to listen to anything Lawrence told me again. Reade was not my primary interest here. Okay, so I wasn't averse to hearing about Reade.

"Hah, bulls-eye!" Jim said, pointing at me. "The ladies do like

Reade, and he likes them. He's a handsome devil. Too bad he's not gay."

"I wouldn't know, because we're not involved," I stated for the record. As if anyone gave a hoot. Jim & Bob's eyes met, eyebrows lifted. "Is it difficult to be gay in this town?" I asked, as if conducting an interview for my high school newspaper.

Jim acknowledged a man across the room before answering, "Let's just say they got used to us. So you want to know about Reade. Sorry we can't help. We go way back, but we're not buddies. He's a hard man to know."

77•

I didn't learn anything useful after that. Jim, Bob, and I talked about musical theater and the business. The kind of stuff disgruntled, washed-up opera singers discuss. How no one can afford to pursue a career nowadays. How aspiring singers in the 40s used to be able to afford daily voice lessons—the only real way to make progress. How, unless you're a natural and find a patron, you might as well give up. Agents were looking for young flash-in-the-pans, who were usually pretty and had small voices, so that the BIG, exciting voices that come in big, less-exciting bodies weren't given the room to develop over time. I refrained from saying, that's okay, because opera is a dying art. For a long time I've felt there are more singers than classical music fans. *Genuine* fans, that is.

Old-fashioned gentlemen that they were, Jim & Bob offered to escort me back to the hotel, even though their Civil War-era farmhouse was within hollering distance of the bar. The moment we set foot into the cold night air, we heard sirens coming from the direction of the hotel. A fire truck whizzed past.

"Looks like trouble at the Lodge," Bob said, stating the obvious.

"At least it doesn't seem to be the opera house," Jim, the optimist, responded.

"Don't be insensitive!" Bob scolded, smacking Jim on the arm.

That slight reprimand almost set him sprawling. He was drunker than he appeared. "Debbie is staying there."

"I don't have much to lose," I said, not wanting to upset anyone. Truth was, after my car was totaled, I had begun to detach from all my possessions. It wasn't as if I had brought my favorite clothing or jewelry with me. In fact, I couldn't afford to own anything that might qualify as favorite clothing. My concern was for Reade. That was soon alleviated. He walked right up to us.

"Hi guys," he said, as if we had all gathered to watch fourth-of-July fireworks.

"Hi Reade," I said. "What's happening?"

"Someone set fire to the hotel," he said, as if it happened every day. "All that's missing is you running down the street naked."

This got Jim & Bob's attention. "Oh, really?" I said. "Sorry to disappoint. Where will I be staying tonight?"

"There's not that much damage," Reade said. "Except from the sprinkler system."

"The EEE, I presume?" Bob inquired.

"That's the claim. Small fires, nothing major."

"Interesting," Bob commented. "Why not the theater itself? That would cause the most havoc in our elitist little world."

"Hell if I know," Reade said. "As I said, token arson. Water damage, mostly."

"Law of unintended consequences," I said.

"Huh?"

"They didn't bargain on your sprinkler system," I said, "so the damage is worse than they intended."

"Huh," Reade replied. "Who the hell knows what they intended? Anyway, your possessions are probably okay. We'll see to that tomorrow. Tonight I'm ferrying everyone up to my place."

"No kidding!" Bob remarked. Jim was silent. He appeared to be at that stage of inebriation when it required all his concentration to stay upright.

"Where is that?" I asked.

"Up in the hills," Reade replied. "Come with me, Debbie. Teresa's already waiting in my car."

78.

"It belonged to the Comte de Bragelonne," Reade explained as his mansion came into view, a turreted Victorian behemoth lurking among the Ponderosa Pines. "It was totally decrepit when I bought it."

"It certainly is purty now," Teresa said, giving Reade's arm a squeeze. She had claimed the seat next to him in his gunmetal-gray Jaguar convertible. As the third wheel, I sat in the back.

The Vicomte de Bragelonne of Dumas fame had lived in 1625 during the reign of Louis XIII, so the architecture was all wrong. Don't be too impressed by my memory for dates and names. Ville d'Aurore's weird mix of poufy seventeen-century French elegance, Victorian fussiness, and rugged frontier artifacts had piqued my interest, inspiring my latest Internet search.

"Was this guy related to Dumas' viscount?" I asked, trying not to drool as we rolled down the long private road leading up to the driveway.

"That vicomte was fictional," Reade replied, keeping his eyes on the road.

"Most of Alexandre Dumas' novels were historical fiction," I said. "He could have existed."

"Even if he did, the founder of this town was a pretender, a self-proclaimed count. With the gardens he took a stab at historical accuracy. The chateau, however, is a Frankenstein's monster. The design was dictated by the availability of building materials as much as the count's fevered imagination. I don't think he did a lot of research. Obviously he was a fan of Dumas. Not surprising, considering how popular those novels were at the time. The house is pretty cool, though, isn't it?"

The word cool seemed like the understatement of the century, but I managed to curb my enthusiasm. "When was it built?" I asked with the merest hint of breathiness.

"1878," he said. "About the time that other mining baron, Horace Tabor, was holding court in Leadville, Colorado."

Reade, overplaying his role as country gentleman, opened the car doors for Teresa and me and ushered us into the main foyer. The flowered wallpaper, oriental rugs, heavy furniture, and velvet drapes that dominated the interior stayed mainly faithful to the Victorian theme. The parlor—almost as large as the main lounge at the Ville d'Aurore Lodge—easily accommodated a concert grand piano, a billiards table, two hearths, and several large mirrors. A series of nineteenth-century oil paintings depicted someone's aristocratic relatives, probably neither Reade's nor the Count's.

Several of the works in the gallery were elegant landscapes of the house and the surrounding area, too naturalistic to have been painted within the last 120 years. I wondered if this Comte de Bragelonne had commissioned the paintings from Albert Bierstadt or Thomas Moran. I knew something about nineteenth-century landscape artists from viewing the permanent collection of Seattle's Frye Museum. You didn't need to be a connoisseur to appreciate works such as these.

"James will take it from here," Reade said. "It might be a few minutes before he attends to you, so have a seat. I need to get back to the Lodge to find the others. Sleep well! I'll see you tomorrow." Teresa's and my eyes followed him forlornly as he walked back to the car. We might have been lapdogs abandoned by our master.

"Well," she sighed. "I've had enough excitement for one night. Who is James and where are we supposed to find him?" She picked up a magazine and settled into a throne-like armchair. She looked in danger of being swallowed alive.

I had had my fill of Teresa for one day, so I chose a hallway and started walking. After several minutes of aimless wandering I opened a random door, flicked on a light, and was blinded by a blaze of copper kettles hanging from the ceiling. Martha Stewart would have been right at home in this fully-equipped modern kitchen. I shut the door so quickly that it slammed. I needed to abort this stealth mission. What if I accidentally happened upon

Reade's bedroom? Okay, so the odds were against it, considering the size of the place.

According to my watch, a full ten minutes had elapsed. I tried to retrace my steps, only to discover that I was hopelessly lost. I recognized the kitchen door and lingered there to get my bearings. As I debated which route to try next, a portrait caught my eye, more modern in style than the others. The subject was a lovely brunette wearing a white, high-collared dress decorated with a broach of embossed gold. I immediately thought of the object that had demolished my bicycle tire and fished it out of my purse. Could it really be the same piece? Difficult to say, considering the damage. No, that would be a ridiculous coincidence. It must be that this particular design was the accessory du jour in this woman's day. I would have to ask Reade about it.

"Deborah?" a man's voice called out. "Are you there?"

"Yes, I'm here!" I said, trying not to sound as if I had been caught sifting through the contents of Reade's underwear drawer. "I'm afraid I got lost," I told the sixtyish gentleman, who looked like a bespectacled, scholarly version of my weather-beaten Great Uncle Fred, a farmer in Duluth, Minnesota.

"It happens frequently," he said, completely neutral. I wondered if he meant that visitors regularly snooped or went missing. "May I show you to your room?"

I didn't know about the other rooms, but mine had been updated to include a Jacuzzi, a bidet, and a fainting couch. No television. An hour later I heard Sven, Corabelle, and Lisette chattering in the hallway, so I knew they had to be staying close by. I could have joined their impromptu party, but I had just emerged from the Jacuzzi and was bundled up in the XXL luxury bathrobe I had found hanging on the bathroom door. From Sven's booming tenor, I picked up enough to conclude that they knew little if anything beyond what I had already heard from Reade.

The whereabouts of Camille, Ulrika, Angelo, Lawrence, Hugh, and Teresa were unknown. In the car, Teresa had snuggled up to Reade like a baby penguin fleeing the arctic chill between its daddy's legs. Had she spent the night between Reade's? He hadn't acted like a man in lust. That didn't prove anything. At his age and in his position, I would expect discretion.

Was I a tad obsessed? I hoped I wasn't about to go off the deep end and start trailing after Reade, playing Donna Elvira to his Don Giovanni.

79.

Sunday was a day off. At 9:00 a.m. I drew the velvet curtains of my suite. There was a pattern of raindrops on the window glass, and the grove of Ponderosa Pines across the way was dripping wet. I took my time showering and dressing in the same jeans and sweater I had worn the night before. When I ventured out an hour later, not a creature was stirring in my wing. I could have waited, ears pricked, but I was hungry, and for all I knew my wing-mates were already up and about.

The staff had set up a buffet in the formal dining room. Teresa and Corabelle sat at the far end of the long mahogany table. I helped myself to a blueberry scone and scrambled eggs before joining them. "Good morning!" I chirped, pouring myself a large coffee and refilling the cups of the others. "How did everyone sleep?"

"Best night's sleep in ages," said Corabelle. "Reade's armed guards patrolled all night. This place is secure as Osama bin Laden's cave."

"I guess I slept all right," Teresa said without conviction. She looked as tired as you can look in your early 20s. In other words, droopy but not appreciably worse. At least she didn't have the swollen mouth and self-satisfied languor of a woman who had made love all night. The day suddenly seemed a whole lot brighter, despite the drizzle.

"Lousy day!" I remarked brightly.

"The rest of them have the right idea," Corabelle said. "Sleep the day away."

"How's Sven?" I said. "He said he was coming down with something."

"He's fine!" Corabelle said. "He was just feeling asocial. If you want singers to keep their distance, tell them you're fighting a cold. He loves to sleep late."

Teresa stood, unsteadily, and said, "I think I'll go back to bed?"

"You do that, honey," Corabelle said. When Teresa was gone, she said, "What will you do with yourself today, Debbie? You don't look as if you need rest. In fact, you look downright peppy."

"Coppelius must be your optometrist," I said. "I haven't slept a full eight hours since leaving Seattle. Normally I'd take a bike ride, but unless my bike has been incinerated or stolen, it is still keeping company with the employee bikes at the Lodge. I guess I could take a walk. Is that the sun I see?"

"Yeah, it's supposed to clear," Corabelle said, taking another large gulp of coffee. "There's not much to see. The foothills aren't that interesting. Lots and lots of Ponderosa Pines. I prefer climates with more variety."

"Where are you from?"

"Vancouver, B.C. As a fellow Pacific Northwest native, you know what I'm talking about. I love the cornucopia of evergreens in our forests: Blue Spruces, Grand, Noble and Douglas Firs, Cedars, Hemlocks. You've got every shade of green, including blue-green, various sizes and shapes of needles. Some branches that are stiff, some droopy. It's the Miss Universe Pageant of trees. At the Miss Idaho pageant, you see white girls, nothing but white girls. When was the last time you saw a black or Asian around here? This is the tree equivalent, as far as evergreens go. You've got Ponderosa Pines and Douglas Firs, period."

"Wow," I said. "That was quite a speech for this early hour."

"It's Reade's ambrosial coffee," she explained, pouring herself another cup. "The others better rise and shine soon, or I'm going to finish off the entire urn."

I checked to see who might be lurking about before saying, "So, have you forgiven Camille and Ulrika, or are you plotting your revenge?"

"Fuck 'em," Corabelle said dispassionately. "I'm sure they will apologize. Say they were quoted out of context. That's what they all say. I know that reporter. What a piece of work! Probably convinced them they were off-the-record. Really, they're a couple of hare brains. The damage is done, so what's the point? Reade told me to let it go, so here I am, letting it go." She extended both arms as if preparing to be frisked.

"I'll take your word for it," I said, and we both laughed.

"You've been a trooper," she said. "If all the crap you've been through had happened to me, I'd be a raving lunatic."

"I don't think so," I said. "From what I hear, the last go-around wasn't a picnic, either."

"You mean *Carmen*. Yeah, this place is cursed, and I'm not talking about ghosts. I hope Reade learned his lesson about hiring solely on the basis of talent. My mistake was not filling him in on all the personal shit that went down last time. He makes a show of getting to know his singers up front. In truth, he keeps his distance."

80.

"He keeps his distance?" I repeated. "That's not what I hear."

Corabelle narrowed her eyes. "Don't tell me you've been listening to Lawrence! The rule is, whatever he tells you, assume the opposite."

"How well do you know Reade?"

"We met when we were both living in New York. I directed some stupid showcase he was in with a silly little company. A group of wishful thinkers had named it Manhattan Grand Opera. We did an unintentionally hilarious, Wal-Mart version of *La Bohème*. Let me tell you, that garret has never looked so tacky. You expect poverty, but a group of artists like that would at least have had taste! Reade was Marcello."

"Nice voice?" There was no way I was going to admit that the

Manhattan Grand Opera was one of my better credits.

"Gorgeous! Ooh, and did he ever make a handsome Marcello! Our Rodolfo couldn't hold a candle to him."

I smiled. "So to speak."

"Yes, the candle-lighting scene would have been a lot hotter if it had involved Mimi and Marcello. Mimi was panting to service his candle, let me tell you. She was pretty, too. But Reade wasn't having any. Strictly business. He dated society girls, none of them in the profession. I don't know how he got in with that crowd. The one he married introduced herself after one of his Juilliard performances."

"Married?" I repeated, choking on a section of grapefruit.

"For about a minute. Actually a year. No children. She left him when his sister was killed and he decided to become a cop. After he won the lottery, she looked him up again. By then, he had her number."

"Do you think he could have made it as a singer?"

Corabelle shrugged. "Who knows? He was convinced his voice was on the small side. I think it would have filled out nicely if he had hung in there another five years."

"Who should have hung in there?" It was Juergen, fortunately. I didn't think Reade would have appreciated hearing his talent assessed in his own home.

"Reade," Corabelle said.

"Yes," Juergen said, "he was really good." He filled his plate with goodies, took the seat beside me, and dug in.

"How did you meet him?" I asked.

"New York," Juergen said, covering his mouth as he chewed. "Same as Corabelle. I was the rehearsal pianist for that stinking production of *La Bohème*."

"With the three of you, how bad could it be?"

"Gloriously bad," Juergen said. "No budget, so the orchestra was terrible. The strings sounded like bilious hornets. Whoopee cushions would have been better than those horns. Musetta was the producer's wife. Pretty but almost tone deaf. Luckily there was no publicity, so no one saw it. Our reputations were preserved."

Corabelle stood and tossed her napkin on her plate. "Well, I'm off!"

"Me, too," I said, jumping to my feet.

"Come on, you're not done yet," Corabelle said, pointing to my half-filled plate. Either that or you're shamefully wasteful! Keep Juergen company for a few minutes. What if Camille and Ulrika come in?" I sat again, reluctantly.

"I can handle them," he grumbled. "Haven't I proved that?"

"You were fortunate your leading ladies didn't commit hara-kiri after that first run-through," Corabelle said, miming a ritual disembowelment with a butter knife. "Sven told me about the bloodbath."

"Yes, I was a bad boy," Juergen said with an evil grin.

81.

"I had to put those ladies in their place," Juergen continued, "especially Camille and Ulrika. That pair is bad news in combination."

"Kind of like you and Ludovic," I said, without thinking. Damn! When was I going to learn to keep my lips buttoned?

Juergen, however, laughed uproariously. "Ho!" he bellowed. "He does make a good, how do you say it—?"

"Henchman," I said.

"Sidekick is the word you're looking for, I think," Corabelle said, giving me a swift kick under the table.

"Henchman will do," Juergen said. "Anyhow, I knew they would recover, and they did. Reade told me to cool it, but he didn't have to. It is not to my advantage to have leading ladies with no confidence. I can do without arrogance, however. Those two! Strangely enough, they are surprised no one likes them. They are like those people in Florida who build big houses in the Everglades and then wonder why they are plagued by snakes and alligators."

"See you later," Corabelle said. Again I attempted to follow suit.

“Wait a moment,” Juergen said, holding fast to the sleeve of my sweater. “Why are you afraid of me?”

“Why wouldn’t I be?” What was this? Had someone slipped sodium pentothal in the coffee?

“Because I am harmless,” he said, wide-eyed, the Artful Dodger passing himself off as Oliver Twist. “I know what you overheard. I was there, remember? It might interest you to know what really happened. Originally, Camille approached me. I responded, yes. She is pretty, and I was free. Then she said I harassed her. With Ulrika, I made the first move, but I’m not a Dummkopf. When she didn’t respond, I left her alone. These two use poetic license. Frankly, I was surprised. I know men do that in bars, exaggerate their conquests. I didn’t realize women could be worse.”

He stopped speaking, and we both feigned a sudden interest in the silver coffee urn. “Anyway,” he went on, “I have a girlfriend now.”

I felt my shoulders relax. “That’s nice,” I said, inanely.

“So I am not approaching you,” he continued.

“Good. I mean, I didn’t think so. Well, Juergen, I’m glad we had this little chat.”

“It’s not that I don’t find you attractive,” he went on, relentlessly. “You are smart and musical. Pretty, too.”

“Well, thanks,” I said. “Juergen, I hate to eat and run, but I—drank too much coffee. You understand.” A crude but effective excuse. I fled to my room. Why had I drunk all that coffee? Here I was, on an ideal napping day, exhausted from a string of sleepless nights and all hopped up like a nine-year-old who had gorged on Halloween candy.

Apparently no one had anything bad to say about Reade. He was a talented singer, and, according to Corabelle, the furthest thing from a star-fucker. That didn’t explain what I had seen with my own two eyes at that party. If Juergen were to be believed, no one had anything to fear from him. *The man doth protest too much, methinks.* Both Corabelle and Juergen had gone out of their way to assure me they were too mature to carry grudges.

Back in my room, I mentally ran through my parts, including the blocking, while bonding with the heavenly pillow-top mattress. At around 4 in the afternoon, curiosity drove me to see what the others were up to.

82.

Down in the parlor, gathered around a roaring fire, Sven, Corabelle, Lawrence, Hugh and Angelo sprawled about in strange positions like exotic throw rugs, tossed carelessly this way and that. It was a study in ennui.

"What about Five-Card Stud?" Corabelle proposed from her place closest to the fire.

"Only if it's Strip Poker," Sven said.

"If I beat the pants off you," she said in a languid voice, "I prefer not to do it literally. I've seen more than enough. I still have nightmares about that thing."

"One man's nightmare is another's dream," Sven responded.

"Strip Poker is about humiliating your enemies, not getting a thrill," Lawrence said. "But if we're going to strip, I will need to change my underwear."

"That is so much more than I want to know," Corabelle said, covering her eyes with her hands. "That does it. We keep our clothes on. Penny ante."

No one moved. Lawrence alone registered my presence. "Debbie!" he said. "Would you like to play?"

"I'll just watch," I said. "I know a little about the game, but I've never been interested enough to learn how to hold my own against experts."

"Ha!" Sven said. "Not us. You mean you never watched those celebrity Poker shows?" he said, as if I had admitted to never opening a newspaper.

"Nope," I said, unapologetic. "No reality shows, either. And I haven't once tuned into *American Idol* or *Dancing with the Stars.*"

"God, who can tolerate that?" Hugh groaned. "The humiliation!"

"What do you do for entertainment?" Lawrence said, rolling onto his side.

"Read," I said. "Listen to music."

"Not opera," Lawrence said.

"Of course not. Lute, Spanish guitar, Chopin. Nothing with voices. Not as background, anyway."

"Amen to that."

The game finally began. Sven let me share his hand. Angelo, as unlikely a cardsharp as he was an opera singer, proved to be the dark horse. If the game had been Strip Poker, he'd have made the parlor look like the hospitality suite at a naturists' convention.

At around 5:00 p.m. Ulrika and Camille wandered in. "What's up?" Ulrika said, as if we were all best buddies.

Corabelle stared, incredulous, for an excruciating minute or two before saying, "These are called playing cards. We are engaged in an amusing little game called Poker."

"Can we join in?" Camille asked.

"Do you cheat?" Lawrence asked without looking up. "Because, all things considered, I'd be astounded if you didn't."

"Tell me, Camille, what were you thinking?" Corabelle said. "Hit me, Lawrence. I mean, don't you know better than to tell reporters what you really think about the operas you're in?"

"Corabelle, I couldn't be more sorry," Camille said. "Ulrika, too." She indicated Ulrika, who nodded vehemently. "That reporter played dirty. We were sure the interview was over, that we were—"

"Off-the-record," Corabelle said, giving me a significant look. "Yeah, yeah, I've heard it all before. (I fold.) Goddamn it, Angelo!"

Angelo's hand was an Ace-high flush. He laughed diabolically and claimed the pot, which wouldn't have paid for an hour of parking in Seattle. Sven dealt the next hand.

"You've told me worse on-the-record," Lawrence said to Camille as he frowned at his new cards. "Hit me! Hmm." He paused. "Raise you. What was that term you coined for Corabelle?

Idiot-savant-garde?"

"I'm amazed anyone tells you anything," Hugh said to Lawrence. "It is either passed on to the person you would least want it to reach or entirely inaccurate." His lack of irony didn't bode well for Lawrence's romantic ambitions. Pretending to concentrate on his cards, Sven wore a secretive smile. For a Poker hand it wasn't much. Either he was bluffing or reflecting on something other than his cards. Aside from the present match, it was clear who was winning that particular game of love and chance.

"Uh, Sven," Corabelle said, "Let's deal Debbie in for the next hand."

Sven looked up. "Huh?"

"Should be a hoot. She has the worst Poker face I've ever seen."

83.

I'll never know exactly what Corabelle thought she saw in my expression, but she was right about one thing. I was too transparent. My amazement at watching our group deal the evil divas into the game was too pronounced not to register on my face.

Although Corabelle and Sven had their moments, no one could dethrone Angelo. Reade, like the Beast in the fairytale, didn't make a personal appearance. At 6:00 p.m. his for-all-practical-purposes invisible staff prepared us a healthy buffet so that we might graze at will. A miserable failure at Poker, I retired to my room to make a few phone calls.

"Debbieeeee!" Frankie said. "You still in one piece?"

"Yes, especially now that I'm in a safe house."

"What? Does the Lodge have an armed guard? More importantly, is he cute?"

I sank back onto the mattress and shut my eyes. "I'm told there is an armed guard or two. If he shows himself, I promise to give you my personal assessment of his assets. Although it's the last thing on my mind."

"What *is* on your mind? Seriously. No more attacks?"

"Not on me, though the EEE is still on the case. It, or they, destroyed Teresa's costume and threw a rock through her window. Then they set fires around the hotel. That's why we're all in Reade's mansion."

"You gotta be kidding! Come on, admit it. You're shittin' me."

"I wish I were. The Lodge wasn't badly damaged. In fact, it's open for business, but Reade wants to keep us all secure. Maybe now I'll be able to sleep."

"Are those two screaming meanies holed up with you?"

"Yes, in a different wing of the house."

"My, my, the house has wings."

"Flying buttresses as well. Now I'm really confused. First Camille and Ulrika were going out of their way to alienate and humiliate. Now they're making nice. I have no idea what turned them around or if it's even real. And at this point I'm too tired—" I broke off to yawn, "to care."

"All right then! See you day-after-tomorrow!"

"Thursday? Opening night is Friday."

A pause. "Well ... Sven told me about the understudy dress rehearsal. You never know. I might pick up a few unpolished jewels."

"Yeah?" was all I said, stifling a tasteless quip about polishing the family jewels of amateurs. Personally, I planned to skip the understudy dress rehearsal. The last thing I needed was to start imagining that every one of these voice students could out-sing me, especially if it were true.

My mother, in lieu of leaving me a traditional message, had warbled the first few lines of the Mother Superior's ballad from The Sound of Music: "*Climb every mountain, ford every stream! Follow every rainbow, till you find your dream!*"

That night, in my dreams, I scaled a mountain—a sheer cliff. A few feet shy of the top, I was gripped with paralyzing terror. Then, oddly enough, a window formed in the rock directly in front of me. I climbed in.

The clock read 10:00 a.m. I had slept a full nine hours. In the shower I was inspired enough to belt, "*We Shall Overcome!*"

84.

As usual, Reade was long gone by the time any of us came down to breakfast. I descended just as Corabelle and Sven were heading out for a walk in the forest. I ate quickly, determined to avoid any more weird confrontations that would distract me from singing well. I spent the rest of the morning stretching, warming up my voice and marking through my part.

At noon I came down to grab a sandwich from the buffet. Lawrence was pawing the merchandise. "Looking for hidden razor blades?" I asked.

"Not a bad idea," he said. "But no, I'm angling for tuna fish."

I pushed the tray around and found a note that said, TURKEY. "I don't think you'll find it here," I said. I waved the card labeled TUNA triumphantly in his face.

"You're in a good mood today," he accused.

"And you're not," I said. "I can't help it. I finally slept through the night." I didn't bother to explain about the dream. He didn't look as if anyone else's good fortune would interest him.

"Good for you," he said, munching sullenly on the tuna sandwich.

"What's with Camille and Ulrika?" I whispered. "Did I miss a revival meeting where they dedicated their lives to the Lord?"

"Beats me," he said. "Either that, or they're hatching some new plot. At least this time everyone has her own leading role. There's no need to filch."

"Everyone but Teresa."

"Yes, Teresa will have to wait until next time."

"Is that what happened last time?" I said. "Role filching?" I helped myself to a bag of chips.

"How do you stay so skinny?" he grumbled. "I've gained five

pounds since I returned to the Land of Buffets. I hope I still fit into my costumes."

I had noticed he was packing it on, so I tried to get us back on topic. "Did Camille really get lured away so that Juanita could take her role?"

"There's no proof," Lawrence said, "and lately I've been accused of disseminating false information. So, no comment."

"Come on."

"She took a drive on the day we opened. She was wearing, in the middle of winter, stiletto heels and a pencil skirt. One guess as to who she thought she was meeting."

"Sven?"

"Duh."

"What about Lisette?"

"She got sick. No one planned that. Not unless we have a resident expert on germ warfare. Most likely she picked up the virus from Ulrika, who recovered in time to take over Lisette's part. That had to smart."

85.

At half-past noon, a van arrived to transport us to the orchestra-tech rehearsal.

Although less excruciating than the piano-tech, this go-around still promised to be a tedious affair. The show was heavy with special effects, and none of them seemed to be working properly. It was difficult to see how this coal-fueled freight train was going to magically upgrade to a bullet train in two days.

Angelo's magic tricks in the Doll Act constituted the first roadblock. As the evil inventor Coppelius, he was supposed to perform some simple sleight-of-hand. He is the provider of the Doll's supernatural eyes, and during his aria, he attempts to sell Hoffmann a pair of enchanted glasses:

See these eyes, living eyes
Eyes that burn like glowing coals.
These eyes, they see through lies
They see clear to the depths of your soul.

In the end the effect worked, though it was just as well Angelo had not tried to trade in his pop star's microphone for a magic wand. Some of the eyes were snaps, firecrackers that explode on contact with the floor, like the ones Fred Astaire used in his fourth-of-July dance in Holiday Inn. Far from equaling Fred's finesse, Angelo threw the snaps down as if they were nasty bugs. He then hopped away, features contorted with fear, scrambling about like a cowboy getting his feet shot out from under him.

"Basta!" he yelled, forcing Juergen to bring the music to a halt. "I will not do this! It is dangerous." A random giggle was soon stifled. Everyone, including Angelo, knew it came from Ulrika. Jason Bell, prop master as well as set designer, pulled Angelo aside. He must have found the magic words to reassure him, because after a few minutes we were back in business.

As the rehearsal dragged on from day into evening, disaster was averted more than once. The picture frame, where I was stationed as Antonia's mother, jammed suddenly, nearly pitching me forward into empty air. I tripped over the bottom of the frame, catching myself at the sides just in time. Though teetering precariously, the frame held, sparing me a ten-foot freefall. Hardly life-threatening, though I might have sprained an ankle.

Then, at the end of Act II, the gondola lost a wheel. Lawrence caught Camille just in time to prevent her from falling overboard. They were both shaken. "What if that happens during a performance?" Camille complained. "I could have been killed!"

"It was a fluke!" Jason insisted.

At 6:00 p.m. Reade arranged for pizza and salad to be served in the ballroom. Lisette and I sat together at a round, hand-carved table whose chairs had wrought-iron backs and round, burgundy velvet-cushioned seats.

"The White Lady would feel right at home at this table," Lisette said. "So what do you think? Is she up to her old tricks?"

I snorted. "Oh, come on!"

"How else do you explain all this?"

"Sabotage?" I proposed.

"The EEE hasn't claimed responsibility, and none of us has sufficient motive."

"Not like during *Carmen*," I said.

"*Carmen*?" Lisette said, disoriented. "Nothing like *this* happened."

"You don't think someone arranged Camille's car trouble?"

"Oh *that*," Lisette said, nibbling at her pizza. "Juanita, of course."

"Of course?"

"I always assumed it was Juanita," she said. "That girl was completely unscrupulous. I'd go so far as to say amoral."

"Do you think her car accident was arranged?"

"It wouldn't surprise me. She made a lot of enemies in her short life." Lisette pointed at Camille and Ulrika, conversing easily with Corabelle on the other side of the room. "Speaking of women with loads of enemies, I wonder what happened to make those two see the light? I've noticed they've been minding their p's and q's. I wonder ..."

"What?"

"If they've been threatened. You know, anonymously."

Camille, as if sensing she was the topic of our discussion, peered in our direction. We quickly averted our eyes. "If that were the case, wouldn't they tell Reade?" I asked.

"Not necessarily. Maybe they realize they've gone too far. Neither would have been so cocky on her own. There's safety in numbers. You know, mob mentality."

"Juergen said something like that at breakfast the other morning."

"Oh?" Lisette raised her eyebrows and leaned in closer. "Do tell. You had a morning tête-à-tête with Juergen?"

I laughed. "Nothing like that. He was rather sweet. Assured me I had nothing to fear from him. Told me his nasty little performance at the run-through was a one-time lesson in humility."

"Huh," Lisette said. "He might have spared me!"

"Perhaps you got caught in the crossfire," I suggested. It wouldn't do to remind her that she was the only one who had earned his censure by missing the high note at the end of her aria.

86.

Two dress rehearsals took place the following day, one in the afternoon and one in the evening. The first was informal. We wore costumes but skipped the makeup and marked to save our voices. The second—in full costumes, makeup, and voice—played out in front of an invited audience of wealthy patrons. Both proceeded with deceptive ease.

Thanks to a sound sleep the night before, I had been in excellent voice for the rehearsals. In bed that evening, however, I began to panic in earnest. Everything had gone too well. That didn't bode well for opening night. A mixture of exhilaration and dread kept me awake. I avoided looking at the digital clock. Finally I gave up and read. Why fight it? I had the next day off and was sure to sleep the following night.

If only I had known!

The next morning I came down to breakfast at 8:00 a.m. looking, I'm sure, like I had been detained on an airport runway for eight hours before a transatlantic flight. There, lingering over his coffee and *New York Times*, sat Reade. Rossini could have composed an opera in the time that had passed since we had spoken. (He did work with amazing speed!) "I was hoping to run into you," he said brightly. "Wow, you look awful."

"Thanks," I said.

"What's wrong? Yesterday went like a dream."

"You, of all people, should know that a great dress rehearsal isn't the most positive of omens, especially taking into account recent events."

"Me, of all people?"

"You went to Juilliard!" I blurted. Damn it, I'd have killed for the opportunities he had thrown away! "How could you stop singing?"

"How can you keep singing?" he said. "It's easier to give up when you've had a little success. I could see far enough into the future to know I wasn't going to get rich or even particularly enjoy being a professional classical singer. I like being rich. Singers never get rich, especially the ones with a pleasant, smallish instrument like mine. I wasn't interested in a career in early music."

"So you went into law enforcement? Loads of money in that."

"I had my reasons, which you must know, now that you're so well informed. Getting rich stopped being a priority at that juncture. I didn't know what I was missing. Once I got rich, I grew to like it. Men like to win. Having major money means you get to win a lot. I like having nothing to prove. When you're a singer, you're upholding your reputation every time you open your mouth. Your entire career is dependent on winning the approval of the right people, who are, more often than not, ignorant assholes."

Not knowing how to respond, I busied myself by heaping my plate with scrambled eggs. Meanwhile I digested his words. If I had gotten to first base in my career—say, won a competition, done Santa Fe's Apprentice Program—would I have seen enough to make me want to quit? This experience was teaching me that the career wasn't all it was cracked up to be. Everyone acted as if their lives were on the line, yet this was a neighborhood puppet show compared to the Met or Chicago Lyric. Their *lives* might be on the line, but not their livelihoods.

"You're quiet this morning," Reade finally said.

"I'm mulling over your words of wisdom."

James saved me from further explanations by appearing in the doorway holding a portable phone. "There is a call for Ms. Deborah de Lille," he said.

I had forgotten to turn on my cell. The butler handed me the phone.

"This is Deborah de Lille," I said, in a formal voice fit for narrating a Ken Burns documentary.

"Debbie!" My mother said. "Thank God. There's no room at the Inn. What are we supposed to do?"

87.

"Maaaahm!" I remonstrated. "You can't be serious! You didn't make reservations?" The words stuck in my throat.

"We assumed you would."

"You did?" Reade gestured for me to hand him the phone.

"Mrs. de Lille?" he said. "This is Reade Phillips. Yes, I'm the general director. Where are you?" He listened, patiently. "How many of you are there?" Another pause. "Uh-huh, you, your husband, your son Roland and his girlfriend. Who else? Winston Dixon?" I groaned audibly. Reade narrowed his eyes in my direction before returning to the phone call. "Tell the taxi driver to take you to the Bragelonne Estate," he said. They all know how to find it. We'll be expecting you," he checked his watch, "in about a half-hour." He ignored my frantic pleas to repossess the phone.

"Why didn't you let me speak to her again?" I said in despair.

"Because I had this feeling you'd object to my putting them up. Where else are they supposed to stay, since you didn't make reservations?"

"They never asked! I figured they'd make their own. And I didn't expect them until tomorrow. This is a disaster!"

"Why?" He said, observing me as an alien might an abductee. "And, by the way, who is Winston? I assume he's not the family dog."

"Oh God, Winston!" I groaned. "He's been lying low for months. Why would he surface now?"

"What is he, a CIA operative? Come to think of it, we could use one of those!"

How could he joke at such a moment? "He's a family friend," I said.

"Your fiancé?"

"Hardly!"

"Animal, vegetable, mineral, man, woman, child?"

"Animal and...man."

He sat back and blew out a puff of air. "Well, at least we've established that we're playing a game."

"I hope it's fun for you."

"Oh, now you're going to pout! And after I've done you this amazing favor."

"Says who?" My God, what was I doing? He had done me an amazing favor! "I'm sorry, Reade, you've been incredible. I didn't want to entangle you in my complicated personal affairs."

"Gee, thanks," he said. "And now, if you don't mind, I'll let the servants know they need to make up rooms in the East Wing." He left the room.

I turned on my cell and punched in Roland's number. "Dweeb!" he said. "We're coming up the drive. This is no time for regrets."

"Rolly, you know damn well I didn't set this up!"

"Oh, come on, it will be a hoot. Freesia is absolutely thrilled."

"Freesia?"

"You'll like her. Listen, I'm happy to be present at your one and only professional job. You don't have to thank me."

"I can't believe you brought Winston," I said through gritted teeth.

"We didn't. He's driving up on his own."

88.

"Mom invited Winston," Roland explained. "Sort of. She sent out a group e-mail, and he responded. He's in Spokane taking a deposition. Some bigwig Mormon is getting divorced. So don't start concluding he's seen the light. I bet he wants to get laid." I heard my Mom's voice in the background, remonstrating. I could just make out Roland's voice, saying, Mom, you're dreaming. "I'm back," he said into the receiver, "and we're here. See you in a few. Say, this place belongs in Disneyland! Who the hell is this guy?!" He ended the call.

A few minutes later James, toting two suitcases, accompanied my little entourage in. "Nice place you got here," Roland said. "Debbie, meet Freesia."

I shook hands with a Hispanic woman about my age whose bosom rivaled Salma Hayek's. "You're the opera singer. Roland has told me next-to-nothing about you."

"Likewise," I said. I liked her already.

"Mom, Dad," I said, kissing them each in turn. "I'm overwhelmed."

"Debbie, I'm so sorry," my Mom said. "I know we've sprung this on you, but the cards said it would all be okay. Have you noticed that Mr. Phillips' butler looks just like Uncle Fred? A little more intellectual, it's true—"

"Did the cards tell you to invite Winston?" I said, my tone turning icy.

"Not exactly," she said. "I included him in my e-mail, but I never expected—"

"Okay, okay," I said, trying not to overreact. "How come you can't be a Luddite, like everyone else's mother? When do you expect—?"

"Sorry to interrupt," Freesia said, shifting side-to-side, "but where's the bathroom?"

"Follow me, Miss," the butler said. "Mr. Roland, I'll show you both to your room so that Miss Freesia can freshen up." Where did Reade get this guy? He had obviously graduated from the *Masterpiece Theatre* School of Buttling.

Roland and Freesia exited at the precise moment the doorbell rang. "That must be Winston, now," my mother said, turning expectantly. Winston appeared on the threshold, looking right at home—as if he owned the place, in fact. He was wearing a gray business suit, top-of-the-line. A Mickey Mouse tie provided the right touch of insouciance. Six-feet-tall, salt-and-pepper hair closely cropped, regular features, gym-slim, he would definitely make the grade as a TV lawyer. His aura of danger intimidated everyone but me. My parents retreated a few steps, as if by reflex.

"How are you, Deborah?" he said, bending to kiss my cheek but finding my neck instead. "Ready for your professional debut?"

I was spared the effort of coming up with a suitably flip response to his exquisitely condescending question by the arrival of Reade. The sight of Winston did not give him pleasure. It was the sort of expression you'd expect to find on a referee about to call foul.

"I'm Reade Phillips," he said, shaking hands all around. When he got to Winston, I could have sworn he applied extra pressure. It was a recap of a scene from *Ben Hur*—the confrontation between Charlton Heston and his traitorous childhood friend just before the chariot race, except with no gay overtones. I wasn't surprised that Winston held his ground, but Charlton himself couldn't have set his square jaw more fetchingly than Reade.

"Thanks so much for putting me up," Winston said.

"I'm happy to put up with—I mean, put up all of Debbie's entourage," Reade replied.

"No need to go to any trouble," Winston said. "I can stay in her room."

"She's performing tomorrow," Reade said. "She gets her own room. Whatever private arrangements you make are your own business. My concern is for the good of the company. You understand, I'm sure."

"Of course," Winston said. A score for Reade. Winston looked as if one of his slick clients had poured him corked wine.

In the manner of an unusually gentle shepherd, the butler herded the three of them in the direction of the East Wing, leaving me alone with Reade. "Wow," I said. "This is the best gig, ever. I didn't have to do a thing."

"Don't you forget it," Reade said. "Now, if I were you, I'd make myself scarce and figure out how to get them to leave you alone until tomorrow night." Just when I could have sworn Reade was on the verge of asking me to dance, Winston, with his uncanny timing, had come along to crash the party.

89.

Like any creature under siege, I retreated to my hidey-hole. As I burrowed into my bed, my cell phone started to trill in rising scales. It was as though every moment I failed to answer, the stakes got higher.

"Give me directions," Winston said without preliminaries.

"Huh?"

"To your room. This crib is bigger than the White House! How do I find you?"

"Winston, I'm trying to conserve my energy."

"I get it, like athletes. No sex before the big game?"

"Something like that. Winston, don't you need to get back to your deposition?"

"I have to be in Spokane all day tomorrow, but I'll return in plenty of time to catch the show. Tonight I'm taking you and your parents to dinner."

"Uh—"

"Look in the hallway."

"You're not there, are you?"

"Unfortunately not."

I sighed with relief to find the hallway empty, save for a small package. "Uh, Winston, if you can't find me, how did this get here?" I asked.

"The butler did it," he said with no irony.

The box contained a little black dress, exactly my size, no doubt. Exquisitely simple. Winston had always had impeccable taste.

"Winston, it's lovely, but I can't—"

"Meet you downstairs at six," he said, ending the call.

I stared at the phone. What was I supposed to do? Refuse to have dinner with my parents, just because Winston was hosting? At least Winston had a reason for being in the area other than me. I could hardly fool myself that he had rushed to my side the minute he realized that he wanted to spend the rest of his life with me and that he wanted the rest of his life to begin right now. You know, like Billy Crystal says to Meg Ryan in *When Harry Met Sally*. Unlike Billy and Meg's characters, Winston and I had never been friends.

At 5:45 p.m. I descended to the parlor. I should never have tried on the dress. It was a perfect fit and made me feel gloriously feminine after weeks of male impersonation. I hoped Winston wouldn't place too much importance on my wearing it, but frankly I didn't care. He owed me, after everything I had put up with—the broken dates, the endless waits, the lovely loving and the hateful hates … Unlike in the Rodgers and Hart song, I *did not* wish I were in love again.

Down in the main parlor, I found Corabelle staring at one of the landscapes, lost in thought. She wore a skintight T-shirt, her pierced bellybutton revealed amid an inch of taut, exposed skin. Her old Levis appeared to be applied with a brush. With a body like that, you didn't need to invest in designer jeans with cool, baffling names like Seven Degrees of Supplication or Two Moons for the Multitudes. When I entered the room, she put a finger to her lips. She then directed me to twirl and gave me a thumbs-up. "Who's the guy?" she whispered. "He's in there," she said, jerking her head toward the other room.

"Either my brother or my ex," I said, matching her conspiratorial tone. "If he's short, bald, and self-important, it's my brother. The tall, well-coifed, self-important one is Winston."

"Winston, huh? He looks like a cigarette. Tall, slim, hair the color of ashes. A fancy one. I hope he's smokin', because there would have to be some major payoff for hanging out with a jerk like that."

No use defending him. "There are compensations," I admitted. "There *were*, anyway. He's about as addictive as nicotine. At the moment all I've got is the taste of ashes in my mouth."

"So you've taken up the habit again? Guess that explains where you've been all afternoon."

"That's n-not—"

"None of my business!" she broke in, throwing up her hands. "Have a nice evening!" Thrusting her hands in her pockets, she strolled away, whistling.

90.

Winston was helping himself to the port in the decanter. "Good stuff," he said, toasting me. "Reade recommended Fugiamo's," he said, finishing off his glass. "You look fabulous," he said, drawing me in to plant a soft kiss on my lips. "What is this? Have you lost weight?" He spanned my waist. "You're too skinny."

My parents appeared at the doorway. Their attire would have been perfect for a nice evening out in 1986. My mother wore a blouson-type silk dress, a size too small, and my father wore a form-fitting three-piece suit, made for a smaller form than his. They looked like recruits for a flea market fashion show.

Fugiamo's was a rich man's Olive Garden, Americanized Italian food at top prices. Lucky for me, the great service guaranteed a brisk rather than leisurely dining experience. Winston ordered a hundred-dollar bottle of wine, which my parents chugged like two-buck Chuck. They were visibly dismayed when their entrees arrived looking more like miniature rock gardens than actual food. When the dishes proved edible, they sopped up every drop of sauce with bread, leaving the basket empty. Winston, increasingly desperate, broached a variety of subjects until he finally hit upon one that put a nickel in my mother—past-life regressions. The ensuing monolog lasted about a half-hour. I didn't care. It was Karmic payback—a small taste of Winston's customized Hell, if such a place exits.

When I spoke, it was to egg my parents on. I may never know what Winston hoped to achieve by his Herculean efforts because—in his mind at least—getting me into bed was a sure thing. All I know is, the evening ended earlier than I dared hope. Naturally Winston insisted on accompanying me to my room.

"Well, thanks for dinner," I said, in my best Doris Day style, "and the dress! I'll see you tomorrow, after the opera."

"Goodnight, then," he said, folding me in his arms. It was always that way with Winston. Before I knew it, we were kissing, tasting, melting. Only this time I had too much at stake. I refused to let nature take its course. I stepped on his instep.

"Oops. Sorry!" I said. "God, I'm clumsy when I'm tired! Before I do any real harm, let's call it a night." I shut the door firmly in his face.

91.

When I came down the next morning, my parents were finishing breakfast, flanked on all sides by Camille, Ulrika, and Lisette. "You have such nice colleagues!" Mom enthused. "They've been telling me all about that rehearsal where everything went haywire. Thank goodness all the bugs got worked out!"

I couldn't believe my eyes. Here was proof positive my mother had no psychic ability whatsoever.

Lisette says there's a ghost in the theater. She told me the whole sad story. I thought I'd go down there this morning and see if I can pick up any vibrations."

"That sounds great, Mom. Knock yourself out."

"I guess you need to rest? I could use a ride."

"I do, sorry. I didn't sleep too well last night." What an understatement. "Besides," I added, "I don't have a car."

"What happened to your car?" Oops. How to answer without spilling the beans?

"It's in the shop," Reade said, appearing out of thin air to come to my rescue once more. "Ville d'Aurore can be such a small town! For foreign cars they often need to order parts."

"You're twenty minutes from Spokane," Mom countered. She had a point. "And it's a Honda."

"An old Honda," Reade said. "Almost vintage. I'm not sure it's even fixable."

"What a shame," my Mom said. Phew.

"Come on," Reade offered. "I'll give you a tour of the theater. How was dinner?"

"Yummy!" my Mom said. "And so artistic!"

"We'll see you tonight," Hoffmann's three lady-loves trilled as they filed out, wholesome as the sisters on Petticoat Junction.

92.

In the afternoon I napped, or rather passed out, from sheer exhaustion. A sleep so deep it took me a few minutes to realize where I was when I came to.

My alarm clock was a call from Frankie. "Debbieeeee!" How are tricks?"

"Tricks are for kids," I said. "I'm feeling every one of my thirty-two years today."

"Great understudy run-through yesterday," he said. "I may sign a new client."

"Yeah?" I said, warily.

"The chorus Antonia is fab. A baby Callas without the vocal issues. What an actress!"

"What about the men?"

"Disappointing," he said. "No one's the total package."

"You mean, no one has a great package."

"Go back to sleep, Grumpy," he said. "You need an attitude adjustment. I don't sleep with clients."

"Not even Sven?"

"I would definitely make an exception. But he's not askin'. It'll be a hot day in heaven if he ever does. But really, are you okay?"

"Yeah, sure. I'll see you after the show."

The evening got off to a rough start even before I left for the theater. So far Roland, Freesia, and Winston had avoided meeting face-to-face. And, lucky girl that I am, I was there when push came to shove. Here is how it played out:

Roland and Freesia were chatting in the parlor, and I was sharing a light meal with my colleagues, when Winston/Odysseus came home from the wars. You'd have thought Freesia was Penelope.

"What are you doing here?!" he remonstrated. No words of greeting.

"What are you doing here?!" she responded.

"Who is he to you?" Roland asked, hackles, and the pitch of his voice, rising.

"Who is he to you?" Winston said. It was not dialogue calculated to win writing awards on soap operas. The acting was convincing, however.

Before they came to blows, Reade intervened. "I see you've met," he said.

"Winston is my attorney," Freesia explained. A bit more, I conjectured.

"It's a small world," Reade said. "Where are you planning to go for dinner?"

Teresa, sitting unnoticed by the fire, rose and said, "Why not break bread with us?" She gave Roland a fetching look before sashaying into the dining room. As usual she was the personification of spring in a flouncy skirt and peasant blouse, silky blond hair streaming down her back.

"Great idea," Roland said. Freesia and Winston, skating on thin ice, followed.

Corabelle patted the empty seat next to her. "Why don't you sit next to me, Freesia? Ever done any stage work?"

"I once played the Countess in the *Marriage of Figaro*," she said, giggling.

"You're a singer?" Corabelle asked.

"No, not me! It was the Beaumarchais play," Freesia said, blushing.

"Caught between an unfaithful husband and an amorous teenage boy," Corabelle said. "Was that a stretch for you?"

"Not the unfaithful husband part," Freesia said. "Winston can attest to that." Winston looked as if testifying on Freesia's behalf or granting any other favors wasn't on his agenda. I didn't think she'd be wise to count on him in the foreseeable future.

Roland, on the other hand, was rallying more quickly, thanks to Teresa. "So you're Deborah's brother!" she said, fluttering her colorless lashes. "She's a wonderful performer. Wait till you see what she can do."

"Lucky me!" said my brother, already a besotted idiot. "I'll also get to see you in action."

"Well," Teresa simpered. "You'll see me, that much is true! You won't hear me, more's the pity. I do have a little ol' walk-on role. As far as singing goes, I'm the general female understudy. Everyone's hale and hearty, meaning I won't have much to do."

"She looks charming in her costume," Sven said as he entered the room.

"Sven, this is my brother Roland, his, um, *friend* Freesia and another, um, *friend* of mine, Winston," I said. "This is Sven, our star tenor. Just wait until you hear him."

"He certainly cuts an impressive figure," Freesia said, instinctively thrusting her chest forward. "If you can sing anything like you look, Sven, we're in for a treat."

"He's a treat, all right," Corabelle said, relishing the way Roland and Winston bristled.

Sven enfolded me in a warm bear hug. "Get some rest, darlin'?" he asked, petting me with his large paw. "Her room's next to mine," he explained to the others. "Sometimes I hear her thrashing around and moaning in her sleep when she's having bad dreams."

"You do not," I protested. "The walls are thick enough to

entomb an elk."

"Who knows what secrets lurk within these walls?" Sven said, a wicked gleam in his eye. "That doesn't mean what's hidden behind them is safe." How sweet! Sven was making a thinly veiled attempt to prevent Winston from propositioning me again.

Although I had already lost my appetite, I forced down a chicken breast and some mashed potatoes. I hoped I had consumed enough to sustain me throughout the long evening.

93.

There was no warm fuzzy feeling of shared anticipation as we sat backstage at our lighted makeup stations. Forced proximity in Reade's mansion had necessitated a detente of sorts. That didn't mean that our group was actually bonding. More like every man for himself.

Mary Jo had two assistants to help the three female leads create their individual looks and two to help the men. Opera stage makeup is so extreme that Teresa could have been made up to be a dead ringer for Camille, Ulrika, or Lisette. What looks like a Halloween mask up close is exactly right for most opera stages. You might call it amplification for the appearance.

"This is your fifteen minute call!" a harried Peter announced as he jogged by our dressing rooms. "The audience can hear you," he warned Hugh, who was testing his high notes. Hugh was unrecognizable in his extreme attire, but not as grotesque as Lawrence, positively ghoulish as Spalanzani's creepy servant Cochenille. As I stepped into the hallway, Lawrence cried "Boo!"

"Lawrence?" I said, recoiling. We were supposed to be in our complete costumes at the final dress rehearsal, but Lawrence had obviously gone with a much toned-down version.

"Yes," he sighed. "It's me. You think this is bad. Wait until you get a load of my Franz costume! It's right out of *The Rocky Horror Picture Show*. You look fabulous," he said, fingering the buttery leather of my vest. "All the lesbians in the audience will be a-twitter."

"Great!" I said.

As he lurched in character down the hallway, he said, "At least someone will find you attractive."

For the Prologue, Sven's only concession to Hoffmann's age was a gray wig. There wasn't enough time between the Prologue and Act I to erase three decades worth of wrinkles.

My sex change was accomplished with relative ease, thanks to my long face and slender body. Boy makeup outlines the planes of the face, in my case already pronounced. Otherwise, I thinned my lips, darkened my eyebrows, and skipped the mascara. Sven gave me a slow onceover. "Hey, stud," he said, nodding his approval. "You're lucky I'm all tarted up or I'd pull you into a dark corner."

I struck a Jolly Green Giant pose, legs spread and arms akimbo. "I bet you say that to all the boys," I said in my lowest speaking voice.

"To some of the girls, too," he said, winking. "Merde! In bocca al lupo!" These are the preferred opening night blessings among singers. Merde means shit in French, and In bocca al lupo is Italian for in the mouth of the wolf. Like the tired old break a leg, it's a reverse magic thing. Superstition dictates that wishing singers or actors Good Luck will have the opposite effect.

"Five minutes to places!" Peter announced as he prowled the dressing rooms.

Lisette emerged, a dead ringer for Madonna in the '80s. She had lost at least another ten pounds in the past week. "*Borderline,*" she sang in an amusingly operatic style, "*seems like I'm going to lose my mind!*"

"Okay, Madonna," I said. "It's all right for you to joke, but I really am losing my mind. I feel like I'm about to throw up."

"You'll be fine!" she said, cheerfully. "Better than fine. Just don't let the White Lady mess with your costume. Ta ta!" She pranced, Madonna-style, down the hallway, disappearing around the corner.

"Places!" Peter squawked, rushing through the hallway like Chicken Little, waving his hands about. If he'd screamed *the sky is falling!* I would have believed him.

94.

The brief overture ended, followed by the strains of the Spirits of Beer and Wine, sung by an offstage chorus. Angelo, as the evil Councilor Lindorf, had two scenes now. In the first, he bribes Stella's servant, played by Hugh, to give him the note intended for Hoffmann. In the second scene, he reveals his evil nature in an aria:

Poetry is not my forte
Using force is better sport

I forced myself to breathe deeply, pressing against my diaphragm to monitor its exaggerated movements. I buzzed into my sinuses, stifled a yawn to relax my throat and felt the sound release. My voice was nice and clear. Why was I so worried? Chances are, the reviews wouldn't even mention me. Or say something like, *it can certainly be said of Deborah de Lille, as Nicklausse, that she was having a wonderful time.* The kind of vague, condescending comment that is useless for press releases.

My shirttail was out. How had that happened? I tucked it in. This time I felt something, or someone, pull it out again. I looked around. No one. My pulse quickened. "Sven?" I whispered.

"Yes?" he said.

"Leave my shirttail alone!"

"What, are you crazy? I didn't touch you."

Lindorf's aria was in its second verse. I made slow circles like a dog chasing its tail, determined not to let anyone or anything else mess with me.

"Goddamn it! Keep still," Sven complained. "You're driving me nuts."

Arms clasped about my waist to keep my costume in place, I went back to concentrating on taking low, even breaths. The chorus of students was well into the drinking song:

Bottoms up, up, up, up up, Master Luther!
Hell's own beverage!
Give us more wine, give us more beer, fill it to here!

Sven led the way onto the stage in full swagger. My throat was closing and my breath was coming in short gasps, but somehow I followed, my movements a stiffer version of Sven's. By the time I joined the chorus of Hoffmann's ridiculous Kleinzach aria, however, I had hit my stride.

Just as I was starting to enjoy myself, a chorus boy seized the opportunity to clap me on the back in a needlessly painful demonstration of comradeship. I held my own. The unrehearsed bit of stage business infused me with the energy of anger, which sure beat quaking in my boots.

Wait a minute! My slaphappy comrade was a disguised female, like me. Her boy's short bob was her own, not a wig, and her hairline was so low it concealed most of her forehead. I recognized her as my chorus understudy. When had she been given permission to join the male chorus? I figured out quickly enough how to dodge her meaty hands. Fortunately the blocking kept me close to Sven, who had gleaned what was happening enough to run interference.

Lindorf reenters just as the chorus is asking Hoffmann about his newest love. Of Lindorf, Hoffmann says:

Each time my path crosses that of this devil,
Terrible things start to happen in spades.
My luck goes sour; I am betrayed!

I'm not going to keep quoting lines from scene to scene. These in particular would take on special significance. Not that I suspected Angelo of being the source of evil, or at least malicious mischief, among us. One of us was responsible, however. That person was bound to reveal him- or herself in some small way if I paid attention.

Speaking of paying attention, I almost missed my cue. "*What do you mean by three fair ladies?*" I sang in the nick of time. I had to stop letting my mind wander, even though retrieving the name that hovered just beyond my reach now seemed of paramount importance.

The Prologue was ending. As I exited into the wings, Corabelle grabbed my sleeve. I was infinitely relieved to find out she wasn't the White Lady.

"Are you okay?" she said. *What, hadn't I sounded okay?* "I mean, all that backslapping," she added. "What was up with that? I'm surprised you didn't double over in pain."

"Did I sound all right?" I asked.

"Sure, of course!" she said. "I was worried, that's all. That will not be repeated, I can assure you!" She stormed off in the direction of the dressing room where the female chorus was holed up.

Mary Jo was attending to Sven. He looked like a Duran-Duran clone on steroids. The set had been rearranged into a Studio 54-type disco, an effect mostly dependent on several revolving crystal balls the size of melons, dangling from the rafters and reflecting colored lights in every direction. Hoffmann and Nicklausse are guests of the inventor Spalanzani, played by Bob Alter in a zoot suit. Bob was channeling David Bowie in his coked-up, "Thin White Duke" persona. Hoffmann has fallen in love with Spalanzani's mechanical doll, believing her to be human.

Olympia (Lisette) reclined seductively on her couch, supposedly asleep (in reality more like in sleep-mode) as Sven sang her a love song. I was waiting for my cue, the last three chords from the orchestra.

CRASH! The deafening explosion gave rise to a horrific shattering of glass.

95.

The source was the crystal disco ball that hung directly above Lisette. The soprano, reflexes superbly honed by her conditioning, had jolted herself off the bed and rolled, narrowly escaping the ball's deadly impact. Within seconds the curtain fell, leaving us all frozen in shocked silence as excited chatter filled the packed house.

At the moment of impact, Sven had been standing several feet outside of the ball's fallout zone. After I saw that Lisette had also escaped harm, I couldn't help but curse my luck. Damn it, right before my big scene and only aria! What choice did Reade have now but to shut the show down?

Lisette, cool and detached as the automaton she played, stood up and brushed crystal slivers from her costume. Her arms and face were flecked with blood. "Don't you dare shut down this show!" she told Reade. "I'm fine. A few cuts and bruises, that's all."

There was a fifteen minute break while the tech crew removed the remains of the shattered disco ball and secured the others. Reade made a short speech to reassure the audience, and the curtain rose again as if nothing had happened.

I don't know if Lisette's accident was the deciding factor, but Angelo did not detonate a single snap during his first aria. It was just as well. If he couldn't carry the effect off with aplomb, his Coppelius risked looking more like a cowardly crackpot than an evil magician.

Lisette outdid herself. She had never sounded better, including the high E at the end of her aria. When the evil Coppelius destroyed the doll to avenge himself on Spalanzani for refusing to pay for Olympia's eyes, the audience rose to its feet as one entity and applauded with such fervor that the remaining disco balls shook ominously. The cast cleared the stage as if fleeing an earthquake.

"That was exciting!" Lisette said once we had all collapsed in the dressing room. "There's nothing like a little disaster to take your mind off your high-note anxiety! I hope I can do it again tomorrow without the benefit of another life-threatening accident."

"You're a cool customer, I must say," Ulrika said. "That could have been sabotage!"

"That's no concern of mine," Lisette said. "I'm done."

"Places for Act II!" Peter called out, hopping hither and thither as if fleeing Mr. McGregor's rake. As we waited in the wings, I caught sight of Lisette leaning inconspicuously against the wall in a spot that provided a clear view of the gondola. She had to be feeling enormous relief to have come through that difficult and unexpectedly hazardous scene in one piece.

"How does it feel to age ten years in fifteen minutes?" I said to Sven, in an effort to lift the pall that had settled over the wings. Then I recalled the five years he had officially shed and blushed.

If he understood the cause of my embarrassment, Sven didn't take offense. He petted my wig and said, "No wrinkles for you, dear Nicklausse. Wouldn't that be nice? This business isn't as brutal to the aging as classical ballet, but more so than you'd think. The new guy is always breathing down your neck." Hugh brushed against Sven as he passed by. "Hello there, Hugh," our star tenor said. "How's it hanging?"

"This blasted hump is a pain in the—"

"Back?" Sven suggested, patting Hugh on the ass. "Here, let me help you." He reached over to make an adjustment in the hump. Nothing but an excuse to touch Hugh, if you asked me. Not that Hugh seemed to mind.

Act II opens in Venice. Corabelle's Venice was the re-imagined one that exists in Las Vegas. A clever touch on her part, considering that our setting was a casino/whorehouse in the early 90s, the last gasp of that particular Age of Greed.

Camille and I mounted the gondola. The spandex negligee had been replaced by a flowing chiffon version that clung only at the bodice. This design suited Camille's fuller figure. In fact, like the deadly disco balls, the scene was now in danger of becoming all about Camille's breasts. We sang our famous duet while a wind machine caused the soprano's wild red wig and gauzy garment to flutter provocatively. Meanwhile the gondola rolled slowly amid the billowing bolts of blue silk that represented the canal:

Starry night, oh night of love
Smile fondly on our mad follies,
Night far sweeter than the day,
Oh beautiful night of love!

The gears of the gondola squealed, and the contraption keeled toward the audience. Camille and I were catapulted forward and spent a harrowing moment airborne. I hit the ground tucking and rolling down the raked floor toward the audience. Who knew that the semester of stage combat training at USC would pay off so spectacularly? At least I hadn't landed on my duet partner.

Camille was not so lucky. Her fall ended in an ominous thud and crack.

96.

Once again, the curtain fell on our shell-shocked troop.

I was already on my feet and dusting myself off, so Reade tended to Camille. "Can you move?" he asked her gently.

She looked up at him with large, sorrowful eyes. "I think so," she said, wiggling her foot experimentally. She attempted to roll onto her front. "Ow!"

"Lie still," Reade said. "We've already called the paramedics." They arrived within five minutes, put a brace on Camille's neck, and loaded her carefully onto a stretcher.

"Don't shut down because of me," she pleaded. "I'll be all right. I sprained my ankle and wrenched my neck, that's all. I'll be good as new in no time. Maybe not by tomorrow, but next Wednesday for sure. If you drop the curtain now, it might be curtains for the whole run!"

"She has a point," Reade said, to no one in particular.

No one was corny enough to say, *the show must go on*. However, if ever there were a reason for it not to, this was it. Unlike Lisette, I had not been energized by my narrow escape, nor was I out of the fray. What further hazards lay in store?

On the chance that the show would go on, Mary Jo had dressed Teresa in record time. Her costume, the spandex original, revealed her figure in all its flawless splendor. Teresa reminded me of Natalie Wood in *Gypsy*. She wouldn't have looked like a whore or even a courtesan if you dressed her in a peek-a-boo bra, a garter belt with fishnets, and a g-string. And yet, wasn't the illusion of dyed-in-the-wool innocence exactly what was required in a courtesan seductive enough to steal men's souls?

Ann Baxter's Eve had nothing on Teresa. She tackled the role of Giulietta as if she had been the one rehearsing day and night. And Sven, released from the strain of feigning love for a woman he loathed, threw himself into the heightened passion of the moment with a conviction and self-assurance worthy of Corelli himself. Certainly no one watching would have dreamed of stripping him of his award, had he fudged ten years off his age.

Angelo, caught up in the general fervor, once again surpassed himself in Dapertutto's aria, at least from what I could hear over the monitors. According to Lawrence, a shoulder seam on my jacket was gaping open in the back, so I went in search of Mary Jo to see if she could sew it up before my next entrance. I found her in the female leads' dressing room attending to Ulrika. The soprano sat at her dressing table, staring glumly into the mirror, as Mary Jo fastened twists of her hair into pin curls that would hold the wig in place. Ulrika looked so down in the dumps that I almost pitied her.

"What are you staring at?" she snapped. So much for my pity. May you choke on your high notes, I cursed silently. Mary Jo reached for the wig. "Not yet!" Ulrika commanded, as if she was Cleopatra and Mary Jo, her slave. "Leave me!" she commanded. The elegant lady bristled but managed not to rise to the bait. "I need a moment to myself. I'm not putting on that gloomy fright-wig until I have to."

"If you wait until intermission, I won't have time to help," Mary Jo said, her voice admirably even.

"Then I'll fucking do it myself!" Ulrika said.

I followed Mary Jo into the hallway, apologized for my timing, and handed her the garment. She whipped out a needle and thread and closed the seam with dizzying swiftness. "Come on," she said as she helped me back into the jacket. "Let's go listen to Sven and Teresa's duet. I've had it up to here with that bitch."

Lisette, a thoughtful expression on her face, was in the wings already, tracking Teresa's every move. I heard a floorboard creak and, fearing more interference by the White Lady, swerved to find only Ulrika, her pin-curled head still wigless. She hung back but listened just as attentively.

The end of the duet was my cue to reenter. Nicklausse warns Hoffmann again to flee (in vain, of course) and then joins Sven, Teresa, Hugh, Lawrence, Angelo, and the chorus in a long, complicated Septet. It was the highlight of the evening for me, the closest I would come to joining a choir of angels. Dramatically the septet is a road block. Right before the climax, the action stops dead for about three minutes, while each character tells the audience what is on his mind. Yet any true opera fan would scream bloody murder if you cut it.

I wasn't the only one worried about the sword fight between Lawrence and Sven. Each man openly examined the blunted tip of his epee for signs of tampering. Although the rest of the performance surpassed what we had witnessed in rehearsal, this climactic fight failed to deliver. Both tenors were terrified of inflicting real injuries, endowing their thrusting and poking with a comic ineptitude that belonged in a Mel Brooks movie. Watching that sorry fight scene convinced me once and for all that Sven and Lawrence were harmless to the core.

The curtain fell on Act II, accompanied by a blood-curdling scream.

97.

The entire cast seemed to converge on the dressing room of the leading ladies. I'm ashamed to say that I elbowed my way to the front. At this point there was no love lost between me and the chorus.

Lisette, one hand covering her mouth, pointed frantically at Ulrika, lying prostrate on the floor, her face an alarming shade of red and swollen almost beyond recognition. Her breathing was a tortured wheeze. The paramedics, who had to be on Reade's speed dial by now, performed an emergency tracheotomy before whisking her off.

"I couldn't find her Epi-pen!" Lisette wailed. This was the first time all evening I had seen her lose her cool. "She always carried it in her purse. It wasn't there!"

"Calm down, Lisette!" Reade urged, enfolding her protectively in his arms. "Tell us what happened." The entire cast closed in, about as helpful as a cloud of gnats at nightfall. "Out of here, this minute!" Reade commanded. "That means the chorus!" Reluctantly, they complied.

"She was stung by a bee!" Lisette whimpered. One false eyelash was askew, and black eyeliner tears streaked her cheeks.

"A bee?" Reade repeated, taken aback. "How did a bee get in here?"

"It was in her wig," Lisette said. "Don't ask me how it got there!"

"Pardon me?" Teresa said, raising her hand like a school girl. "Shouldn't someone inform the paramedics?"

Word of the latest catastrophe spread quickly. "I always knew she had a bee in her bonnet," I heard one of the chorus girls remark.

This was how Teresa came to perform two roles. To no one's surprise, she made a fetching Antonia. I could only imagine how much time she must have spent going over the blocking on her own for the act to proceed so smoothly. There had to be more to that girl than the sunny exterior. Who else had so much to gain from disabling all three divas? Even though I had fallen overboard along with Camille, I didn't believe I was a real target. More like collateral damage.

It took real courage to trust the mechanism of the portrait frame, after the way it was gone awry in rehearsal. Oddly enough, it worked like a dream.

When Teresa appeared on Angelo's arm as Stella at the end of the opera, the audience leapt to its collective feet for a standing ovation that lasted more than ten minutes. Meanwhile the male chorus pawed the ground, impatient to sing the final reprise of the drinking song. Juergen finally told them to sing over the applause so we could get to the bows, which, predictably, went on and on. By the time the furor abated, it was midnight, one hour past the projected finish time.

98.

There was some talk about canceling the opening night party in the ballroom, but Reade wouldn't hear of it, especially after word came down from the hospital that both divas were out of danger.

"I had no idea opera was so exciting!" Freesia remarked, flushed with bloodlust.

"I bet you'd love a good bullfight," Sven said, his hand finding the small of her back and rotating sensually.

"Never seen one," Freesia said, taking Sven's measure. "You're probably right, though. There are few things more exciting than watching people risk their lives. This was my kind of opera! Except your swordfight of course. That was anti-climactic, under the circumstances." Sven withdrew his hand.

Corabelle, who had been eavesdropping, thrust an imaginary sword into her rock-hard stomach. She was one of few women I had ever seen who managed to look feminine in a tuxedo, perhaps because this one was tailored to hug every curve. "You walked into that one, buster," she said to Sven. "I'm going to fetch you another glass of champagne!"

"Who is that unpleasant woman?" Sven said, making a face.

"Corabelle?" I said.

"Ha, ha. You know who I mean."

"Oh, that's Roland's girlfriend, Freesia."

"What kind of a name is that?

I shrugged. "I think she's also Winston's ex. He almost lost it when he saw her. She didn't look happy to see him, either."

"Does that bother you?"

"It might have, a month ago."

"What has changed?" Sven asked, looking first at Winston, absorbed in conversation with Hubert Silvertone, then at Reade, besieged by his board of directors.

Corabelle reappeared, balancing a tray of champagne flutes. "Has someone changed?"

"Apparently Debbie. A change of heart."

"Preferences?"

"Don't get your hopes up," Sven said.

"Speaking of high hopes," Corabelle said, scanning the ballroom, "where's Hugh?"

"Still expunging the last remains of the dwarf Pittichinaccio from his person, I'd imagine. Talk about casting against type … Young as he is, he has to take what he can get. But he's not going to end up like Lawrence."

"He could do worse," Corabelle said. "Lawrence is a first-rate comprimario tenor. His Franz practically stopped the show. Ugh, bad choice of words. I'm never going to hear the word *showstopper* again without thinking of tonight. What a waste! My beautiful concept, down the drain."

"What do you mean?" I said.

"Do you really think there's going to be a second performance of this production?" Sven said. "First off, there will be a full investigation. I, personally, am not setting foot on that set again. Who knows? Perhaps the White Lady herself is behind it all!"

"She wasn't so much as tugging on sleeves tonight," Corabelle said.

"She pulled out my shirttails twice before the Prologue," I said. "Sven swore up and down it wasn't him."

"It wasn't," he confirmed.

"If she wanted attention tonight, she must be disappointed," Corabelle said. "She had too much living, breathing competition."

"Don't tell me the EEE has struck again," Sven groaned. "If Camille and Ulrika weren't so badly off, I would have sworn they were responsible somehow."

"How could anyone wreak so much havoc without leaving clues?" I said. "Someone would have seen something!"

"Debbie, aren't those your parents?" Sven said.

99.

"Wow," Sven exclaimed. "Your father looks like Sean Connery with hair. If I were twenty years older—"

"Any resemblance is purely superficial," I broke in. "Once he opens his mouth you'll see what I mean."

"Hey, Dweeb!" Roland said. "Nice work! I was really proud of you."

"Yes, sweetie," Mom said. "You're a real deviant now."

Sven guffawed. "Ha, Ha, HA!"

"Diva, Mom, and I told you, this isn't a diva role. If I ever play Carmen or Delilah, you can call me a diva."

"Ooh," Sven cooed, "I can see it now! Deborah de Lille as Delilah."

"So can I, Babela!" Frankie said, laying a hand on my bare shoulder.

"Frankieeeee!" I cried, delighted to see my loyal friend and supporter. "What did you think?"

"Fabuloso, girlie!" he said, enclosing me in a bone-crunching hug. "You knocked their Dockers off, baby. I was hot for you myself."

"I'll bet," I said, beaming.

Frankie leaned over to peck my parents' cheeks. "Hey, you two! Glad you could make it. And you, you big stud," he said to Sven, "What can I say? I worship at your shrine."

"Yes, excellent work," My Dad said in his flat, Midwestern accent. "Both of you." At the sound of Dad's rusty voice, Sven flashed a grin in my direction.

"Nice to meet you, Mr. Conn—, I mean, de Lille," Sven said. "Are you an opera fan?"

"Not really," my father said. "We're here to support our daughter."

"Harold!" my Mom protested. "We're here because the cards told me it was going to be a rocky night. I knew Deborah would need her family at her side." She must have seen me tense up, because she quickly added, "What we didn't realize was just how talented our daughter is."

"Bravo!" Corabelle said, clapping. "Please, adopt me!"

While Corabelle introduced herself to Frankie, I seized the opportunity to slip away. I needed fresh air, more champagne, and plate-loads of food to soak it up with. Halfway to the bar, I was waylaid by Ludovic, of all people.

"Excellent performance, Deborah," he said. "How did you all manage to keep going? I'd have dug in my heels and refused to continue."

I was dumbstruck. Here was a guy I had never exchanged two words with—a reptile who spent the entire rehearsal period squirming at the piano, supposedly hating every note he heard—acting like a genuine human being. "Why, Ludovic," I said. "I'm amazed you know my name."

"It's true we've never been formally introduced. I'm afraid I'm not a social person. It must be the champagne!" He lifted his empty glass.

"Well, Ludovic, I always wanted to compliment you on your playing, but you never looked very ... accessible."

"It's been a rough month for me," he said. "My father died a week before rehearsals began. Also, I could hardly contradict Juergen. I'm counting on him to get me in a few doors in the future." He paused and cleared his throat. "Deborah, will you do me a favor? Since I seem to be in this rare, foolhardy state-of-mind, would you introduce me to Lawrence?"

"Sure," I said, looking around. "If he's here." Ludovic pointed out Lawrence, who was talking to Hugh. From the looks of things, it wasn't a happy exchange. "Looks like bad timing," I said. "Oh, what the hell. Lawrence!" I called out. He whipped about, prepared to disarm a mugger. "Come here a minute!" I said, pretending to be too tipsy to pick up on nonverbal clues. Before Lawrence could bite my head off, I said quickly, "Ludovic is eager to meet you. He recently had a death in his family, so he really hasn't been up to socializing." Now remember, Ludovic is quite a dish when he isn't scowling. Lawrence was not insensitive to this, nor was he blind to the power of jealousy. If Hugh thought he had a rival ...

My work done, I continued on my quest for sustenance. Had I witnessed the start of a beautiful friendship? Then, across the room, leaning out the White Lady's suicide window, I spied Lisette.

100.

Judging by her faulty sense of balance, Lisette had been indulging in serious drinking. She was wearing some seriously treacherous stilettos.

"Lisette, are you okay?" I said, coaxing her away from the open window.

"No," she said. "I almost died tonight."

"But you didn't, and you sang like an angel!"

"Is that what it takes?" she said bitterly. "Thanks kid, but I'm going to bed."

"Before you go, let me tell you, you looked wonderful tonight. And now! That's a beautiful dress, and what a gorgeous necklace!" She did look good. The low-cut black sheath showed off her slimmed-down figure, and the small diamond pendant that hung from a silver chain and rested in the hollow between her breasts was the perfect accessory.

She caressed the necklace. "It was a gift from my ex-husband," she said. "Good night, Debbie," she said, kissing me on the cheek. "I hope I drank enough champagne to knock me out." She weaved slightly as she walked away, passing right by Hubert Silvertone without incident. Hmm, that was strange. You'd think at least one quick, guilty glance …

"Hi Debbie," Reade said. "You were great tonight."

"Well, we got through it, didn't we?" I said. "I feel lucky to be alive."

"And I feel lucky that you're—"

"Reade!" a voice boomed. Another board member. "Might I have a word?"

"Surely," Reade said, bracing for the next round of recriminations.

Alone again, I grasped a full bottle of champagne and sought out Sven and Corabelle. "Wow, where did you go?" Sven said, his voice slurred. "Your family took off. Said they would see you at breakfast tomorrow. Say, do you know where Frankie is?" he said as he cased the room. "That guy's not only a hoot but a lot cuter than I remember."

"Anyone would look good to you at the moment," Corabelle said, taking custody of the bottle. "Let's move the party to my place. I've got a big bag of chips stashed away. I'd rather slit my own throat than accept another false compliment." From the looks of her, food was a good idea, not more champagne. However, this was definitely a good night to get wasted.

We hailed one of the fleet of limos Reade had commandeered to deliver us all safely to his mansion. "What happened to Hugh?" I said.

"I don't know," Sven whined woozily. "I thought we had an understanding."

"There's time," I said. "He doesn't want Lawrence. That I know."

"What do you know?" Sven said. "No, don't answer that." He clapped his hand over my mouth. "I don't give a shit anymore, anyway. Now Frankie ... but he didn't make any moves."

I was too drunk to be annoyed. I pried his hand away and said, "Are you kidding? Of course Frankie has the hots for you. You're a scary person! If I were him, I'd need a clear green light before putting myself on the line."

Sven clipped his forehead with the heel of his hand. "Damn! Why didn't I think of that? Well, too late for tonight."

"Freesia didn't go home with Roland," Corabelle commented.

"Who did she leave with?" I asked. It couldn't be Winston, who had been monopolized by Hugh Silvertone, apparently his new client. Lucky for me, money was Winston's first priority. I just hoped he didn't plan on coming knocking later on.

"I don't know," Corabelle said. "But I wouldn't kick her out of bed. And I had the feeling … No, that must be wishful thinking."

From the way this conversation was going, it was a good thing no one was driving. We pulled up in front of Reade's mansion and pushed and pulled each other in the door, Three-Stooges-style. The chauffeur seemed to be debating whether to lend a hand. In the end he left us to our own devices.

We stumbled into Corabelle's room and fell across the bed, bodies entwined. I was the center of the sandwich. "I wish I had a TV set," Corabelle whined. "We could watch bad infomercials."

"Or ..." Sven said. We stopped talking and looked at each other.

101.

In our drunken state, we must have liked what we saw. First Sven touched his lips to mine; then I turned to Corabelle to pass the kiss on. Sweet, cool, firm lips. With my eyes closed, they felt exactly like a young man's. A loud rapping on the door broke the spell. We all looked at each other, the three little pigs fearing the wolf at the door. We might be forgiven a little paranoia.

"Who is it?" Corabelle yelled. No answer. She rolled off the bed and peered through the peephole. "Freesia!" she said, throwing the door open. "Care to join the party?" Freesia took a few timid steps before hesitating. She hadn't bargained on an orgy.

"I thought this was your room," she said.

"It is," Corabelle said. "Welcome to our after-hours club." Freesia kicked off her stiletto heels and curled up next to Corabelle. Another knock on the door. This time Sven looked through the peephole. "It's Frankie!" he said, and opened the door with unabashed enthusiasm.

Frankie took a few tentative steps as if suspecting a trap. "What's going on here?" he said. "Debbieeeee! What are you up to in here, girl? I thought this was Sven's room!"

"Next door!" Sven said, cheerfully. "I'll show you." Another knock. We all laughed. Sven's Ha! Ha! HA! trumped everything else.

"Who could that be?" I said in a voice that reverberated around the room. Every singer knows that one of the keys to projection is relaxation, and no one is more relaxed—or loud—than a drunk. By the time I made it to the peephole, the hallway was deserted. "Oh well," I said. "Now that I'm up, I'm going to bed. I'll see you all in the morning. The *late* morning."

I stumbled back to my room and collapsed, face first, on the bed. Then I rolled over and watched the ceiling sway, back and forth, back and forth. I must have drifted off, because a loud knocking woke me up. Good thing I hadn't fallen into a deep sleep. I was still wearing my little black dress and stockings. Oh no! What if it were Winston? If so, I would pretend no one was home. I tiptoed to the door in the dark.

"Debbie?" a man's voice whispered.

It was Reade.

102.

"Just a minute!" I called out, sobering up quickly. I raced to the bathroom to brush my teeth and do a quick fix on my raccoon eyes.

By the time I opened the door, Reade had almost rounded the corner out of sight.

"Reade?" I called out, as if nothing were amiss.

He retraced his steps. "Are you alone?" he asked. "I thought I recognized your voice in—" He stopped himself. "I know it's late, but may I come in? I'll only stay a minute."

It was then I noticed the bottle of Dom Pérignon. "Were you planning to christen me with that?" I asked. Speaking slowly and distinctly required considerable effort. "Because, if you were going to offer to share it, you're too late. I'm past appreciating a bottle of that vintage, and I don't believe in wasting good champagne."

"Neither do I," he said, grinning. "We'll save it, shall we?"

"I could use a bottle of water," I said. "I have a feeling I'm going to be a tad dehydrated tomorrow."

He whipped out his cell phone. In half a minute two liter bottles of Pellegrino were left at the door by invisible hands, along with a large crystal bowl of blue corn chips.

"I didn't expect you to be here," he said, as we sat side by side on the bed, the corn chips between us.

"Oh?" I said, chasing a chip with a large swallow of sparkling water.

"I thought I heard you in Corabelle's room."

"That was me," I said, "but it wasn't what you're thinking."

"What am I thinking?"

"Listen, if you didn't suspect something nasty was going on, why didn't you wait for me to answer the door?" I was acting awfully self-righteous, under the circumstances. I didn't allow myself to imagine what might have happened if our visitors hadn't arrived when they did.

"You got me."

"All right then," I said. I was about to reach for another chip, when I found his mouth over mine, moving in for a kiss. His lips tasted, parted, and trailed across my cheek and down my neck. I think I said something idiotic, not that it mattered. No one was critiquing the dialogue or judging the grace of our choreography.

"That's one thing I don't have to be nervous about," I said, as he helped me out of my dress.

"What's that?"

"You already know what I look like naked."

"Not really. I was too much of a gentleman to stare."

"Thank you for that."

He ran a finger along the curve of my naked hip. "I saw enough to know you wouldn't be a disappointment."

Afterwards, his body pressed snugly against mine, it dawned on me that I should have played hard-to-get. Not that that had been an option. Men like him seem to want women who are hard-to-get.

"Debbie?"

"You're not going to tell me you want to go back to your own room, are you?" I said, painfully vulnerable. "Because I really want to fall asleep with you."

He gathered me into his arms. "God, no! I'm only leaving if you kick me out. But first, I have something to tell you. Camille and Ulrika are dead."

103.

I sat bolt upright. "My God!" I squawked. "How did that happen? Last I heard they were out of danger!"

It was then I noticed, on the hearth, a pile of white, folded objects. I stood, naked limbs unsteady, and went over to investigate. Four origami swans lay scattered. I looked up, not surprised to find three on the mantle. "On the night we first met, Lawrence joked about …" I paused to catch my breath, "Agatha Christie's Ten Little Indians. Ever read it?" Reade shook his head. "With each murder, the killer knocks another Indian figurine off the mantle. We were discussing the mystery of Juanita's death. I suggested our story would use swans, because swans supposedly sing one last song before they die."

I counted them off on my fingers. "Juanita, Camille, Ulrika, and Willy. It was during that Get-Acquainted Party. The entire cast was there, except for Angelo and Mrs. Wooley. Anyone might have overheard us and recounted it later to those who were absent. But Reade, tell me, how could Camille and Ulrika be dead?"

"Complications," Reade said. "They seemed to be out of the woods, but Ulrika was far more allergic than anyone realized, and she just … died. Camille not only had a severe concussion, but she miscarried. Who knew she was pregnant?"

"Did you sleep with her?" I said. "During *Carmen*?"

"Hell, no! What makes you say that?"

I looked straight into his eyes. He didn't appear to be lying. "Lawrence—"

"Lawrence!" He practically spit. "You listen to Lawrence? That's sillier than believing in ghost stories told around the campfire. I wouldn't dream of sleeping with any of my leading ladies!" After a guilty pause, he added, "Unless I was really serious about them."

How I wanted to believe him! "I saw you picking up Ulrika at the party," I said. I couldn't help myself.

Reade struck a match and knelt to light the kindling in the fireplace. The flame lit up the bulging muscles of his naked body. He looked like one of the Greek statues in his gardens. Well, not exactly. More like a Greek statue that had been dragged through a briar patch. He had enough scars to shame Travis McGee. I hoped I would know him long enough to hear the stories behind the scars.

"You have a tendency to jump to conclusions," Reade said as he tended to the fire. "I wasn't picking her up. Perhaps I was more flirtatious than absolutely necessary. I was trying to assess her mental health. She had a nervous breakdown after *Carmen*, and I was concerned about her ability to handle another role under those circumstances. Frankly, her husband begged me, or I wouldn't have taken the chance. She is—*was*—a fine singer, but who needs it? If only I had realized all the shit that went down during *Carmen*. My fault, for putting on blinders. Some detective! It's just as well that I retired. God, but you look lovely in the firelight." He reached over and pulled me tight against him. "What will I tell Hermann Mannschliesser now? How the hell did a bee find its way into her wig? They're social insects. There's no such thing as a lone bee!"

"It must have been planted," I said.

"Then what about those other accidents?" he said. "After the gondola misbehaved during orchestra tech, I had it tested a zillion times. And the disco ball!"

"Sabotage," I said. "What other explanation is there? Do you think it's the Enemies of Elitist Entertainment?"

"The EEE? Please! That's a load of B.S. It's got to be a front for someone in the company. But who?"

"I don't know," I said. "Everyone has a motive."

"They do?" I was amazed this had never occurred to him.

"Take Sven. He hated both those women. Camille claimed to be pregnant with his child, and Ulrika was threatening to tell the awards committee that chose him for the Corelli Competition that he lied about his age."

"Do you think he did it?"

"Only if he's a psychopath. But I guess anyone who commits murder would have to be. As for Corabelle, they both trashed her to that journalist."

"Angelo?"

"They spread the word far and wide that he's impotent. He despised them, yes, but he's still a long shot. Someone who is afraid of a few snaps would never have the nerve to rig all those booby traps." I was holding Reade's hand and counting off the suspects on his fingers. "Then there's Lawrence." I chose my lover's pinkie. "Both ladies seduced Sven during Carmen. That infuriated Lawrence."

"Lisette?"

"She wanted Ulrika to pay for taking over the role of Micaela and getting all the glory in the review. Only, she was a target herself and seemed genuinely distraught at the party."

"Granted. Teresa?" He gave me his other hand for counting. "I guess that one's obvious. Her career is made after tonight, even though I'm afraid there will be no more performances in this run. But it can't be her." He took the hand back. "I've known her all her life. I'd swear on the Bible she was innocent. What about Juergen?"

I nodded. "Very possibly. They teased him mercilessly. Except that he already got his revenge at the first run-through. When I spoke with him at breakfast the other day, he appeared to have moved on."

"He's still a good suspect. Anyone else?"

I remembered the bizarre encounter in the basement. "Rudolf the janitor? He likes Teresa, more than *likes*, and he despises the others. Plus, he's weird and scary."

"Too obvious," Reade said, shaking his head. "Mary Jo?"

"Not unless she turns out to be Teresa's birth mother. Why else would she bother?"

"It can't be Hugh or Jim & Bob," Reade said. "Hugh's a newcomer, and Jim & Bob are too mellow to be murderers."

"Peter Haas, the stage manager?"

"That nervous little bunny?" Reade lifted me into his arms. "Let's sleep on it," he said, "if we can. I'm sure we'll get a few hours in, eventually."

We did. Eventually.

104.

When I woke the next morning, the last thing on my mind was whodunit. At around 9:00 a.m. there was a knock at my door. Reade had just stepped into the bathroom.

I peered through the peephole before opening the door a crack. "Just a minute," I told Lisette in a low voice. I pulled on drawstring pants, a T-shirt, and sandals, then stepped into the hallway and shut the door behind me. "What's up?"

"Are you alone?" she said.

"Of course." I didn't want to compromise Reade.

"Listen," she said. "I need a big favor. I lost my diamond necklace last night. You know, the one you commented on? It must have fallen off somewhere in the ballroom. If only I hadn't been so wasted! I'm not even sure how I got home. Anyway, I really don't want to go back there on my own. Will you come with me? It's silly, but I'm nervous about the White Lady."

"Won't the theater be locked up?"

"The butler gave me a key," she said, waving it in the air.

I rubbed my throbbing temples. "My bike is at the Lodge," I protested. "Besides, I'm a little worse for wear."

"Me, too," she said. "Don't worry. I'll drive."

"Okay," I said with a sigh. "Let's go." I didn't go back into the room. Reade might be milling about in his birthday suit. He would wonder why I had left without saying goodbye. Oh well. Time enough to explain later.

Damn, but Lisette was a fast driver! "I'm sorry," she said, noting my greenish pallor. "That necklace means a lot to me. Let's get this over with quickly so we can have breakfast."

I was moving too sluggishly for Lisette, who basically shoved me up the stairs to the ballroom. "I'll look over here," she said. "You take the other side."

"I think I see it!" I said, triumphant. The diamond gleamed in a spot of sun beneath the open window, the one from which the White Lady had flung herself into the courtyard. I leaned over to pick it up. My next thought was, how did a goat get in here? That's what it felt like, being head-butted by a goat.

105.

I listed, nearly regained my balance, and whirled about in time for Lisette's palm to connect more forcefully with my chest. I didn't actually scream. To my ears, the cry sounded like a sorry attempt to sing an unsupported, whole-tone scale of ahs. Whether or not I made a sound, I fell heavily out the window, like a tree in the forest, only with less grace.

I would surely have been a goner if my T-shirt hadn't caught on a hook left over from a holiday light display. It kept me captive long enough to rearrange my limbs into a jumping, rather than diving, position. I heard the dismayingly distant flop of my sandals as they hit the pavement far, far below. I hung, suspended, until the T-shirt gave way with a sickening rrrrrip, releasing me from my temporary new sideline as a decorative banner.

I flailed wildly. When sanity returned, I was swinging monkey-style from the pole where the American flag proudly waved. I blessed my yoga classes for strengthening my arm muscles and Reade for being a Republican, although you may have guessed I'm not one myself.

I was naked from the waist up, not having had the foresight to wear a bra—or panties, for that matter. Our mothers are right: you never know when you'll be in an accident and wish you were wearing clean underwear. Most mothers of Lillian de Lille's era didn't consider the possibility that you'd leave the house wearing no underwear. The flag provided moments of decency. Mostly it flapped maddeningly in my face. It was like being chastised repeatedly by the fan of an outraged eighteenth-century noblewoman. Talk about wrapping yourself in the American flag!

Lisette leaned out over the ledge. "What the fuck?!" she cursed. "Oh, come on, Debbie, give it up! You're just prolonging your agony." She leaned over to expedite things, but her reach wasn't long enough.

"Why are you doing this?" I cried, craning my neck sideways in a vain effort to dodge the offended flag. "I thought you were my friend!"

"It's women like you that make this business a living hell," she said in a level voice. "I starve myself and bicycle until I'm blue in the face. Then you steal my husband."

"What?!"

"Juanita did," she said bitterly. "She was another one. Ate whatever she pleased, like you, and never gained a pound. Except that she had breasts. And that scrawny Ulrika! If I hadn't been dieting, I wouldn't have caught her cold. Then she recovers and takes my part, and I'm left to skulk home with my tail between my legs."

"Camille was worse off than you," I said. I shook with fatigue, unable to defend myself further against the flag's relentless flapping. "She missed out on her own opening night. Why punish her?"

"Blame Juanita for that! With Ulrika's help, she rigged the car and forged a note from Sven to lure Camille away. Too bad she didn't realize I was in the car behind hers on the road back from *Der Rosenkavalier*. I was Sophie, you know."

"You were the ingénue in *Rosenkavalier*?" I said. Why hadn't I Googled that production?

I couldn't hang around like this much longer! Ignoring the burning in my arms, I inched close enough to the wall to plant my feet. I trudged upward, brick by brick, until I could loop first one leg then the other around the Grand Old Flag. This human-swing shape allowed for an even distribution of limbs, a position that might allow me to hang on another ten minutes—as long as my weight didn't dislodge the pole, which creaked ominously.

106.

Lisette, assured of my imminent demise, had assumed a cinematic pose on the window ledge, as though preparing to sing "Moon River" for the cameras. "Camille was the Marschallin," she went on. "What a pain in the ass she was to work with! Plus, she also made a play for my husband."

I got the picture. Lisette's husband was the one making the plays. Not that I was in any position to set the woman straight. "What about the EEE?" I said in a shaky voice.

"The Enemies of Elitist Entertainment? Oh, it exists! Thanks to me. I ferreted out a few female malcontents in the chorus who were handy with a wrench. Anonymous calls planted the idea. I must say, they really ran with it. Thanks to a mole in the tech crew—a devoted boyfriend, I think. They wanted to replace as many female leads as possible with chorus understudies."

"But they attacked you!"

"Yeah. Their plans were less ambitious than mine. They only planned to replace one star at a time. Any more, and the show would close down. And that's what happened, didn't it? Unfortunately they chose to begin with me. It made sense to start with Act I, I suppose. I didn't see that coming. Well, I did see it coming, thank God, if you know what I mean. Only, I didn't *fore*see it. I'm no psychic, like your Mom. Too bad her powers are limited." Her tinkling laugh pealed out into the courtyard.

"Yeah, you're a psycho!"

"Ha, ha. Give it up, Debbie. Just- let- go." She divided these last three words, turning them into a travesty of the Nike slogan, *Just Do It!*

"What about Mrs. Wooley? What about my car?" If I was going to die, I might as well know the whole story.

"Mrs. Wooley? I didn't want her around. She knew too much. She was Annina in *Der Rosenkavalier*. The car business was Ulrika's doing. Her mechanic husband taught her a few basics. My idea, naturally. Once again, it was only intended to shake you up. Talk about overkill! As for Juanita, she panicked. I only tailgated her a little. She drove herself off that cliff. And Camille! Yeah, I arranged that second little spill from the gondola. No one suspected that I was working on the rope while I watched from backstage. But who knew she was pregnant? It's not my fault she miscarried.

"Ulrika. Holy shit! How can anyone be *that* allergic to bees? I still wonder where she stashed her supply of Epinephrine. I was going to inject her and save her life. They all made their own beds. I had a small hand in it. Fate did the rest. You know, The Law of Unintended Consequences. Only, I really didn't bank on Teresa getting all the glory. Well, good for her. I have nothing against her. The EEE tried to scare her away. I'm sure their next moves would have been more destructive, given half a chance. They really needed her out of the picture so she wouldn't be able to cover any roles. Lucky for her, their ingenuity had limits. And who knew Reade would take her under his wing like that?"

"Why me?" I groaned.

"How else to put this matter to rest so I can get on with my life? If I could resolve it another way, I would, believe me. I need a scapegoat, and you have as much motive as anyone. Those two treated you despicably." She leaned farther out the window and smiled sweetly. "Now, do us both a favor, will you, and fall? I would kill for some coffee."

"You didn't sleep with Hubert Silvertone, did you?"

"Nope!" she said cheerfully. "He had the bad taste to choose Ulrika. So yes, I confess, I was the ghost in your room. Careless of me, I admit."

"You were too careless this time." It was a man's voice—Reade!

107.

"Oh shit!" Lisette yelled.

The next thing I knew she was standing on the window ledge, swaying. When the fear in her eyes changed to resignation, she leapt.

As Lisette fell, she grabbed, catching me about the waist. Her additional weight bent the flagpole another 45 degrees. Miraculously, it held. I kept my grip despite sweaty hands. Unfortunately for her, Lisette's conditioning had concentrated on her lower body, leaving her arm muscles unequal to the task at hand. Her weight dislodged my legs so that I hung once again by both arms. Her claw-like fingers slid down my waist to my hips, the drawstring of my pants came untied, and she fell, taking the pants with her. There I remained, stark naked.

Reade tossed me a rope. "Done any rock climbing?" he yelled.

"No!" I cried. "And I hated climbing the rope in high school!"

"Step into the noose," he instructed. My foot found the opening just in time. The pole slipped out of my grasp, and I fell backward, my head slamming against the brick wall. It hurt like the dickens, but my skull is hard as a cocoanut fresh off the tree. I stayed conscious. My leg felt as if it were being pulled from its socket as Reade reeled me in. This painful, inelegant process gave me plenty of time to view Lisette's body. Blood pooled around her head. Otherwise she appeared to be in one piece, if posed at an odd angle.

Like a broken doll.

108.

Reade wrapped me in his leather jacket and held me in a tight embrace. "God, my God," he kept saying. An ambulance pulled up below.

"When did you call them?" I asked.

"On my way here."

"How did you know I was in danger? Did you hear us talking?"

"You were too quiet. Opera singers can't usually speak sotto voce if their lives depend on it. I wish I hadn't decided to take a shower. I would have arrived here a lot sooner! Then, once I realized it was you hanging from the flagpole, I had to find a rope. Luckily, no one had bothered to discard, or confiscate as evidence, the one that had originally been attached to the gondola. Whoever cut it—Lisette, I presume—left it exactly the right length."

"But how did you know where to find me?" I asked.

"It was the note that tipped me off," he said.

"I wanted to leave a note, but I could hardly—"

"Lisette left a suicide note," he said. "With your signature. A confession. Said you were going to join the White Lady. That's how I knew where to find you. I'm not familiar with your handwriting, but considering Lisette's attention to detail, I assume it would pass muster."

"Shit. That explains what happened to the postcard! I was writing to my parents right before the ghost dropped by. When it was over, the postcard had disappeared. It was Lisette all along. But damn it, when did she have time to slip the suicide note under my door? If she had done it while I was changing, wouldn't I have noticed it on way out?"

"Unlikely. You were too rushed. You know, when that ghostly visitation thing happened, I immediately pictured Lisette dangling down from her room. She had the easiest access, and she was in great shape."

"How come you didn't mention it last night?" My teeth were chattering.

He rubbed my back as he held me tight against him. "I couldn't believe it. She was your friend, or at least she did a good job of faking it, and you argued so convincingly in her favor. I'm supposed to be a detective. I should have figured it out. She was a superb actress, a better actress than a singer. Except last night. Wow! She's never sounded better. What a swan song that turned out to be."

"Swan song," I repeated. "How did she get those swans into my room?"

"Easy," he said. "She knew how to access the keys. She obtained a key to the theater, didn't she? It's not as if James knowingly lent it out."

"But we were awake most of the night," I protested. "She must have come in then."

"I gather she chose our brief interlude of sleep," he said. "We're goddamn lucky she didn't notice me, because she would surely have devised a more foolproof plan."

"She didn't expect to see you," I said, "so she didn't. She was sure I was too much of a sexually-ambiguous loser to seduce anyone."

He laughed. "Well, she underestimated you, and she certainly didn't understand men. By the way, how come you're always naked when I come to your rescue?"

109.

"In case you're wondering," I said as we walked down the staircase. "I forgive you for being a Republican."

Reade gave me a playful slap on the rear. "I'm not a Republican. Where did you get that idea?"

"The flag."

"God, how I hate that!" he said as he helped me into his car. "The American flag belongs to everyone!" This was the best news I had heard all day. Although it's true, it wasn't yet 10:00 a.m. "Wait a minute," Reade said, wrinkling his forehead in thought. "Let's say I never arrived, and you were found dead on the pavement, as planned."

I gulped. "Let's not."

"How did that bitch expect to get away with it? How would she have explained her presence? Chances were good that someone would have seen or heard her car leave my house, or at least return."

"If I had really wanted to defenestrate myself like the White Lady," I said, "I would have needed a ride. No car, you see? Lisette would probably have revised her story so that I was the one who lost something at the party. She would have claimed that I made a mad dash for the window before she could stop me."

"Defenestrate," Reade repeated. "Nice word. I hope neither of us has any cause to use it again. Anyhow, that sounds like a plausible explanation, although, naturally, I wouldn't have believed it for a second."

"Even if you had been in bed with Teresa instead of me?"

"Ridiculous!" he proclaimed, screwing up his face in distaste. "She's a baby!"

110.

Back at Reade's mansion, word had spread of my final ordeal. At least we hoped it would be the final one. An anonymous tip revealed the identities of the EEE. The two choristers who had orchestrated the "domestic terrorist group" (as the police called it) were Camille's and my alternate understudies (if Teresa was incapacitated), also lesbian lovers. They had recruited Ulrika's understudy, who had convinced her stagehand boyfriend to help. Lisette's alternate understudy claimed she had been blackmailed into joining the cause. All of them professed horror at the outcome. What had been intended as relatively harmless pranks quickly got out of hand. All of them had been furious to discover how easily they had been manipulated.

Reade's cell phone rang as we were about to go down to breakfast. "Really?" he said, after listening for several minutes. "That's fascinating. Listen to this," he said after ending the call. "According to my private detective, Mary Jo *is* Teresa's birth mother, and Rudolf's obviously obsessed with her. His wall is plastered with her photographs. So they both would have made excellent suspects. It's lucky for everyone that our murderer confessed. Because I'm no Dick Tracy."

"How about Travis McGee?" I said. "Uh, never mind. Did I tell you about my experience with the White Lady? It was while I was waiting for my first entrance. She kept tugging at my shirttails. I'm pretty sure it wasn't Lisette."

"Maybe our ghost was trying to warn you," Reade said. "After all, you were the only one who had a clue that something was afoot."

"Maybe I'm psychic, like my Mom."

"We're kidding around, right?" he said, looking worried.

"If you say so."

"Because you have many gifts," he said, moving in for another kiss, "and I'm planning to discover them all. I just hope you're not too much like your mother."

I laughed. "Don't worry about that," I said. "Speaking of gifts, I look forward to discovering more of yours."

Suddenly I thought of the portrait of the lady wearing the broach. "I just remembered something," I said. "That oil painting near the kitchen, the one of the pretty brunette—"

"The one dressed in white?" he said. "That's the White Lady. No one told you?"

111.

"How could anyone have told me that was the White Lady in the portrait?" I said. "It's practically hidden. I'm fairly sure no one even knows it's there. You didn't exactly give us a tour when we moved in. In fact, you left us almost entirely to our own devices."

"Just trying to give you space," Reade said.

"How did you get a portrait of the White Lady?"

"I painted it," he said. "I worked from her publicity photo, which I found along with other memorabilia from that early period. I still haven't decided if it's good enough to hang in the theater."

"Are you kidding?" I said. "It's a masterpiece! By the way, I think I have her broach. Hang on." I ran to my room, returning minutes later with the mangled finery. "Do you recognize this?" I said. I held the broach out for his inspection.

He took his time examining it. "Nope," he concluded.

"Could you lead the way to the painting?" I asked. "I doubt I can find it on my own." Once there, I held the real piece next to the painted one. "What do you think?"

"Where did you get this?" he asked.

"That's what popped my bike tire," I explained. "I've kept it as a good-luck charm ever since."

"Some good-luck charm," he said. "If the White Lady meant to protect you, she certainly was asleep at the wheel half the time."

"I'm alive, aren't I?" I said. "Maybe she simply tried to give me a heads-up."

As we passed the other pictures, I asked, "Are those landscapes your work, too?"

"Guilty," he said.

"They're beautiful," I said, "but I think you know that." I paused to consider. "From those pictures, I would have guessed you were a traditionalist. And yet you hire Corabelle."

"Keeps life interesting," he said. "Come on, I'm starving."

Reade kept his arm around me at breakfast. My parents looked on in wonder. "You told me he was married!" my mother protested.

After Winston assessed the situation, he made a hasty getaway. Had he stopped by my room during the night? If so, he would have gotten an earful.

Hugh, Angelo, and Juergen—bewildered and hung over—looked like waxen replicas of themselves. As for the rest, they only had eyes for each other: Corabelle and Freesia, Lawrence and Ludovic, Roland and Teresa, Sven and Frankie.

Could a fortune teller more skillful than Mom have predicted all of this? Only if she had a tarot deck with more than one card to represent The Lover.

Cat Melodia is the nom de plume of a Seattle-based mezzo soprano and voice teacher. Like her heroine, she often wears the pants on stage. Three of her opera adaptations/ translations have been performed at community colleges. She has a Bachelor's Degree *cum laude* in German Literature from Princeton and a Master's in Music. You can find Cat on the Web at: **DingDongDiva.camelpress.com.**

8774968R0

Made in the USA
Charleston, SC
13 July 2011